THE ABBOT

by

Tony Rycroft

Published by

**MELROSE
BOOKS**

An Imprint of Melrose Press Limited
St Thomas Place, Ely
Cambridgeshire
CB7 4GG, UK
www.melrosebooks.com

FIRST EDITION

Copyright © Tony Rycroft 2005

The Author asserts his moral right to
be identified as the author of this work

Cover illustration and design by Bryan Carpenter

ISBN 1 905226 10 1

Printed and bound in Great Britain by:
Bath Press Limited, Lower Bristol Road,
Bath, BA2 3BL, UK

Following the 9/11 terrorist attacks in New York, the British government commissioned research into developing anti-viruses for anthrax, fearing a terrorist attack on the UK mainland involving a biological weapon.

When the chief scientist working on the experiments steals the most deadly virus ever created, he sparks a massive operation involving the police, the military and a tiny village in Cambridgeshire.

But when it is stolen a second time and no one knows who was responsible, things turn from bad to impossible.

For my two Dads, both of whom we all miss.

Prologue

The cold was amazing and though not unexpected, it was becoming a problem. The sky was completely clear, not a cloud could be seen and the light from the moon shed an eerie glow across the desert.

There was no way they could move at all during the day, too easily seen; they had to move a night, if for nothing else, to keep warm.

Having landed 2 days earlier, they had already covered over 60 miles, lying up during the day in positions where they were concealed and pushing on at night.

In 3 days the team had to cover another 90 miles across the desert, carrying all of their equipment and personal kit with them. They were a black team, a covert operation, in a foreign country, acting illegally. If they were compromised, they would have to fight their way out, and if caught would be shot as spies. No one would admit to having sent them.

Coleman was the team leader and had undergone extensive desert training and training in deep covert operational tactics. The command was his first. The ten other men had been hand picked for their skill.

Ahead of them lay their target, a small abandoned town; no more than a few of the buildings remained intact; 150 miles deep into this foreign country, an enemy's country where somewhere in these few buildings were the hostages.

The operational orders given to the team were to land, make their way to the town without detection, rescue the hostages, and then escape the same way they had come in. If they were caught, they would be abandoned. They would not be helped.

Coleman and each of his team knew that they had to succeed and failure would be certain death. Each was willing to die if necessary; that is what they did.

The hostages were taken 7 days ago by people they believed to be the Israelis. There were three people, civilians, and not military personnel. Israel was now acting across foreign borders using their own black teams. Coleman's team was sent in retaliation.

The fight against terrorism, in the last 5 years, has been pushed home in the Middle East far harder by Israel than by any other country, including the USA. The continued failure of not only Israel, but the whole of the world, to stop terrorist attacks against the Jewish people had forced Israel to go on to the offensive, mimicking the USA and their war on terror.

The three hostages, or detainees, depending on your point of view, were people who could be forced to reveal information that perhaps Israel should not know. The only answer was to rescue them, or, if this was not possible, to kill them.

A small fishing boat had carried them to within 500 yards of the coastline, then drifted a further 400. Quietly they moved it on further towards the coast, and then just as quietly, ten men moved over the side. Using their backpacks or bergens as floats, they swam in to the shore.

They landed near a large dense shrub that had grown down from the shoreline above them. It was clearly visible as they approached the beach and provided the cover they needed.

The first man came ashore, hid his pack in the shadows and took a defensive position to protect his comrades as each one slowly came out of the sea. They moved up the beach and, in the dark of the shadow from the shrub, removed their weapons from the backpacks.

They all carried a large burgen. It containing the equipment they needed for this mission and nothing else, explosives, sleeping bags, food, ammunition and the radio. Each had an AK 47 assault rifle across their arms, a side arm holstered, and knives strapped to their thighs. Two of them carried large belt-fed machine guns. No insignia were on their uniforms; they were blackened with paint on the faces, they could have been soldiers from any country.

If the weapons had been seized, they could not be identified. All marks, serial numbers and other identification had been ground away.

Time was short, there was 150 miles of hard ground to cover and it had to be done within 5 days. As each man gathered his load, he said just 'ready' when he was ready to move off. The last man to leave the shadows of the shrub broke away a branch and used the foliage to brush the sand and remove the trace of the team landing.

From the beach they moved inland, boxing around the edges of a small fishing village, avoiding any contact. They made their way on a preset heading, following their every move with GPS positioning. Their plans for the next few days were hard and they had to move as quickly as possible to keep the appointment they had with the hostages.

Walking along a waddy, a dried-up riverbed, they stayed close to the northern wall. It was about 10 feet high and the shadow thrown by the side in the moonlight provided perfect cover. In single file with about 10 feet of space between them, close enough to hear each other, far enough apart to stop two men being hit by the same gun when, rather than if, they were fired upon.

Coleman was using a night sight to help see further along the waddy and into the darker areas ahead. This slowed them down a little as he would stop and crouch down carefully. As he crouched down, his hand went up and the rest of the team crouched too, each one defensive with his own arc of fire to look after.

Once clear, they would move on again at full march pace, they had to achieve the distance in the time, otherwise they would fail, stopping only to check their position on the map with GPS.

Their aim was to get within 10 miles of the target, hide their kit away and prepare for the assault on the town. The Israelis would be expecting an attack to release their hostages, and Coleman knew that he must get everything right. He had to think as they would think and plan his attack looking for their defences and weaknesses.

As the waddy flattened out into the desert, they became more obvious and began to move quicker, to get into shadow and away from the moonlight. It was freezing at night and they could not allow themselves to rest for long, when they did stop.

When first light started to appear, they searched for a place to lie up during the day. The desert was full of crags and caves, and large masses of rock, each providing cover for them, and shelter from the sun.

A small cave suited them well. Coleman did not have to organise his men. They each knew what to do, equally as well as he. Their kit was stowed in positions where they could get away quickly. One of them stood guard near the entrance whilst the others got their heads down and some sleep. This was changed four times during the day; each one would have their time as guard, looking after the others. As the light started to fade, they sat together and discussed the plans for the assault. The next days and nights were a repeat of the same: moving carefully, but quickly, each night and resting, hiding each day.

Now 40 miles away the small town lay at the eastern side of a large waddy. It was elevated from the riverbed by about 15 feet, almost on a ledge. Road access from the north was the only possible way into the town, and out, unless you crossed the riverbed.

The back of the town was up against a large, almost cliff-like, face rising up about 100 ft. It must have been a perfect defence from attack then; it had only one road to protect and the front across the dried riverbed.

When it was build over 400 years ago, it was a formidable position, the centre of the trade in opium into North Africa. The Israelis had stopped here with the hostages. They were waiting for the air searches to stop before making a run for the border.

Leaving no sign of having been in the cave, each took away everything they had brought. No one so much as pissed on the floor, it went in a bottle and they took it with them, brushing over the sand with broken branch again to hide any marks.

Moving out when the night was dark enough, they continued on the bearing towards the target. Tonight, they had to reach their forward operating point, ready to make their raid.

The night was less cold and the sky was obscured with clouds. These were far better conditions for moving quickly with less chance of being seen. Coleman again took the lead, and the others followed, quietly, deliberately placing each foot on the ground, making no sound.

After about 5 hours marching, suddenly Coleman froze and the line came to a stop. Each man crouched and remained completely still. For 15 minutes Coleman watched, using the night site. He could see a vehicle and four men up ahead, parked on high ground. They had a perfect view of the approach Coleman was making. For now the dark was hiding his team. To his left and right the walls of the waddy rose too steeply to allow them to box the position and get round and away from the threat.

They had to go forward or back. There was no time to waste, as he had to move the team forward. With a gesture of his arm he beckoned the second man forward and spoke in a whisper.

"We need to move forward onto their position and see who they are and what they are doing. If they are Israelis and we kill them, they will be missed."

Coleman knew that, if they were Israeli troops and did not return or meet a radio check time, the alarm would be raised and their mission would fail.

"Move forward with me and go to the right of the vehicle, I will go to the left. Do not move unless I move." He was as cool as the night itself.

Coleman and his number 2 shed their big backpacks, and very carefully laid them in the darker areas close to the waddy walls. They moved out on their bellies, moving like snakes in the dust. Slowly they edged towards the four men some 100 yards to their front.

The others took up covering positions overlapping their arcs of fire, checking behind and forward.

Each knew what had to be done, if they were Israeli troops, they would be forced to retrace their steps for at least 5 miles and then box around the position. If they were not troops, Coleman would do what he thought best under the circumstances.

It took over 20 minutes to crawl to the place where the four stood. They were leaning against a land cruiser looking towards the direction that the team were coming from. They wore no uniform, and did not act like, or seem to be, soldiers. They did not hear death approaching them.

Coleman gestured again, making a sign, drawing his finger across his throat. Together, they moved slowly forward again, moving round to the back of the land cruiser. Surprise was to be their greatest weapon. Splitting up, one at each end of the vehicle, they both pounced from nowhere taking two of the four by the neck and cutting their throats in one clean cut.

As they fell, blood pumping from their necks, the other two cried out. Before they could react, they too were dead, cut cleanly, lying in their own dark pool, next to the car. Hopefully it would be blamed on local tribal feuding and not be linked to any undercover operations.

Moving back to the others, they gathered their packs, their hands sticky with blood. They moved forward, passed the four dead men and on into the night. It did not bother anyone that they had just killed four people, it was their duty, and it was their belief.

The planning had allowed just 4 days to get from the drop-off point to the forward position 10 miles from the town. They had one further night and one day for recon. use, and then they had to attack. If successful, they had to move the hostages back to the drop-off point in 5 days.

The boat would return and wait for 4 hours. If they were not there, it would leave and they would be forgotten.

The GPS registered a point 10 miles from the target at about 3 am in the morning of the third night. This was 2 hours ahead of schedule.

He had to make use of the extra time and Coleman sent out four men, forward towards the town. His instructions were that they should get within sight of the town, find a position where they were concealed for the day and observe, take notes and then return after dark.

Each man went off in the direction of town and peeled away in their own directions to find their place to watch. They did not expect any sentries or guards this far out, but as they closed on the ruined town, they changed their methods, moving like animals, slowly, deliberately, making use of all the cover available.

For the next day they each lay in their hides, motionless, watching, counting the people, memorising positions, vehicles, guard points, and looking for the hostages. They had to know as much as possible, and remember it. What they reported back would affect the whole assault.

The remaining part of the team concealed themselves and prepared for the attack. Removing their packs and storing away unnecessary items, they fitted their weapons and ammunition on themselves and prepared to move out.This was the time for them to eat and drink; it could be some time before they were able to do either again. If they had to run, they would need all of the sustenance they could get.

One hour after dark the first of the recon. patrol returned. No one heard him approach; he appeared like a ghost from behind a rock. The others followed within the hour. Sitting in a tight circle, they shared the information with everyone.

The hostages were held in the largest building on the right of the church, or what remained of the church. Two men guarded them and they were changed every 4 hours. There were approx 20 men in the town including the guards. Two gun positions overlooked the road into the town, a further position looked down over the waddy. Each position had two men, another two men sleeping would eventually relieve them. That was 12 men.

Two guards, changed every 4 hours were seen guarding the hostages. Another four men. They had seen another three moving around the town at will, patrolling where they could, and the final man was the officer in charge.

The three hostages were in the building next to the church. It had one door to the cliff side, hidden from the sight of two of the gun positions.

The rest of night was devoted to setting up the attack. Four of the team left with small packs on their backs, moving off towards the town. They split into pairs, one pair heading to the road above the village, and the others moved towards the top of the cliff above the town.

They would lay charges during the night and feed the command wires back across the riverbed to their own lay-up points, and wait.

The charges were set to blow the road, blow the cliff top above the town, and cause panic.

"We attack just as the light comes, when it is difficult to see clearly, when they are tired, and sleepy, when most are off duty."

The night passed slowly and Coleman slowly felt the adrenalin rush starting within him. He would spend some time praying before he committed his men. Would he succeed? He had to, he would if he caught them off guard.

The two machine guns were set within 150 yards of the town, trained on the Israeli gun positions. Following the explosions, whilst they engaged the machine guns, the men that set the explosives would move forward and engage loose troops on the ground. Coleman and one other would go for the hostages.

For now, he waited; his team waited too, their guts tied into knots, each one prayed to his God. There was no need for any further orders; each knew his place in the attack.

As first light glinted above the far horizon, the stillness of the night was lost to the sound of two huge explosions, the first destroying the road to the north, removing their only exit, the second brought tons of rock from above, smashing into the old houses where some of the Israelis were asleep.

Instantly, the two hidden machine guns started firing, controlled blasts, aimed, and deadly. Moving the gun from stop to stop on its swivel, each stop marked the enemy gun position. Within minutes the Israeli positions fell silent.

Picking up the guns and moving forward, they engaged and killed the relief guards that were asleep, woken in a start and cut down as they tried foolishly to help their comrades.

Coleman moved on towards the church, and flattened against the wall of the next building. His back-up was behind him, protecting the opposite direction.

Slowly around the corner, they moved towards the main door, a big timber door, and placed a small charge against the two flat iron hinges. Seconds later it was gone, and both rolled into the building. The two guards were stunned by the blast that removed the door and disorientated. Coleman cut one down with a short three-round blast and the second died at the same time, shot by Coleman's second in command.

The hostages were in a bad state, beaten, frightened and crying.

"Get up and run, follow us, don't talk, don't stop, or we will kill you," he yelled, grabbing the only female by her arm and pushing her forward.

Five minutes later they were gone, back into the darkness of the night. Out of 20 Israelis, 12 were dead and three were wounded, out of the 10 of them, three were dead.

Coleman pushed the hostages forward without compassion. His orders were to get them out or kill them. He would kill them if they became a risk to his men or himself. They moved along the riverbed back to the rally point, chosen earlier for its natural cover. Once again they sank into the darkness, fell still and silent. They would rest. If the counting was correct, there will be no follow-up from the Israelis.

Coleman sat, peering across from the darkness into the town. He could see the remaining troops trying to help their fallen friends.

"I have done that, I have killed them." Coleman stared at his success.

"We need to move on, 10 minutes to clean up, then we go. If they can keep up, then shoot them."

They moved out of the rally point back into the waddy and started forward, moving away from the scene that was now the old town, and death combined. They were now seven in number, three went at the front and four at the rear. In-between walked the hostages, all very quiet, and walking for their lives.

In the distance a faint 'thump thump' could be heard; the unmistakeable signature of helicopter rotors. There were two, the beat from one was interfering with the other.

"Move, back into the waddy, get into cover, gunships! Somehow they have called for help."

Two helicopters circled in from the west and hovered over the town. Large searchlights scoured the remains of the buildings, finding the bodies of the dead Israelis. Slowly they moved out from the buildings and then along the waddy, moving towards their position.

They all instantly sank into the night pulling the hostages behind them, and hid.

"Bring the two big machine guns," Coleman snapped, "Now! They will not take us."

They set the gun up in a small clearing allowing sight upwards, and primed it ready to fire, The big searchlight found them and the gun responded firing just a few rounds up towards the aircraft, but the helicopter did not move away to protect itself, nor did it return any fire.

"Coleman," announced the PA System on one helicopter, "Hold your fire, Coleman. You have completed the mission, it is over, your exercise is over now."

"Exercise, what exercise?" He recognised the voice, but was unsure what was happening.

In the heat of a Bedouin tent at, midday Coleman sat with his commanders being debriefed. He did not believe what he had just heard.

"This was a test, Mr Coleman. They were not Israeli troops you have just killed, they were our own people, and they were training, just like you. It was them, or it was you. Kill or be killed. There is no room for sentiment in what we do.

Each man had been told to prepare to fight, you Mr Coleman were told to attack and rescue our friends. They were told that someone would try to rescue our prisoners, and they must defend them.

17

What better way of finding the best out of the people we train, someone would lose, tonight it was them. We needed to know if you were really one of us, and ready to die for what you believe in; ready to kill without question."

"I was! – I was ready, I had killed for them." He thought.

1. The Stranger

It was the third time that this stupid man had come into the pub, and he was acting just as weirdly this time as the last.

"I like Guinness and I like Stella," he announced to Jimmy behind the bar.

"What shall I have tonight?"

"Have what you like, mate," replied Jimmy, who suffered fools badly. "So? What do you want?"

"OK, I'll have a Guinness first."

The stranger had a slight clip in his voice, as though he was a foreigner, but it was only just noticeable.

Jimmy was on his guard following this person's last visit and the locals sitting at the bar were also watching this guy very closely.

He was about 6 ft tall, a little plump, had his dark hair combed forward and was wearing a pair of suit trousers and nice shirt with a fleece cardigan over the top.

He seemed a bit of a retard, not sure what he wanted, and talked to himself most of the time.

About 6 weeks previously, the same man, now christened 'Pervy' by the lads in the bar, had arrived at the pub around 8.30. He came in carrying a large sports holdall, and was holding it close to himself. People noticed him immediately, and became curious, without being obvious.

He stood at the bar at the same place he was standing now. He would order a drink, and quietly stand there and drink it, holdall in his left hand and drink in his right. If someone walked by, or the bar staff came closer, he would always try to start a conversation with them.

After the first three pints, he became a little louder, more confident and less attached to his holdall; eventually laying it on the floor and moving over to the pool table. He then started a game of pool against himself.

The game was completely normal; he actually played against himself, in every sense of the word, taking turns with his imaginary friend sticking rigidly to the rules.

This began to really fascinate everyone. All of us mess around sometimes, and knock a few balls back and forth, but to play, against yourself, and properly, was really weird.

Because of the size of his stomach, Pervy found it a little difficult to lean over the table, and take the lower, or longer, shots during the game. As he tried to lean, it was obviously annoying him, or bothering him that it was a little difficult.

"Can you tell me if the table is regulation height?" Pervy asked.

"I've no idea, mate," replied Jimmy, " Is there a regulation height for the table?"

"Oh yes, and I think this is too low, It is difficult to reach some of the shots."

The game continued; Pervy and his imaginary friend taking turns at the cue ball, until, half-way through the game, he informed everyone, to their great amusement, that he was playing to the Romanian rules, and he was a pool expert.

The table was too low and was affecting the game he was playing. By this time the first 4 pints must have been hitting him, more so as he was drinking Stella.

The Abbot was a typical village pub, one of two in the village of Abbotsley. It was situated right next to the church, separated only by the graveyard. The original part of the building, now the main bar and cellar, dates back almost as far as the church itself. It was rumoured that it may have formed part of the main sleeping quarters of an old monastic establishment. Not quite a full blown monastery, but had obviously had some importance in the area at the time.

The Abbot was quite a large pub and had recently been divided by the installation of a removable wall. Since Jimmy had got his entertainments licence, the wall had been installed to provide some defence against the bands and discos that became more and more frequent.

By removing five screws, the partition wall could be moved easily, door as well, creating a much larger area. In the event of a function being booked for a lot of people, Jimmy could take down the wall and increase his usable area.

It boasted oak beams, fireplaces and an old wooden bar, but the rooms were modern, made to look old with plenty of space. The original building, made from yellow sandstone matching the church, was almost indistinguishable now, with the various extensions and improvements added over the many years.

The outside of the pub had been plastered at some time in the past and was now the traditional white painted wall and black beams that attracts so many people to a country village in the summer.

By far the best feature of the pub was its commanding position over the village. Although Abbotsley was in Cambridgeshire, almost on the edge of the fens, and should be flat, there was a hill more or less in the middle of the village, rising about 100 feet in 100 yards and falling away the same to the east, west and north, but more slowly to the south, directly behind the building.

The Abbot, perched at the top of the hill had one of the best views available to any property around the area. A clear view could be had for almost 270 degrees, looking out from the front and side windows.

About 1 mile away across from the front of the pub the land rose again about the same amount, a small gentle ridge. In fact it was only 30 years ago that Anglian Water wanted to flood the small valley and create another reservoir. The area was short-listed and a massive local fight began to save the village.

Had it gone ahead the pub now would be on a small peninsula surrounded on 3 sides by water, and probably one of the best-situated alehouses in the country.

The separation of the bar area by the removable wall allowed the restaurant and drinking area to be kept more individual. The bar had the usual huge TV, and it was huge. There was a pool table, and a couple of slot machines in the corner. Seating was comfortable but basic, easy to maintain, or clean up.

In contrast, the restaurant area, whilst still keeping a small part of the bar just behind the wall, has the leather chesterfields, nicer décor, and the tables for meals set out nicely throughout the room, a totally more relaxing atmosphere.

At the same time as the wall was installed, pine shutters were hung on the insides of the windows. These were for decoration mainly, but would help keep out the cold in the winter. The old building did not boast any insulation and could get cold easily.

Jimmy was a trained London chef and had moved to this area with his parents and bought the Abbot. He had tried many different ways of selling food to the local area. The restaurant was very good, a limited menu, but what you could got was excellent. He did a very good fish and chip supper with mushy peas for £5.00 and it included a pint.

The full menu was also available to take away. In fact, Jimmy would also deliver it to anywhere within a 5-mile radius. This service proved very popular and Jimmy was building a good reputation and business supplying the residents of Cambourne, the new township built to serve the expanding Cambridge business parks.

It seemed, since the wall went up, the locals never went in the restaurant unless they were eating. They started to congregate against this new wall, being able to watch everything else that went on in the pub. Pretty typical behaviour for locals in their pub.

Pervy, having announced to the world that he was now a Romanian pool expert went back to his game against himself, having reloaded his Stella glass.

Tom, a local from the village was in the bar with his wife Lynn and all of his children. This was really unusual for Tom, as William was away at university most of the time. The younger two would only come with them sometimes, as the demands of school and homework took precedence. This night, Wednesday, was mid-way through half term and they were allowed.

As with many of the villagers, one night each week was a ritual visit to the pub for a few beers and a chat with everyone, catching up on life around the area. Tom and his wife always came on a Wednesday.

Sitting patiently waiting for the pool table to become clear, Anthony and Jane were starting to really crack up laughing at the antics Pervy was now up to. William was watching from near the bar and had already pointed out the stranger's behaviour. Realising he had an audience, he began to play to them. He was useless at pool, even against himself. But with the Romanian rules he was playing, he claimed every mistake was not a mistake just a demand of the game.

Jimmy's attitude to the children was very good. He had no objections to them being in the pub. He would not allow them to drink any alcohol, but realised they were also part of the community, and his future customers. William was obviously over 18, Anthony was almost 17 and Jane was 14, so they were not a problem.

The guessing had started as to where Pervy was from: escaped from a local home for the bewildered, let out for half term from a secure hospital? By this time the whole pub was fascinated.

His attention was also now turning to the ladies in the pub and he was openly making remarks about the women and girls in the bar. The remarks were more banter, and the type of comments made between lads after a few drinks. To make them openly and directed at the ladies, was a concern.

By now, at about 9.30, the bar had the normal 15–20 folk for a Wednesday, all transfixed on Pervy.

Tom decided to offer to play against him, which he accepted readily, provided Tom paid the 50p needed. It was quite sad to see him having to play alone, and only neighbourly to offer to play with him.

It was not a game that Tom played very often, but he did play with the children and some of the other locals, just for fun. Unlike some pubs, pool was a pastime and had not yet become a serious game.

Pervy elected to break and failed to pot anything with his opening shot. Tom managed to claim a colour with his first shot. Under the normal rules, you then keep the colour you first pot.

The conversation from Pervy was very rude and his comments about the ladies in the bar became more of an embarrassment than distasteful. Bending over to take his shot, near to Jane, Pervy said,

"Just scratch my bollocks will you whilst I am bending over."

Jimmy had overheard what was said and he knew Tom was not happy. Pervy had no idea that Jane was his daughter, but anyone would object to a comment like that.

"You want to throw him out Tom, go ahead," said Jimmy.

Potting one of the colours, one of Tom's balls, Pervy claimed the pot. He was now suddenly 'colours' leaving Tom with the 'stripes' and had changed over mid-game. Obviously another rule from Romania.

The game continued in much the same way. Tom. along with most others, just hoped this fool of a man might move on when the game was over.

After 4 pints, eventually Pervy took himself off to the loo, leaving his holdall open, and lying on the floor next to the pool table. This again was strange, he took the cue into the toilet with him, but left the bag. After being so protective of it, it was now unimportant.

Kids being kids, Anthony and Jane decided it would be a giggle to take a look in the bag and together sneaked a little closer to open the bag, Anthony or 'Ant' as his mates called him keeping one eye on the toilet door to make sure Pervy did not come back too soon.

"Oh my God!" screams Ant, whilst he and Jane moved very quickly back into the fold of the locals, still leaning on the partition.

"There's a big knife in his bag," Ant tells his Dad, fighting his breath, obviously a little panicked.

"Did you see it Jane?" asks Tom.

"There is something in the bag long and silver, it looks like a knife," blurted Jane in less than 2 seconds.

Intrigue had now turned to concern, and Tom quietly spoke with Jimmy, who was in the kitchen at the back of the pub, dealing with some meal orders.

"Seems our friend may have a knife in his bag, and a big one at that."

"Oh Shit! Get the kids away from him and see if Paul will take a look."

Paul lived almost opposite Tom. Built like a brick house and had the temperament of mouse. He stood about 6'4" and must have weighed in at 22 stone. During the spring he had lost over 3 stone for charity, but still was a big man. not fat by any means, just big and powerful.

Without any hesitation Paul just picked up the holdall and took a look inside. The *Financial Times*, today's date and an umbrella with a silver point and shaft. No knife, the kids had seen the brolly and thought it was a knife. Nothing else at all.

The kids were perhaps expecting to find something sinister, and Jane did not see it too clearly. Considering the contents were harmless and there was very little in it, why was he so possessive of the bag?

After a great deal of relief and laughing at the wall, Pervy emerged back into the main area, and back to the pool table.

The table was more or less in the middle of the main pub area, perhaps 20 feet from the locals' wall, and 12 feet from the bar. The fireplace sometimes obstructed a shot, as there was not too much room between it and the table. A window to the break end of the table gave a glorious view over the village and surrounding farmland.

To the right side of the window, which was set into a small alcove, was a built-in seat able to take two people and a small table.

At the pool table you could see anyone else in the pub, and when unoccupied it sometimes became another leaning area for people to congregate.

Pervy was back into his stride, now hitting stripes again, a second change of colour. Eventually, even with Romanian rules, Tom won.

Gathering up his holdall, Pervy said he was going, and took off. Just like that, he was gone, everyone watching out of the windows where he went.

What bothered Jimmy most is that he had by now sunk 4 pints of Stella and had just got into his car and driven off.

A white Citroën AX on an R plate, nice car in nice condition. A typical rep's car, but Pervy gave no indication of being a rep or salesman. It would have been more understandable a local ambulance coming to pick him up, not him driving himself away, and pissed.

Jimmy is very strict over the problem of drink and driving, resorting many times to actually driving his customers home; well, the more local ones. After a discussion with the local police station, we all settled down to discuss the strange visitor.

☼☼☼

So this was the third time Pervy had made a visit to the pub, and tonight he was drinking Guinness.

"What's up with Stella tonight?" asked Jimmy, knowing that he had a difficulty making his mind up.

"Nothing, but Guinness reminds me of the desert at night, cold and black," came the reply. "My name is Derek," he suddenly proudly claimed, "and I'm a doctor."

"Really!!" Daft Derek seems to fit well, Jimmy thought, moving down the bar to tell the lads.

It was Thursday night and Tom with Lynn came into the pub, stopping to review Daft Derek as he was now known, on the way. Tom had been working late on the Wednesday and so not wishing to miss the ritual, they came up to the pub on Thursday.

25

Derek's holdall was back, and sticking to him like glue again. The pool table was empty and Derek had no interest.

"Perhaps Doctors don't play pool," Paul said. "What was all of that shit about the desert?"

"No idea, mate, beats me, he's off his trolley."

He was drinking pretty fast again and had consumed about 5 pints of Guinness before he made motions to leave. His actions were still strange tonight but in a different way, not so bold and loud. He did spend a while discussing something with himself and had also developed a flick, moving his head to the left, just like a girl flicking her hair from her face.

"Just going to the toilet, then I am leaving," Derek informed us.

"Tom, you got your camera in the car?" John enquired. "Yes".

"Well go get it and let's get a picture of this prat in case the police need it sometime."

John was also very tall, again about 6'4"; his job involved drilling holes in buildings to allow cable and pipe installations. He spent most weekends doing gardening jobs and small building jobs around the village. A popular person in the pub and village.

He did not have the bulk of Paul, but not many would argue with him.

Tom shot out to his car, having driven the 400 yards to the pub, and grabbed his digital camera. The problem he had was that from where he was sitting, it would have been obvious to Daft Derek that he was having his picture taken.

"John, make like you're messing around taking a picture of yourself, and shoot the camera over your shoulder. You should get him full in the middle," Tom said passing the camera to John.

Tom went into the restaurant area to look through the window and get the number of the car Daft Derek was driving.

There was room for about three cars to park directly at the front of the pub, and only just room for another car to pass. At the side of the road, the grass immediately started to fall away down the hill. About half-way down the hill, or the village green as it was know was a tall oak tree about 30–40 feet high.

Why they called this bit the village green was a mystery. The slope was very steep, but it was central to the village and, believe it or not, the annual fete was held on the green. All village events on this piece of grass were fun to attend.

Derek had parked his Citroën here tonight instead of parking in the normal car park between the pub and the graveyard.

The picture was bad and unusable but they did get the number plate. Then, after his, what now seemed to be regulation, four pints, Derek took his leave. He left the village in the opposite direction from last time.

There were only three ways in and out of the village. The main B1046; from St Neots east to west. Both of these routes are totally visible from the pub for about 1 mile in each direction. There was a small unclassified road from the village green to the south, passing over the top of Tetworth hills. Although some of this road was visible, not all of it could be seen as clearly after 50 ft.

Jimmy again informed the local police, and passed on the information about the car.

The second visit had been more normal. Derek had come into the pub with a friend, a foreign-looking man. They sat and ate a meal in the restaurant area, before moving through to drink his Stella at the bar.

His strangeness was not so obvious this night, perhaps as he was able to talk with his companion. On several occasions he was heard to be talking another language, just what language was unknown.

The friend was not British from the look of him; very dark hair, heavy shadow on his face. He had trouble with the language and Derek had spoken in what was obviously his friend's tongue.

The holdall was with him again, and kept very close. They both left earlier this time, and drove away in separate cars in different directions.

Derek had now become a familiar site in the pub, and a talking point for everyone. Nobody knew exactly who or what he was, other than that he acted very strangely. His mannerisms and his bag had become accepted. At the time everyone believed he was a bit 'one short', but in fact to do what he was doing was quite clever, and we all missed it.

2. Abbotsley

Abbotsley is a small village, sitting to the east of St Neots and midway between St Neots and Great Gransden. The village boasts only 450 residents and has a very sought after reputation with the local estate agents. With very little land available for building, property values have rocketed in the last few years.

The B1046 passes straight through the village from west to east. Apart from the bends in the middle of the village, this is a long straight road. It has been the focus of many campaigns to have the speed limit reduced. Boy racers seemed to believe that it is acceptable to roar through the village at crazy speeds. In fact, some of the residents also seem to be arrogant enough to disregard the speed limit.

From the village, travelling west for about 1 mile, there are sets of double bends, which, to the satisfaction of the residents, eventually claim most of the idiots that cannot control their speed. It is a weekly event for those who have land rovers to pull some smashed up hot rod out of the ditch.

In the opposite direction the road is equally as straight, and apart from a minor humped bridge, ends at a T-junction almost exactly 1 mile from the village.

The local authorities are deaf to the problem, using their indicator for justifying speed restriction measures; the village would have to have someone killed. This may seem totally bizarre, but it is actually true. The Cambridgeshire County Council along with many other authorities in the country measure the road safety problems in the community by the number of deaths or serious accidents.

Unless some poor unfortunate child is actually killed in the road, in the village, the council will not act. Their opinion is that someone has already been killed or seriously hurt elsewhere, and their attention is needed more at this location.

Someone was knocked down, some time ago, as they tried to cross the road. It could be that they did not look properly, but we should be able to expect some form of respect from motorists that pass through.

When the bypass was built, taking the busy traffic on what was the A45 and is now the A428 around St Neots, the relief to the town was amazing. The long queues passing through the town centre were gone, and traffic could easily pass to the south of the town and on towards Cambridge. The road was long overdue and is now a very busy link from the M11 to the A1.

To create the bypass the road had to pass under the main north–south railway from Edinburgh to London. In the past the famous Flying Scotsman would speed along this stretch of line. Nowadays it is a more sedate route for the town's many commuters.

The bridge that was created was not built correctly; it was not high enough. This presented the local authorities with a major problem of the routing of high vehicles through the south of the county.

To solve the problem, they defined a high vehicle route through the heart of Abbotsley. Not only does this route pass through the outskirts of St Neots, having to negotiate a supermarket, a senior school and the residential area of Eynesbury, but it also passes directly through the village.

This entire route has to have a minimum height clearance, and no obstacles in the road, such as traffic calming. Hence the people of Eynesbury and Abbotsley realise that there is no way they could expect any form of traffic-calming on our roads. More seriously, it prevents any traffic-calming in the road past the school: local planning at its very best.

From the main road through Abbotsley there is a minor road heading to the south along the west side of the Abbot pub. This road can be seen well from the pub for about 500 yards then disappears up a small hill and onwards south towards Gamlingay.

From the vantage point of the pub, elevated in the middle of the village you can clearly see to the east and west for about 1 mile, and to the south for about 500 yards. From the pub looking north there are only houses and fields.

The Abbot had changed hands several times in the past 10 years. It even stood empty for a year.

Previous owners had tried hard and failed to build the level of custom they needed to maintain a living. Jimmy, who took over the pub after it had stood empty for a while, has spent a great deal of time developing the local trade and has managed to pull it off.

The support he has from locals has developed over the few years he has been in the pub to what it is now.

Jimmy applied for, and got, an entertainments licence, allowing him to provide customers with a venue for their parties and family gatherings. It also allowed him to join the growing list of pubs that have live bands playing on a weekly basis. Some of the bands attract a large following of fans, and this is what Jimmy was interested in: the drinking ability of the fans.

Tom had beaten Daft Derek but he was useless at pool. He was a useful person on a computer. Tom worked for himself importing timber for furniture into the UK from Scandinavia. Although this formed the major part of his business and income, Tom had developed some other interests in the IT side and was involved in providing internet access and support.

His office was actually half of the garage at home. He bought the house from a local builder who had built it for his own family. Just before completion one of the farms nearby became available and the builder moved into the farm. The house had stood empty for 2 years before Tom agreed a deal to buy it.

There was a fair amount of finishing work to be done, and at the same time as this was completed the garage was divided into two, and made into an office.

At any time there are always at least three computers running in the office. Tom was a fanatic, providing website building services to business, access to the internet for home and business uses, such as video conferencing or other graphic uses.

One of the things that Tom had developed further was the use of digital music on a computer. He built a machine that is capable of holding the equivalent of thousands of CD records, over 60,000 individual tracks, and playing them back like a juke box.

By attaching this to a huge amplifier and lighting system, Tom had built his own disco unit that could work without a single CD. Any track could be found and played within seconds, and overcame the problem DJs have when their customers cannot remember the full name of the record.

The technology was amazing. If a CD was put into the computer it would automatically dial up onto the internet, establish which CD it was, then write the tracks, including the full track names, onto the computer. In less than 10 minutes a CD could be added to the library, by only hitting one key on the keyboard.

Paul had been a DJ years ago and was interested in the system that Tom had developed. Together, they covered most of the disco requirement for the pub, and local schools. Slowly they were taking more work on, and it was developing into quite a nice sideline for the pair.

Paul's wife, Beryl, was almost forty and Paul wanted a surprise party for her. Beryl was the life of any party or gathering, particularly when in the pub. To date, she has never refused a dare, much to the embarrassment of many local men.

The big problem was making sure she did not find out, but on her birthday she had to work, which gave everyone the day to get the pub ready, the disco set up, and the new wall taken down.

Jimmy was going to open the pub at 11.30 and work could then start on the party to be finished before Beryl came home at 3.30.

The small yellow van had been parked on the top of the village green for about an hour. No one had yet got out, but from a distance you could see that there were four men sitting in the van. One had a thermos flask and was distributing coffee to his mates. On the dashboard, just below the windscreen was a copy of the *Daily Star*, folded, exposing one of the naked girls for all to see.

It was unusual to see any form of maintenance being carried out in the village by the local council. The Parish Council had been forced to fund most of the work that had been completed recently.

They had had the village pond tidied up, some of the ditches had been cleaned out, and some work was done to the village green. No funds were available to improve the children's play area, so the Parish Council had started to organise fund raising events, to meet the cost.

Once a year during July, the village held its feast week, a time when for one week everyone would come together for various social events. These ranged from throwing the welly on sports day, to inter-pub cricket, a kids' disco, the hog roast and more; all designed to have the village people participating together.

A different event would take place each night, culminating on Saturday when the main evening event of the Hog Roast took place. A good hundred people would turn out and try their hand at square dancing in the car park of the eight bells pub.

The biggest attraction of the week, and one of the most famous, was the scarecrows. Each house was invited to build a scarecrow and display it at the front of their house. This was now a huge thing for the village and was featured on the TV every year. There was not any particular theme for the scarecrows to follow; it was down to individual choice. From Elvis to the seven dwarfs had been recreated.

People would come from miles away for an afternoon wandering the village looking at the creations. It proved a good week for the pubs in the village, but the main attraction of the scarecrows did little to raise any money, whether for charity or for the needs of the village.

The van was marked Huntingdonshire District Council on the side of each front door: a completely innocent sight and quite normal of what you would expect of such contractors.

Eventually the men left the van and continued, or even started their work. They split into two pairs and set off in opposite directions along the top of the green. The first pair moved round and towards the road leading south to Gamlingay. After about 200 yards they stopped and examined the ground around a fire hydrant, situated just to the side of the road near to a small corner of boundary wall. It was mostly out of view, but in fact had clear sight across the road.

One of the two started to pretend to pick up litter from the grass area and stuff it into a black sack. The sacked looked half full, but had been brought with them already filled.

Whilst he was busy doing this, the second man crouched to examine the hydrant a little closer. He dug into the pocket of his fluorescent green jacket and removed something, then returned to his crouching position.

The small device, the size of a matchbox, was placed at the foot of the small squat concrete hydrant sign. He held it in position with some gaffa tape then pushed mud around it to hide it from view. Once he had satisfied himself that it was located well, he made sure that the clear glass part of the device was free from mud.

Inside the small package was the electronic guts of an infra-red sensor, the exact same device fitted to the floodlights we all buy in Homebase for the garden. Removed from the familiar semi round housing, the actual electronics are very small. Taped to the back of this was a small radio transmitter. This had been taken from one of the tiny remote control cars available now in any toy or gadget store. This was the transmitter part held in your hand to make the car move. When linked to a small battery, the device became active and would send a signal every time the sensor was tripped.

It was now active and consumed very little current. Without having to change the battery it would last for at least 10 days. Anyone or anything that passed this point would trip the device, and it would then transmit a command signal, but to where?

The two pairs of men continued around the green, placing similar devices at strategic points. Concealing their activities by appearing to collect litter, they were for any one who cared to watch, just council workers.

For over 2 hours they worked collecting the rubbish, and in fact did a good job, whilst concealing the true reason for their activities. When finished, three of them returned to the van, whilst the fourth walked to the far right of the green, passed the first sensor and waited.

The driver flashed his lights, upon which signal the fourth man started to walk. He walked past each sensor in turn, whilst in the van the signal was checked and rechecked. They all worked. Except for one.

It was simple enough to replace, and within minutes, the same procedure having been repeated, they were gone. Their job was over, or this part of it.

3. BBR

During the period when London had housing problems, many towns within 50 miles of the City had to expand and make room to accommodate the 'London Overspill'. Some towns and cities further afield, such as Cardiff, were also obliged to offer housing to London families. Huntingdon, in Cambridgeshire, one such town built the Oxmoor housing estate on the east side of the town.

It was a mixture of normal terraced houses, townhouses and small blocks of flats. Facilities for old people were built and a large new industrial estate proposed. In the plans for the housing estate, shops, pubs and other various community facilities were included, along with infant, junior and senior schools. The town had a new hospital started in Hinchinbrooke Park.

It was an opportunity for local councils to take advantage of extra Government cash and improve the town for everyone, including the new London families.

Pedestrian footways were built, keeping the people and traffic as separate as possible. From the plans you would believe that it would be a model housing estate and a reasonable place to encourage Londoners to move to.

Perhaps at the start it was, but over the years the buildings deteriorated, the neighbourhoods became more like battlegrounds as the kids fought running battles in gangs. Graffiti became commonplace and the estate became a sore on the side of what is a pretty town.

Many initiatives were started to improve the estate, most failed. All had some effect, however, and towards the end of 1999 the overall impression on the estate was improving. The hopes and plans of the community for the new millennium were high.

Housing a single mum and child is one of the priorities of the housing agency, but they mostly get allocated flats or small houses on Oxmoor. This estate was the bulk of the local council's housing stock. It was also the area with the highest turnover of property. During the Thatcher years when everyone was encouraged to buy their council house, very few who lived in Oxmoor took up the offer.

Carol was 35, small, dark haired and rather plain looking. She lived with her son, Sammy, in a two-bedroom flat, which, luckily for her, was on the ground floor of a block containing another 29 similar flats.

She was 30 when she fell pregnant with Sammy, her boyfriend Gary had only managed to stay for 3 months after finding out and then left her to it. Gary was of mixed race, partly middle Eastern and partly British. He was a British subject and held a UK passport, but his ambitions were to leave the UK and move back to one of the Arab countries. As far as Carol was aware, this is where he had gone to escape her pregnancy.

Sammy too had dark colouring, a very striking little lad with jet-black hair. During the time that they were together, Carol was introduced to, and had become very close to, many of Gary's friends and his Arab community. They accepted her openly in their own fold, far more quickly than any white community would accept Gary.

There were many people from the Middle East regions now living in the area. They had a close community and regularly met, using the local halls and rooms available on the estate. Not everyone was an Arab, but the community had grown from a nucleus of Arab people encouraging and accepting anyone into their lives.

She had no money to speak of, but did work nearby at Brampton Bio Research Ltd on a part time basis. Sammy prevented her working full time, but the company did provided crèche facilities. This was unusual, but they found employees hard to keep and did everything to encourage them.

Carol was able to work 4 days a week, including Saturdays. She did not mind weekend working as the other days off made up for it.

Brampton Bio Research lay slightly to the west of Huntingdon, at the west side of the A1 trunk road and is one of the most controversial companies operating in the county.

It is a Contract Research Organisation and had been operating since the early 1950s. Initially working on veterinary and biochemical research, its services to industry expanded over the years to include work on pharmaceuticals, agricultural chemicals and other consumer products and chemicals.

It quickly established a reputation as a world leader in its field. It also recently became the target for the campaign against animal testing. In the last 4 years the company has been the subject of continuous protest, both peaceful and very violent.

As legislation in the 1960s had an increasing impact on Industry, and the authorities became more aware of the potential harm of various drugs or chemicals to public health, BBR grew steadily stronger and moved to the forefront of research It now employed over 1200 staff, 800 of who have scientific qualifications including at least 150 Ph.D.s.

BBR was a good solid company operating well within the law and supporting the local community with many jobs. Although some of the work it carries out is perhaps questionable, it was within the law and therefore legal; they had a right to continue it.

The campaign against animal testing was very strong and had made a target of BBR. Simple demonstrations outside the main gates of the complex were enough to start with, but soon became insignificant. The response was to step up the demonstrations with more inconvenience to the company and their employees.

The protestors would chain themselves to vehicles, preventing their removal, and block the entrance; chain themselves to huge blocks of concrete. All non-violent protest and whereas it was a difficulty to BBR, they suffered it in silence.

A constant group of people from all walks of life kept a presence at the gate, shouting obscenities at the employees as they walked past, or drove past in their cars.

The protest turned slowly into a hate campaign against the company. Resorting to much more sinister methods, the protestors found and targeted employees at home, somehow tracing car number plates. The gatherings outside the complex became bigger and more violent, stoning cars and buses on the way past their lines into the main gate.

Time-hardened people, with no other purpose than to cause damage and physical violence, had now replaced the genuine caring 'normal' protestor. They were more interested in the buzz of the fight than the real reasons for the original protest.

The local police did all they could, but their own resources were stretched to the limit. They had to fund the policing of BBR from the normal budget as Government refused extra cash. It was not possible to ask BBR to help with the costs as the problem took place on the public roads.

BBR responded by turning their facility into a fortress in the middle of Cambridgeshire. What was open house to schools, colleges and young farmers clubs was now closed and ringed with hi-tech cameras, razor wire, and state-of-the-art defence against the animal rights campaigners.

Police presence was now full-time, the layout of the road was altered, and more and more of the staff took to using the company bus provided for their protection.

No one would agree that to cause suffering to an animal could be justified just to produce a new face cream, or make-up product. The rapid success of the Body Shop proved this. The argument against animal testing is very strong and supported by most humane people. It could be argued that testing of some kind to prove a new drug, badly needed to fight disease, is justified.

It is only an argument and not a war. The campaign against BBR was out of hand, being driven by a few people who thrived on trouble and violence. Employees had their homes attacked, their cars fire bombed, and the company chairman was badly beaten one night by animal rights supporters, so called caring people interested in the well-being of animals. They acted like animals themselves, resorting to the rule of the jungle.

They protested to, and lobbied, the company's bankers, holding meetings and protests outside their branches all over the country. Not wishing to be involved or seen to support the work carried out at BBR, the banks pulled out and it seemed as though BBR was going to fail, the protestors would win.

With such an emotive issue, no other bank wanted to offer banking facilities. As with all such protests, you only hear about the bad things going on within the labs. You never get to hear much about the success they have.

How many of the protestors would accept medication, developed using animal testing, for themselves or their children if it was a choice between life and death. The answer is simple, all of them. 'It is only bad if I do not need it.'

Although Gary had gone long ago, Carol continued her friendships and involvement with the group of Arabs on Oxmoor. They held regular meetings, socialised and worshipped together. Carol had wished to become a convert to the faith and even studied the Koran.

It was at one of these meetings that Carol first was introduced to Dr Michael Coleman. He was white and British but, like her, had friends who were Arabic and enjoyed their company.

He was about 42 years old, a little plump, and seemed a little simple. They struck up a friendship that blossomed into more over the next 3 months.

Michael Coleman had told Carol that he had a Ph.D. in biochemistry, obtained at Cambridge in the late1970s. He worked on behalf of many big companies and developed a keen interest in virus manipulation. His work into this subject became of interest to HM Government and he was recruited to work at an MoD Laboratory near Salisbury.

Having developed an interest in things Arabic, Coleman was a risk to the MoD and they terminated his contract. They also made sure he was unable to work in the same field of research at any other EU lab.

In early 2003 Coleman had met up with Carol at the Oxmoor community hall. He was attending an evening where a visitor from Lebanon was talking about the difficulties of the Arab–Israeli conflict. By the end of the evening he and Carol were talking as though they were old friends.

"Why do the Arab people fascinate you so Carol?" Coleman asks quietly. "It is strange to see such a young person involved in such a way with the small Arab community."

"It is because of Sammy," Carols replied, "Sammy's dad was half Arab, his name was Gary. He brought me here to meet people, and to have fun sometimes. He's gone now; he left when he knew I was pregnant. Did not want the responsibility."

"That is unusual for an Arab person. Normally they keep family and children very dear and close to them, Coleman remarked.

"I know, Gary was strange, he had been born in England, in Huntingdon, he lived his life here, and had many friends. But, inside he had some need to visit the Middle East and learn more of his frefathers, and their conflict. He could get so angry about this problem."

A week later he met her at a local Italian restaurant, a rare treat for her. All of her money went on the rent and paying bills, trapped by the stupid rules of income support, she earns £300 per year more than the limit and as a result lost over £2000 of support.

A babysitter, one of the Arab girls, was looking after Sammy. She loved little Sammy as though he was her own, and Carol was happy to leave him.

This was the first of many evenings together and the couple grew closer with every minute they spent together. Coleman started to watch her and learn her routine each day and week. He got to know when she was working, and when she was at home. From their conversations it was obvious that she worked within the secret part of BBR, but Coleman knew this already. Many cold days and nights on the road protesting gave him the opportunity to find out which girls worked where.

The George Hotel in George Street, Huntingdon; formerly the home of Oliver Cromwell's grandfather, was now a very pleasant hotel that once a year staged a Shakespeare play in the open courtyard. This was an event that attracted people from all over the UK, and Coleman had promised to take Carol.

Macbeth was a little above Carol, but she enjoyed the evening and the meal they both shared afterwards in the Hotel's restaurant.

Later Coleman took Carol home and came in, when asked, for coffee.

"That was a lovely evening Michael, thank you," she said, "Coffee?"

"Yes please, black and no sugar, and very strong". Typical Arabic. "Do you ever wish for better things in life Carol, wouldn't you like to have more money, and a nicer place for Sammy to live?"

"Of course I would, anyone would, but how can I pull myself out of this situation?"

Coleman walked into the kitchenette area and took hold of Carol around her waist, gently, and gathered her up into his arms, from behind. She sensed the warmth of the gesture and snuggled into him.

"That's nice, it has been a while since anyone wanted to cuddle me!" as if she felt she was unworthy.

"Everyone deserves a little love in their lives Carol, so why not you, maybe I can help you find a way out."

Turning her round and bending to kiss her on the forehead. Carol moved back slightly and his kiss met her mouth.

Although almost 10 years her senior, Carol and he had grown close, and she had thought of this moment. She had no one in her life, except Sammy, and this was a welcome change.

Carol returned his advances with interest and moved over to the old worn sofa in the middle of the room. Sitting down on the edge, she removed her blouse, turned off the light, and let herself, for once, do something she wanted to.

The next morning she found Coleman asleep next to her on the floor. The cushions from the sofa had been moved during the passions of the previous night. They both fell asleep in a tangle of legs and arms; it was a warm night and the fact they had no covers did not matter.

"Carol," Coleman said sleepily. "If I asked, would you do something for me?"

"I think so, it depends what it was."

Carol was thinking about continuing where they had left off last night. Coleman was serious, and sat up to look at her.

"I need you to help me get something, and you would be paid very well for helping me. You and Sammy could move out and have money for the good things."

"What is there I can do to help you?"

BBR was now in crisis as the banks refused to offer any account facilities, scared of attracting the protestors and bad publicity. Not one would help. The loans had been called in and it seemed as though BBR was about to call in the receivers.

At the last moment the Government granted them a bank account and facilities at the Bank of England, underwritten by the Government. The Company's activities were too important to allow it to die; they were also of interest to the MoD.

Four weeks after the deal was done, the Chairman of BBR was informed that, in return for the favour, his company would be expected to take on a MoD contract, for which it would be paid above the going rate. It was a highly classified contract.

After the problems on September 11th 2001 in New York, the anthrax scare in the USA caused widespread panic. Not just from the public who were ill informed, but at higher levels. HM Government saw this and put into action a plan to help head off such a problem in the UK.

They needed a vaccine, or anti-serum or anything that could deal with anthrax infection, and to find this they had employed BBR, secretly.

A separate block, used in the past to house rats during experimentation, was converted for the MoD work. Being more than 30 ft underground and airtight, the basement lab was the best option. It already had systems installed for air extraction and could be run at negative pressure.

The room is kept at a lower pressure than normal atmosphere, making sure any leak comes in, rather than out.

Using a bank of 300 lab rats, each one was to be infected with anthrax. Not basic anthrax but a new weapons grade of the virus. This had been developed to overcome the difficulties of dispersion. You need a certain amount of the spore to generate the infection, and dispersed too thinly, the virus was useless.

The spores were being held in suspension in a water-based fluid, designed when released to form into even sized droplets. Small enough to carry on the wind, or a hot air current, they would disperse naturally over a huge area and drop as rain. Each droplet carried enough of the spores to infect ten people.

This was the most deadly anthrax virus developed by any Government in the world. Highly classified. It was also the best source to use for developing any cure or vaccine.

A third generation of anthrax had been developed and was due to start testing at BBR in the next few weeks. No one yet knew what this was, or why it was different except for one person.

4. Coleman

Having completed his Ph.D. Michael Coleman was approached by various institutes and offered research facilities to continue his work on virus manipulation. The pharmaceutical industry had been made aware of the progress Coleman had made during his final thesis. The university was quite understandably proud of having such an advanced student, and the results he produced.

They 'leaked' information months ago to these companies and knew that one might take up the research and progress it further. They also hoped, selfishly, that they would fund Coleman in house at Cambridge, thereby supporting the university as well as Coleman's new efforts.

It did work; one of the market leaders agreed and had funded the continuation of Coleman's research for the past 10 years. They shared his progress and adapted these results into other research areas. The benefit to the company was far more than the costs of the sponsorship.

His thesis was based on the idea of manipulating the DNA of a virus and re-engineering it to attack defined parts of tissue cells. His original aim was to develop a 'biological weapon' to use on cancer. If the virus could be changed so that it would only attack certain types of cells, it could be targeted at malignant cancer cells. The patient would develop symptoms like a severe cold, under clinical control in hospital. The virus would be attacking the cancer cells and destroying them.

Over the next 10 years he achieved some success. The laboratory testing of his first attempts proved both good and bad. The cancers were certainly reduced, and in one case destroyed. However the side effects were too large. It was not yet possible to get the virus, once changed, to attack only the cancer cells. It was attacking other cells at the same time. This was a problem and the main focus of his efforts. He was sure that it could be done and was well on the way to progressing the methods further when he became distracted.

Coleman was a very typical professor, not so much nutty but he seemed a little simple to anyone who did not know him. He had spent 3 years working on his degree, 1 year on his masters and devoted 3 more years to his Ph.D. In fact, 1 year may have been enough, but Coleman was a fanatic, and his attention to detail was infinite. He had now completed another 10 years of research in the protected environment of the university.

He was outstanding in his field; nobody like him had come through Cambridge for a generation. They wanted him to remain in the university and offered him a fellowship to lecture biological science and continue his own studies.

This was an honour for Coleman, he had grown very used to living and working within the academic world, and it was comforting to know that his future would be secure. He did long for something different, a challenge, or change of direction. Just where, or in which direction, he was unsure. If he did not have the nerve to change things, at least he knew he had a position at Cambridge.

The Ministry of Defence had by now learnt of Coleman and his efforts. They approached him to head up a research facility looking at ways of countering the effects of chemical and biological weapons. The job, position and salary were very attractive. What Coleman was not made aware of at the time the MoD had talked to him, was that they needed him to improve the effectiveness of anthrax as a biological weapon and once achieved, then find the most effective countermeasure or antidote. He was interested in the job, and liked the idea of being involved with the Government as it provided a secure environment, as he was now so used to.

Before starting any new position he wanted to take some time out to travel and see a bit of the world. Having spent so many years studying, Coleman had arrived at a junction in his life. To stay within the academic environment and take the fellowship, or start a new career working for the Government. He had given himself this time to decide. Both the university and the MoD were willing to wait for up to 1 year for his decision.

The Middle East had always fascinated Coleman and he was very well read about the difficulties throughout the ages in this strange land.

He wanted to visit the area and visit several different countries. There must be common ground between them all, and he wanted to learn more of their difficulties and the ways of life the people developed around such problems.

He planned to travel firstly through Iran and hoped to be able to study their way of life a little, and learn to understand their strict religion. Why did they hide their women away like they do? How can religion rule with such a heavy hand?

This was, to his delight, easier than he ever thought possible. The Arab people are deeply suspicious of Westerners, used to criticism and conflict. They were all too often at the wrong end of their anger, or retaliation for the terrorists' acts. Damned by the West because of the few.

When a Westerner actually asks to be allowed to learn more of their way of life, and their religion, they are very hospitable people and accommodated Coleman. The opportunity to educate a Westerner, someone of Coleman's status in the educational world was not to be missed. Allowing him to see that their life, and ways, were not always as bad as people are led to believe. It was a great compliment to the Arabs that Coleman also wanted to learn their language.

What was planned as a 4-week visit turned into over 3 months, Coleman was absorbed in his hunger for the history and teachings of the Arabs. Being granted access to a temple and the teachings of one of the Ayatollahs gave him the opportunity to find his way into the spiritual side of the people. This too, to Coleman, was an opportunity for knowledge not often available. He took it and made the most of it.

By the time he left, he had developed an understanding of the Arab people and traditions, far better than most time served diplomats had ever dreamed of; an understanding of their problems and their dislike of the West and the Israelis.

The fact that the West had a hand in forcing the Palestinians out of their homeland and replacing them with the Jews, the Israelis, was never, in a 1000 years, going to be forgiven. Generations of Arabs will forever be taught this chapter of the history books, and be brought up to continue the hatred and determination to reclaim Palestine.

He now understood that it was far more difficult for them to live and ignore this great injustice, than it was for them to fight. To fight was natural, to forget was totally unnatural.

From Iran, Coleman moved on to Syria, and spent another 2 months living in Damascus. He rented a small flat, in the outer suburbs of the city and he started to live and mix with the local people. The law prevented him from working, but he did, and easily became understandable in the local language.

Since 1516, Syria had been part of the Ottoman Empire, which held fast until the beginning of the First World War. Britain, France and the Arab people formed a coalition that brought about the expulsion of the Turks. Despite their hopes for independence, a French mandate over Syria was declared by the League of Nations in 1922. This resulted in much hostile feeling towards France by the Syrian people.

A long struggle ensued and when, eventually, the British left Syria in 1946, the country became both a republic and a charter member of the United Nations.

Political instability followed the birth of the republic, with one military coup succeeding another. In 1963 the Ba'ath party came to power and the country began to stabilize. Another coup in 1970 brought to power the then Defence Minister, Hafez al-Assad, who has remained as President to the present day.

The city was very typical Arab, the buildings all constructed from similar pale yellow stone, and had been built as need and life demanded. Here, there was no planning office making sure you did not build anything without their permission. If you had the space and the money, you could extend your house or shop by just building it.

The markets were crowded, not just with the merchants, but with people, a simple purchase taking three times as long as it should, whilst the customer haggled the price to an acceptable level. Fantastic colours, smells, and sounds, the like of which could never be experienced in the West. Even on a holiday nothing matched an authentic experience such as this. He felt at home both within himself and with these people.

Coleman was able to get work in one such market, selling fish and meat from carpets on the floor, most of which had been dried in the sun. The Syrians would carry the dried food in their shamaks, a good source of nourishment at times when fresh food was not available. These were Arabs and they had the blood of Nomads in their veins. It was commonplace for them to go off into the deserts for periods, just to get away.

Following the USA's lead after the bombings in New York, Israel had launched its own war on terrorism, going back into Gaza strip, the so-called new Palestinian homeland.

After World War II, both Jews and Palestinians fought almost continually. Despite Palestinian numerical superiority the Jews were better prepared. They had a working government and also possessed a well-trained and experienced army. The Palestinians were still in disarray from the Arab revolt and most of their leaders had been exiled.

The principal spokesman for the Palestinians, the Mufti of Jerusalem, refused to accept the existence of a Jewish state. The UN's suggestion of partition was rejected by the Mufti, though the Jews agreed to it. Armed fighting by the military broke out and both sides used what is now called terrorism. Nothing had change in all these years.

With brute force the Israelis made sure that President Arafat had pulled up the terror organisations, and stopped them attacking the Israeli people.

This was a good thing, now, 18 months later and 6 months after Arafat had failed to wake up one morning, there had been a peace, a nervous peace for almost 1 year. In fact, the terrorist had gone underground, moving out from what was previously a safe haven, now a potential threat.

The new Palestinian state had gained many things by stopping the suicide bombers of the Islamic Jihad and Hamas. Travel between Israel and Gaza was now easy. UN aid had been granted and the infant country was now growing.

The terrorists were still there, and operational, hiding in the deserts between Lebanon and what used to be their home. Libya had provided training and other facilities for the hard-line terrorist for may years and now continued to offer safe passage. They waited and trained for their final conflict. Small suicide bombs were no longer enough, their effect was no longer enough to rock the established peace between the two countries.

Coleman was granted the visa, required by Palestinian law, and started a 1-month visit to Jerusalem, the maximum stay allowed for any tourist.

This time he rented a small hotel room, remarkably cheap. These people still had no money, and any foreign income was worth grabbing without any haggling. It was a comfortable room, although very bare, white plastered walls, a small balcony looking out over the sprawling town. There were rugs on the floor and the walls. A small room off to one side hid the toilet and a small hand basin. By his standards a little sparse, but to a Palestinian this would be like the Ritz.

He spent time studying the old temples, and the stories of the early Bible. He compared these stories to those of the Koran and it was interesting to him how close they were. The clerics were entertained by Coleman's interest in their religious ways, and found his deep questions food for their own thoughts.

A small bar had become his favourite place in the evenings, it was quiet and shady. It could be seen from his own room, just across the street. The owner's wife home cooked the food, and he would occupy the same table each evening, on the small front terrace, an extension of the broken pavement. They would feed him, like he was family, one of their own and Coleman always paid a little extra. The position allowed him to sit and watch the local life go by.

It was here after only 6 days that he first was approached.

"Good evening, Mr Coleman," a soft voice said from the left, slightly behind him.

"How do you know my name?" Coleman replied, disappointed more than concerned that his anonymity was ruined.

"I am a student of biology at the University of Jerusalem, I have seen you here in the bar, and recognised your face. You have been featured many times in magazines I have read. I was very excited and I have checked it is you."

It was a very striking young woman who had spoken to him. He was surprised that someone knew his name. She was dressed in silk clothes, common to all women in this city. No longer were they hiding their faces. She was beautiful, young, with a body to match and Coleman had not failed to notice.

His experience with women was very small. The life of a research biologist kept him occupied long hours and long weeks. Apart from the women who worked for him, and those whom he taught, Coleman had not gained much first-hand experience. He had one long-term relationship during his earlier years at the university, a postgraduate student helping out for a while. He was warned off by his colleagues, a little too close to being a student.

"May I join you?" she asked politely, and waited while Coleman nodded approval. Sitting down, she gestured at the boy and ordered a coffee, speaking Arabic.

"Would you like more coffee, Michael, may I call you that?"

5. Ella

"To defend the existence, territorial integrity and sovereignty of the state of Israel. To protect the inhabitants of Israel and to combat all forms of terrorism which threaten the daily life."

The whole class were chanting this 'Mission Statement'. There were about 20 young people gathered in a room. At the front of them a severe-looking officer scrutinised each one of them as they repeated over and again the same two sentences.

"You! Ben-Yehuda, come here to the front, girl."

Ella Ben-Yehuda looked horrified; she glanced at her friends, each side of her.

"Yes you, come here."

She walked through the others and to the front of the room, moved smartly to the officer, and snapped to attention. He was standing on a raised dais, a platform where a teacher would normally stand to address his class.

It was Thursday, the day of the week when all students over 16 years of age would come to college dressed in army fatigues. The day would be devoted to the history of Israel and the struggle for peace. From the Battle of the Roads and Operation Yoav in the war of independence; all the way to present day operations and the doctrines of their government.

The heat dictated the college timetable. It was too hot after 2 pm for any work to be done. College started at 7.30 in the morning, and continued until 1.45 pm. There was only a 30 minute break for food at 11.30 am. On a normal day they would return home at 2 pm. Thursdays were different. They worked until 4 pm.

Ella stood, looking at the officer, waiting to hear what he wanted. Had she failed at something, was she to be punished for something? He looked around the room, regarding each one of them slowly and individually.

After what seemed a lifetime, he looked down from his pedestal at Ella then back up and addressed the class.

"You should all be ashamed, your progress is slow, slovenly, your attitude is wrong and it must be changed. Here is the one student who I can tell you is ready, willing, and more than able. Listen.

"Repeat the mission statement for the benefit of the others in the class," the officer barked.

Ella Ben-Yehuda turned about and came to attention facing her friends in the class.

"To defend the existence, territorial integrity and sovereignty of the state of Israel. To protect the inhabitants of Israel and to combat all forms of terrorism which threaten the daily life."

"That is how to recite this statement, no hesitation, not one word wrong. Now, go on, tell us all of the four sources that we draw the spirit of the Defence Force from."

Once again Ella spoke, no hesitation, parrot fashion.

"One – the tradition of the IDF and its military heritage as the Israel Defence Forces.

Two – the tradition of the State of Israel, its democratic principles, laws and institutions.

Three – the tradition of the Jewish People throughout their history.

Four – universal moral values based on the value and dignity of human life."

"Good, excellent, return to your place Ben-Yehuda. This is the standard you should all strive to reach; this is what you owe your country. You will all be called upon at some time and you must all be ready." She was 18 years old then and had been training with the IDF for 2 years whilst continuing her studies at college. She was very clever and both Ella and her family wanted her to go on to university and study chemistry.

Mr and Mrs Ben-Yehuda lived in a modest house in Tel Aviv. It was, to all intents and purposes, a bungalow, built to their own design but also to blend with other housing around them. Almost a bungalow because it had been built on concrete stilts, leaving enough room beneath the main house to construct a second.

Traditionally, this part of the building would be used when the daughters married. The family would stay together and bring up the grandchildren as one unit.

For now, this part housed the family car, some chickens, and household junk.

A middle-class neighbourhood, neatly kept. Most people had a car, worked, paid their taxes, and attended their church as all good Jewish people would.

They were immensely proud of Ella's achievements at college, none more so than her progress in the IDF training. To them it was important. The system, rather like the ATC in some private schools in the UK, provided a basic training. The initial training provided in the schools and colleges laid the foundations for their time when they all had to give something back to their motherland.

When she graduated from college she left with some of the highest marks they had seen for some years. She also left having commanded the school's contingent of IDF for over 6 months.

Ella commenced her degree in biophysics at the Technion Institute in Haifa. The degree was more challenging than the alternative chemistry degree and she felt that this would be more useful when she eventually finished and went to work. Her aims were to continue in education and perhaps lecture herself.

It was law, once she had completed her degree and before she could commence work, that she had to complete her national service. This was unavoidable and Ella was happy to do it, when the time came.

So it was with some surprise, that warm May morning that Mr and Mrs Ben-Yehuda received such a letter from their daughter. Certainly this would bring shame on their family, what on earth would their friends and neighbours think about them and their daughter.

His wife sat on the chair near the window; she was looking into space, weeping uncontrollably. He sat with the letter in his hands, his eyes boring holes through the paper.

"Dear Mum and Dad,

You will be disappointed to receive this letter, I know, and I know you will feel I have let you down. For years I have studied, I have completed all that has been asked of me. I have been true to you and the family name.

But I now feel there is a big injustice in the way we, Israel, treat the people of Palestine and our Arab neighbours. For 2 years I have studied the history of the countries so intent on destroying each other. I believe that it is wrong and it is us and not them that are wrong.

I now have a boyfriend, a lover. We love each other and he is Palestinian. So I am leaving to return to his home to be with him. Forgive me..."

How can he ever forgive her, how can he ever come to terms with this betrayal. He wrestled with his feelings, his loyalty to Israel, his loyalty to his family, but more his love of his only child, Ella.

She was gone, would they ever see her again? "God only knows," he thought.

Two weeks later there was a knock at the front door of their house. It was almost 6.00 pm, the heat had subsided enough to leave a pleasant evening. They were both sitting on the balcony at the rear. No one was expected, they had, for the last days, kept out of sight and to themselves.

At the door were two uniformed officers of the IDF, they asked to come in. They spent 20 minutes talking and departed, leaving behind a postcard for them. It showed a view of Jerusalem. No stamp, but it was addressed to them at home.

"Don't worry, all is well," Ella.

And so it was that Ella was now in Jerusalem.

"Yes I would like coffee, thank you." Coleman ignored her use of his Christian name. He did not care if she called him Michael; he was actually enjoying the flattery of the situation.

"My name is Ella," she offered as if by exchange for using his first name. "How do you come to be in our city, Jerusalem, Michael?"

"Simple really," he responded, " I am travelling throughout this part of the world, I am interested in the culture, the religion, and the problems, more so the cause of the problems between your countries."

"You have learnt our language well, but I too speak English, so we can use either."

They sat talking until well into the night, she was obviously a student, well educated and was asking deep questions of the work he had done. Coleman was transfixed by her beauty and intelligence. He had no idea who this woman was, and why she had chosen to spend her evening with him, other than a shared interest in his area of research.

At around 11.00 o'clock she made a move to leave.

"May I meet you again, Michael, I have enjoyed this evening, perhaps you may help me with my studies?" Again, he was flattered that someone so lovely could want him to help her.

"Yes, of course, I would be delighted. I am here most evenings, please feel free to join me."

For the next week, each night Ella would return and sit with Coleman talking. Mostly about life in general, about their science, and about the conflict of the area. Tonight, as Ella rose to leave, he was blatantly disappointed and Ella noticed.

"Please come to visit me tomorrow, Michael, I would like to cook for you, come to my house."

His heart leapt and he agreed without hesitation, already his mind was wandering from his head to his groin. Could this beautiful woman really be interested in me?

They met the following evening at her apartment; the map she had drawn for Coleman was invaluable as navigating around the small streets of Jerusalem could be difficult.

Ella had gone to a lot of trouble and had prepared a meal, a simple traditional one, using mutton and herbs. This was typical of the area and its people. Coleman, for his part, had been reading some of the work Ella had put into her thesis. She was in a final year of study at the university in Jerusalem.

They spent time discussing her progress towards the degree and Ella had brought out her work from the previous year's study. He read some and asked her about the methods and results she had used and achieved.

He was impressed and was full of praise. It was his opinion that she would achieve a very high result in her examinations. Delighted, she hugged him tight and Coleman just kissed her. She did not pull away.

He was unused to being in this situation but the feelings growing inside him were strong and he started to touch her, not thinking of the possible problems had she complained or been offended. Whilst they continued to kiss he moved his hands slowly from her waist and gently across her breasts, lightly feeling them, an unfamiliar experience to him.

Ella let out a gentle moan and pushed closer to him encouraging his advances. He became bolder and caressed her more firmly, their kissing becoming more intense. Both were still standing but Ella was leaning against the side of the table where they had both sat to eat less than 2 hours earlier.

She helped him a little and loosened the silk wrap top she was wearing, giving him full access to her breasts. He moved slowly, remarkable considering he had no experience, and enjoyed the feel of her warm skin in his hands. Ella moaned again and started to move towards the bedroom at the back of the flat.

Standing next to the bed she removed her top; wearing nothing underneath. She took Coleman's hands and returned them to her breasts, helping him massage her, becoming more and more aroused. Stepping back again, she removed the rest of the silk, and exposed her naked body to him.

They both moved, sitting on the edge of the bed. Undoing his belt, she removed his trousers, shirt and underwear, then pulled him onto her.

Coleman responded, kissing her gently on her breasts, moving his hands now up and down her inner thighs, teasing Ella, gently stroking her femininity. Pulling himself up, above her, across her, he moved her legs apart and Ella guided him into herself.

From this evening on, they became inseparable. Their discussions moved away from the university studies into the history of the Middle East. Slowly Ella was letting him understand that she believed in ultimate action to defend their faith and remove the Jews from their land.

He stayed in Jerusalem for 7 weeks, 6 of them with Ella, and they slept together continually. She taught him to love, and the pleasure of love.

She knew he would now follow her anywhere, he believed as she did.

They flew from Jerusalem to Istanbul, where they transferred to a Libyan Airlines flight to Tripoli. Booking into a hotel, they spent time together as tourists around the great city.

A week later, Coleman was in the desert to the south east of Tripoli and had been for 3 days. They had been collected from their hotel by two men, dressed in Arab dress, and then driven away in a beat-up old

Mercedes diesel. The journey across the desert had taken over 4 hours and with no air-conditioning in the car, it was not the most comfortable journey either of them had ever had.

They stopped overnight at a small Bedouin encampment where they were fed well and provided with a tent to sleep. Coleman noticed how much better the stars were visible from the desert. They seemed so clear here, and as though they were closer.

The following morning, very early, the journey started again, another 4 hours of heat in the Mercedes. The driver informed them that they were near to the camp, their destination, and that soon they would be challenged, checked for security reasons.

Finally they arrived. Built into a large waddy, where years ago a river once rushed past, were a series of caves and buildings that had been fashioned into the rock face. It was mainly sandstone; soft enough to allow the construction, strong enough not to collapse.

From the air it would hardly have been noticeable as most of the buildings were actually modern-day caves. As they approached, concealed guards could now be seen, and they too were protected from aerial view by corrugated iron sheets, covered in smaller boulders.

As they opened the doors of the car and got out, it was clear that they were the centre of attraction to everyone. Ella had told him that they needed his help, but he did not understand what he could do. He was not a terrorist, he was unable to kill, or so he thought. But for Ella he had agreed to meet them and talk.

They were shown to their quarters and given food and water. The camp was isolated for good reasons, stores were not plentiful, and the rations given to them were poor and the water warm and dirty. The plan was to meet after dark and sit with these people to learn what it was they needed from someone like Coleman.

There was one man, an Arab, who was in charge of the camp. He did not claim a military rank, for he did not feel he was a soldier; in his mind he was a servant of both his country and Allah. Everyone called him 'leader', or rather this was the closest translation from Arabic.

They did not waste time in small talk, the point was made clearly and quickly.

"Michael, we know that you have a deep love for the Arab people. We have seen you in our lands, and we have heard of your thirst for our knowledge and culture," Leader said, quietly. "We also know from what Ella has told us that you too are now convinced that what has happened is unjust, and needs to be, shall we say, corrected?"

We need you to help us avenge the interference of the infidels over the many years we have suffered. Our people have been forced into complying with their ways. Look at our so-called homeland. It is completely in their hands, they have made beggars of us all."

"Tell me what it is you think I can do to help, and if I can then I will," Coleman said, not sure what would come next.

"We want a biological weapon, a weapon of mass destruction, to use to reclaim our birthrights. You can do this for us, you can make one for us, we can give you anything you need in return, you can have ten like Ella."

"That is completely crazy, I cannot provide this type of information for you, let alone build such a device for you to use just to forward the cause of your people. Killing is not the answer, it never has been, too many have died in the name of this so-called holy war, attempting to recover your true heritage."

For now, they agreed to discuss the matter, to debate the rights and wrongs, to look hard into what could be achieved if Coleman met their wishes.

Over the next 4 days they appealed to his love of the Arab people, and Coleman soon began to realise that he could perhaps help them. They needed the ultimate weapon. A nuclear device was completely impractical. Anything to do with building this type of weapon was monitored, and very closely. He could develop a biological weapon, or better still he realised he had the perfect opportunity and could steal one. But it must be done in his way, and they had to agree to this, otherwise he could not help.

Coleman informed them that he could help them, he could provide such a weapon, but only under his terms, and the weapon would be used in a way that perhaps would not involve mass loss of life.

Over the next hours he laid his plan out in front of them; it was only an idea at this time, but for a scientist, formulating ideas in your head was almost as routine as breathing.

He added a further condition to his agreeing to help them. He wanted to be trained as one of them. He wanted to learn the art of terrorism, become a shadow of the night, not afraid to die, or kill. Coleman considered this as exciting as being with Ella. They readily agreed and together forged an alliance unholy to anyone's God.

It took 20 weeks of constant training, getting fitter, learning to fight, to shoot, and the art of deception. He started to become a true Arab, learning how to exist in the desert, how to find food, how to stay alive when most people would perish.

Unlike conventional troops or security services, the terrorist must learn to use what was available to him to carry out the job. They were well funded by the Arab Nations, who found it very easy to pour money into an organisation that carried out their dirty work for them. Some things were still beyond their money.

With the collapse of the Soviet Union and their slow move to financial stability, money still bought almost anything: weapons, explosives, information. It could not buy anything to do with chemical or biological weapons. Nor could you buy anything nuclear. The new government was unwilling to risk the wrath of the USA.

The terrorists were taught to adapt and create things that they needed to carry out their tasks; creating surveillance and security devices from normal household or industrial supplies; using domestic or amateur radio products to create detonators. Using standard untraceable items for every conceivable task.

By the end of his training, Coleman was a different man. He had learnt in months, what normally takes years. He had proved he was now able to kill when, during that terrible night in the desert, he and his men had attacked who they believed were Israelis; the terrible moment he learnt he had been deceived, and had killed Arabs.

Coleman realised that he now viewed their lives and his as unimportant when measured against the final ambitions of his newly adopted people.

6. Coleman at the Mod

It was over 2 weeks after he returned to the UK that Coleman finally made contact with the University and the MoD. He wanted 2 weeks to become English again, get used to being back in England.

When he finally did make contact with the university and informed them that he had decided to join the MoD, they were very surprised. The directors asked Coleman to meet them and discuss his decision, over a meal.

The meal was strange; the university were pulling out the stops for him. The venue was the grand surroundings of King's College, in the Masters' dining room.

His old colleagues, however, could see a different man. Gone was the scholar, and the hunger for information, the need to progress his own science, his obsession. Instead, they saw a man who was decided on a new way forward. They were bitterly disappointed.

"Michael, what can you do for your science working with the Government? Their interest in you is not what it seems. They seek knowledge to use as methods of destruction, not to benefit mankind. Your philosophies were against this at one time. What has changed?"

Coleman thought before answering.

"I have changed; I have seen a different world full of unfairness. My ambitions within the university have gone and I wish to follow a new path. I am not sure what work I will be doing for the Government, but I wish to try."

He paused and considered again what else he should add.

"The work I have completed within the university has always been sponsored. A large corporation donates money to keep the research alive. They are no different to the Government in this respect; they

58

have their own agenda, profit. The Government's agenda may not be profit but, in a way, it is just as selfish, with some possibility to benefit others. "

With almost no pause the response was bordering on angry,

"In what possible way could your helping the Government ever benefit others? You will be working with the MoD for pity's sake. Possibly making bombs or something! At least your research here could eventually save lives."

"Quite so," Coleman responded, just as quickly: "But I now believe I can help people in a different way; make it possible for other people to make a difference; allow people to regain their dignity."

They were unconvinced of his reasons, but by the end of the evening they had not changed his mind, and reluctantly had to admit defeat. Coleman was to leave Cambridge and start a new career with the Ministry of Defence.

Even before the meal at the university he had been in contact with the MoD and confirmed his intentions to join them. To his surprise they had asked him to attend an interview again, as they needed some information.

At 8.00 am on sunny Tuesday morning, a car arrived to collect Coleman, as agreed, and take him to a meeting with his new employers. It had been allowed access to the university, right up to the doors of his accommodation building, forbidden under any circumstances. Security was paramount, and it had decided to hold the meeting with Coleman in the safety of a military base, RAF Northolt.

This RAF station, situated just of the A40 in North West London was convenient to everyone. It was used for flying the Royal Family, and VIPs in and out of London, domestically or internationally.

The security was very tight at all times as they could be called on at short notice to prepare flights for any of the Royal Family or Government, or indeed accept an incoming official on the Government's behalf. In the final few days before the funeral of HRH the Queen Mother, the Station had been on its highest level of security, as all of the foreign Heads of State, and Royal Families were received through RAF Northolt.

It also enabled the officials from the defence laboratories, together with military security to arrive by helicopter, which compared to Coleman and his driver was a very good idea. The M25 on any morning between 6 am and 10 am is nothing better than an NCP car-park. They were inevitably delayed.

As interrogations go, this one was very relaxed and laid back. Coleman recognised immediately that he was being quizzed very deeply, in a way that most people would not notice. They obviously needed to clear him once more, after his absence.

"Mr Coleman, we are concerned at the length of time it has taken you to arrive at your decision to join the laboratory and work with us. Could you explain why?"

"Did they know where I have been," he thought very quickly, "or is it genuine discomfort that he took so long to make his mind up?"

Coleman composed himself from within before answering.

"I set off to travel the Middle East, around the Holy Land, and bordering nations. I have a fascination about the parallels between the various faiths, including Christianity. My interest turned into obsession and I spent rather longer than I had intended."

The leader in the desert had arranged for Coleman's passport to show dates of entering and leaving the various countries he had visited, to coincide with his cover story. It would not show any of his time spent in Libya, let alone in the desert.

"The languages of the nations have changed greatly over the years and records, or books were harder to research than I had imagined. The time I have spent studying has been well documented, and you are most welcome to read the notes I have made. Some time in the future I intend to write a book about the subject."

The discussions continued, he was treated well, and nothing about the interview gave him cause for concern. The conversation centred on his time spent amongst the Arabs, what he did, whom he had met, where he had stayed and the timescale. Coleman had prepared for this discussion, as he believed it was inevitable.

"I think there is one matter of which you should be aware at this point."

Coleman had decided to add in a little extra fact of truth that could be verified.

"During my stay in Palestine I met a girl and we have remained in contact ever since. We are very close and I hope that soon she will be allowed to travel and visit me in the UK."

He deliberately kept any comment about the relationship to a minimum; for no other reason than he was embarrassed.

"Her name was Ella, and I have prepared the information about her so that you may check to be sure she is OK."

As he had hoped it would do, this was the final confirmation to his questioners that all seemed to be in order with Coleman.

Towards the end of the afternoon, he was clearly tired, and the day was brought to a close.

"Mr Coleman, you realise that you will be working within a top-secret part of the defence research program and that you will be subject to the Official Secrets Act?"

"Yes, I am aware of that, you have made it clear on many occasions." Coleman responded.

"People in your position will be subject to constant security checks, not just for our sakes but for your own. Every year a review of your own security status will be made. If there is anything that could compromise your or our security, now or later, it would be dealt with very severely."

"You have explained this quite clearly." Again Coleman gave the answers they wanted.

"That's enough for now Mr Coleman, please be ready to be collected next Sunday evening at about 2 pm. The driver will take you home now and return on Sunday. From now on, you are working for us; please do not discuss this with anyone."

They stood and left, all three of them, after satisfying themselves about Coleman's movements over the past year.

The driver was waiting outside the building and opened the door of the car for Coleman to enter. He was a cheerful man, a civilian driver. The journey back to Cambridge was just as frustrating as the morning. Hold up after hold up on the M25. It was perhaps a good idea to make the journey to Hampshire on Sunday, less traffic.

The laboratory was based at Boscombe Down in Hampshire, 20 miles west of Andover at the side of the A303. Coleman was indeed collected at 2 pm, a far more enjoyable journey this time, taking less time to reach Boscombe down than it did to reach RAF Northolt, earlier in the week.

The driver took him directly to the accommodation reserved for him whilst he was working. It was a condition of his employment contract that he lived on the base, close to his work.

The house was obviously an old armed forces' married quarter that had been renovated. Probably built just before the War, it had everything Coleman could need in the way of living requirements: furniture, appliances, linen, there was even a welcome pack of food to get him started.

As he was unsure of his living accommodation, Coleman had brought the bare minimum of things with him. He would send for his other belongings later. They had told him that the house was furnished and fully equipped by the services. His own flat in Cambridge was now empty and in the hands of a local agent to rent it out, not to students, even at Cambridge they lived like pigs most of them. Coleman insisted it should only be let to a professional person.

He unpacked what he had brought with him. By now the time was a little before 7 pm and Coleman had not eaten, so he set about preparing a meal for himself and making himself at home.

Settling down after eating, he considered telephoning his friends and the leader to update them of his progress. This was not such a good idea, as he thought the telephone could be monitored and this concerned him a little. Working from room to room around the house, he looked to see if he could find any trace of a listening device.

Perhaps he was just paranoid. They had no idea of what he been doing in the Middle East, so why would they be checking on him. He retired early, wanting to be up at the crack of dawn to start his new work.

David Wilson was to be Coleman's direct superior. He was a scientist but in what discipline Coleman had yet to learn. It was clear to him that he was not as advanced as himself.

On Monday morning at 8 am Coleman was met and guided through the security procedures on the base. He was finger printed, photographed, his retina was scanned and finally a DNA sample was taken from his mouth. A computer printed out the security tag he was to wear at all times whilst at work on the base. Finally, he was shown through to the laboratory and his office.

"Good morning, Mr Coleman," David Wilson was waiting to meet Coleman at the lab door.

"Do things have to be so formal? Please, call me Michael. If we are to work together, then we should at least be friends and acknowledge each other as such."

"That's fine, Michael, now welcome to your new facility."

It was a bright clean lab, it appeared to have everything that had been agreed, and there were already six staff in the room, watching Coleman.

The scene was one from a sci-fi movie with apparatus covering most of the work surface areas. There were several extraction cupboards, heat cupboards, all with glass fronts and a furnace. Around the edges were many types of computers and other analytical machines to help with his new project.

A gentle hum could be heard continually, the heating and air-conditioning units keeping the room at a constant temperature and pressure.

"Ladies and Gentlemen, I am pleased to introduce Michael Coleman, whose reputation precedes him, and of whom I know you are all very familiar." Wilson was trying to make Coleman feel at home and welcome.

"Thank you I am sure," replied Michael, "but please, this is unnecessary, can we start and get down to working, or at least planning our work together? I have been given this job to help the Government with their research. I am not yet familiar with exactly what it is they wish of us."

Wilson took the hint and ordered everyone to follow him into a small lecture theatre a short walk away.

"The purpose of the new research we have commissioned is top secret and highly classified. I must remind you all again that you have signed and are now bound by the Official Secrets Act. What goes on in this facility is not for public knowledge. You work for HM Government, and your work, in the Government's view, is of the utmost importance."

Wilson droned on for about 20 minutes, making sure they all knew of the backing and support they would receive for the work to be done. All but Coleman still had no idea of what was involved. He knew only what he had forced out of them during discussions about his taking the job. He knew that it was research into a chemical weapon, and he had assumed it to be anthrax.

"Chemical and biological weapons are a reality. They are now a threat on the battle field, and from terrorist attack. Over the past three decades many countries have worked on using anthrax as a weapon, and unfortunately the terrorists too have sought to use this biological weapon against us.

On one side of the balance we need to be able to deploy such a weapon as anthrax, whereas on the other side of the balance we need to be able to respond to an attack with anthrax.

Your work will be to investigate the anthrax virus and develop it into a better form, more suited for weapons' use. It must overcome the traditional problems of dispersal, and it has to be developed in a way that its use can be strictly controlled.

In parallel to your results, another laboratory will be working on anti-vaccines or a method of dealing with whatever you are able to produce. It is not intended to go to war and use the developed anthrax, but if we can develop it as far as possible, under controlled conditions, and then produce a method of dealing with each variant, we will be more prepared for any attack in the future."

There was a silence that lasted for what appeared a lifetime. Everyone was trying to understand the logic behind what was being done here, in England, by us, the good guys!

For anthrax to become totally effective, you need a certain amount of the spores to come into contact with the person. If the spores land on your skin, you can develop the minor skin disease, which, if treated quickly enough with antibiotics, can be controlled and cured.

The more destructive side of the virus is when a person breathes it in. This will quickly result in severe infection and death is almost inevitable. A lot of spores are still required.

Traditional dispersal methods such as aerial spraying would disperse the spore too finely, and contact would be very minimal. The overall effect of an attack in this way would be useless to a war effort. What had to be found was a usable transport method for a set amount of spores. This is where the MoD asked Coleman to concentrate his efforts.

Over the past months whilst training and working in Libya, Coleman had considered the problems of anthrax. He did not know that they would develop an anti-vaccine or serum for each product he produced.

The idea was very clever, not unlike the training exercise he had take part in, killing all of those people. One part works in one direction and another works against you. Something will come out of the middle.

It was also a bonus Coleman agreed with himself and took on this task with reasons other than loyalty to his country.

Over the next months he discovered that, if the spores were suspended in an emulsion, they could be contained in large enough quantities, long enough to disperse and be effective. One droplet falling onto a person would contain enough spores to infect them. By spraying the new emulsion, droplet size could be controlled with nozzle design and maintained during its fall to earth.

Coleman also investigated using nature as his dispersal methods, spraying the emulsion into fast moving thermal air currents, which would carry the anthrax high into the air, and then allow it to fall miles away when it rained.

He also started to look at engineering a cold virus, using his own research from the time when he worked to help cure cancer. If he could combine a simple cold virus with anthrax, it would multiply and spread wildly. Dispersal would be easily carried out to start with, and then nature would take over.

This idea took many months to perfect but Coleman succeeded. He produced anthrax that was cloned into a common cold virus. It worked too! The tests carried out in the lab were very successful. Once one rat had been contaminated, it infected the others, just like a cold.

The virus would last for about 5 days after dispersal. It would spread during this time, but then it died. Coleman did not know why. It stopped, would not spread further. Five days after release, the virus died, wherever it was. In his own mind, Coleman considered this a good thing, but he knew Wilson would be unhappy. Happy that the progress had been made, but unhappy about the short useful life the virus would have. In Coleman's view he did not need to know.

The bottom line was that this development was important. He now had the anthrax in a form that could be delivered easily to a target area, and would be spread by nature. People infecting people infecting people. This was a very very deadly thing he had created.

"Mr Wilson, I need to see you in the lab as soon as possible. We have something that needs discussion and direction from above. Do you think you could join us some time during the day?"

"OK Michael, I have to meet the Minister in about 2 hours, can we schedule a meeting for 10 am tomorrow?"

"Fine," replied Coleman, and hung up the phone, rather distracted.

After almost 6 months of work he noticed that things around him seemed more relaxed. Coleman had not stepped out of line once. There had been no contact with anyone in the Middle East except Ella, his one true love.

He sent an email once every week to Ella. Written in English it was a simple lover's message, showing their affection for each other. To do this without risk of Wilson knowing, he used a hotmail account on the internet. The address to which the message was sent was in Germany, but the email server immediately bounced the message and forwarded it on to another server and bounced again eventually reaching the intended account.

Any trace that was made would show a German IP address and, unless they had a court order, no one could access the forwarded information. If they did get the order, then they would be led to the next bouncing server, and a new court order. In the meantime the account would be wiped with a three-keystroke combination.

Coleman had recently purchased a pay-as-you-go mobile telephone, and using cash had added many extras. He bought the Nokia modem cable and software for his laptop. The name he gave when registering the phone was obviously not his. It was legal and could not be frowned upon by the MoD security people.

This allowed him to send and receive emails direct to his laptop. Unless they were watching him 24/7, Coleman knew it unlikely that they would pick up any transmissions. He also had his regular mobile, provided by the MoD. No email messages were stored on the laptop, just in case. Using hotmail allowed almost total secrecy. To secure this further, the hotmail account was changed every second week.

The message he sent was again to Ella,

"Ella, I cannot stand the loneliness any longer, I need to see you and hold you. Please make arrangements to come to the UK and visit me."

This was a prearranged message that Coleman needed a meeting to discuss something critical. The leader would now arrange for someone to visit Coleman in England. It would be Ella as it was a perfect cover story and Coleman could not wait to see her.

"Good Morning, Michael," bellowed Wilson as he strutted into the lab, "Got something to show me?"

"Actually yes!" Coleman replied, gesturing Wilson to follow him into his office where he closed the door and offered Wilson a seat.

"You are aware of the work we have done to date, and the results we have produced. The emulsion idea is working and has now been sent to BBR for anti-vaccine and serum production research. It will be at least 6 months before this is back with us again for more progress.

Whilst the rest of the lab staff were finalising this project, I started considering another idea in a very small way, which has produced some remarkable results.

My research at Cambridge centred on manufacturing a virus that could be programmed to attack certain types of cell: malignant cells, or cancer. The progress I made was remarkable, even if I do say it myself. Therefore, it occurred to me that we could use a similar method of combining two types of virus, the common cold with anthrax.

This would mean that anthrax could multiply very quickly, with the same speed as a cold virus. It would also allow it to spread by contact, and other usual means, just as a cold would."

"What does this mean, we can spread anthrax like a common cold, infect ten people, and they each infect ten others and so on?" Wilson was actually excited as if he was being told he had won the lottery.

"Exactly right, except for one thing. It means we have no control once it has been released, or could have no control. I may have developed the most deadly thing on earth since the plague."

Wilson's face did not move, he showed no emotion, he was now deep in thought, possibly of promotion or other self-centred results of this breakthrough.

He was sitting thinking about an Armageddon virus that could wipe out most animal life on earth whilst Coleman considered Wilson's use as a guinea pig.

"Good work," he said, "when can we get some to BBR for anti-vaccine?"

"Not yet, certainly not for at least 2 months. This was a lab batch, I have to reproduce the results and create the methodology to allow possible bulk production. I will be able to release a small amount for BBR within 6 weeks."

"That's fine, keep me fully informed, I will update the Minister."

"One more thing," Coleman said, "My friend Ella is coming to visit me next week, she will be staying at my house on camp. I would like you to know in advance. Please inform security."

Wilson was gone, bounding down the corridor. He acknowledged Coleman's information with a wave. "That's fine." And he was gone.

After so long and not hearing anything about Ella from security, Coleman was sure it would not be an issue. In telling Wilson, he brought the possible problem forward. Nothing further was said, and Coleman began to really look forward to her arrival.

Ella flew into Heathrow on a Jordanian flight arriving at 5 o'clock in the morning. It was on time and Coleman waited in Terminal 2, anxiously. Could they be following him, did they trust him or not? There was less traffic at this time of the day and a tail would be easier to see.

The frequency of flight arrivals had now reached the early morning rush. Standing near the back, away from the waiting crowds, he peered at the hoards of bodies exiting the customs hall. His face lit up as he saw Ella, smiling and waving toward him.

She was just as lovely as when she had left him, when he had departed to go back to London. That was a day Coleman had been dreading, a day he had so many times regretted. But now she was here, in London, and all his for the next week. With 7 days' leave agreed in a hurry with Wilson, he was free to show Ella London and England.

One of the best times they could talk business was on the return journey to Boscombe Down, along the M3 and A303 past Andover. Against the tidal flow rushing into the capital, it was an easy journey. He had taken the train to London and hired his car there. The rental agreement was for 7 days, and he would return it when Ella had gone home. This was very deliberate. The car had to be secure and free from any form of bug.

They chatted together in the car about his times in Palestine and the fun they had shared together. Ella had achieved a first rate degree, as Coleman knew she would.

"Michael, I am thirsty, and hungry, can we stop and eat something?"

"Sure, there is a service area not far from here, we can get some coffee."

Fleet services are open 24 hours a day and coffee with sandwiches were purchased and they both sat in a smoking area. Each of them was looking, to be sure they were not followed, and neither had noticed anyone.

"Can we talk here, is it safe?" Ella asked, "Why did you request a meeting?"

"It is safe. They may have bugged my flat, but they cannot control this situation. The car is clear too. I hired it in London, but we need to be careful."

"You are just as beautiful, Ella," Coleman gazed into her eyes, bemused.

"There is time for that when they are listening, Michael, we have to talk now."

"Yes, I know. There has been some progress and I need to start preparations for removing some of the product we have made. Very soon I will be in a position to act and force them to give us what the leader has asked for."

"What is it?" Ella asked.

"That is best left to only my knowledge at this time. It is what I was asked to find, only better. Now listen carefully and do not ask questions. I need money to buy some things to use to obtain it and I need four men to work with me. All must be fully trained, passable in the UK and prepared to die for their belief.

I need to buy some heavy plant, drilling vehicles and other equipment. I need to buy two, possibly three, cars. I have to establish a new routine in a new area, and spend money to buy access. I will need weapons, explosives and ammunition. These will all be expensive but the prize is worth it."

"How much do you need and when?"

"I intend to establish a company working in drilling; for cable and pipe laying. I will buy the vehicles and equipment. It will cost at least one million pounds. Is that a problem?"

"If you are sure, no it is not. But we need to know what you are planning, and how you intend to steal this thing. Then what are you going to do with it?"

"No! I have to be trusted to carry out and complete what I have started. If I tell you what is to happen, it could put you at risk and the leader with his followers. When I am ready to strike, I will inform you by email, with a brief description of what I intend. Once it is done, you will know. Now, the money?"

"It will be available for you 1 week after I return."

Coleman looked at Ella, and again his brain sank to his groin, it had been a long time.

"Ella, we can continue this when circumstances allow. Now, I need to take you home and fuck you."

A wicked smile spread across his face and Ella grinned back at him.

They returned to Boscombe Down and went about their holiday week as any others would. Idyllically placed to visit many beautiful places around the south of the country, they went and did everything they could. They were inseparable. To anyone watching; a normal healthy couple.

His time with Ella was short. No sooner had she arrived than she was gone. He was alone again, but his purpose had been renewed.

Six weeks later Coleman had perfected the first batch of the new anthrax virus and he personally accompanied it to BBR near Huntingdon. It was his wish to make sure that it was stored and treated correctly. He did not want this becoming part of a massive accident.

The virus was transported in a flask made from carbon fibre and almost unbreakable, lined with stainless steel and opened at one end only. The inside looked rather like a vacuum flask, but contained another glass vessel holding the virus in a liquid form.

Each week, one of these flasks would be sent to BBR and they would attempt to counter it, and provide a solution to its effects.

Each week, there was an opportunity for disaster.

The fact that BBR were working on results produced by Coleman allowed him frequent access to the site. He had been there many times and had suffered the humiliation of being heckled by the protestors, so called well-meaning people, protecting animals.

"My God! If they only knew."

For security reasons, Coleman was not allowed any contact with staff at the BBR lab, he was considered a risk to their efforts of countering the new versions of anthrax.

Three months after the discovery of the anthrax/cold combination, Coleman was in his office working recording notes and details of his progress. It was early, as he preferred the quiet mornings to get this part of his work finished.

Wilson arrived and came into the room and looked at him.

"Michael, we have a problem, could you please come with me?"

He had no reason to suspect anything bad was wrong, but immediately became worried when two security officers joined them as the left the room and walked to the security HQ. He was led through the building and into a small room.

In the room were two of the three people who interviewed Coleman at RAF Northolt. Wilson joined them on the far side of an old desk; they gestured for Coleman to sit down opposite them.

"Michael, these people have some questions for you. They need to have answers or explanations. You must co-operate with them. Do you understand?"

"Yes, of course I do, what is the problem?"

The elder of the two men now rose to his feet and started pacing around like some professor giving a lecture.

"Mr Coleman, I work with MI6, and it is our job to make sure that your security is 100% all of the time. This means you are monitored continually, for your own sake; we don't want you being blackmailed, and for our sake; we do not want any information leaking out.

Your were made aware of this when you started your position here.

I have to inform you that our conversations this morning are being recorded. Unlike police procedure you are not allowed to keep a copy of the interview."

Coleman was now concerned at the situation and was becoming angry at his treatment.

"This is completely ridiculous, what on earth is going on?"

"Two months ago your friend Ella came to visit you from Palestine. Whilst she was here, we obviously monitored her, as well as you. The photographs we took at the time were checked and compared to records we have here and at various places around the network.

They were also circulated to the CIA and other friendly agencies.

There was a match on Ella, not a perfect match, but her picture compared to one taken by one of our own agents, working in Libya. This was enough to start a deeper investigation. As it happens, the CIA also flagged up Ella, and had another picture of her, this time with a group of what seem to be trainee soldiers, or terrorists.

I have to stress that the pictures were not clear, and not a complete match."

"Ella is a typical Middle Eastern girl; there are many similar in appearance to her. This is stupid. What are you saying, she is a terrorist?" Coleman now knew he could be compromised.

"Not exactly, no. However, in the second photograph from the CIA there is one of the so-called soldiers, sitting at the back of the group that has your build and similar facial structure. We cannot be sure, but we are concerned it is you."

"Oh, so now I am a terrorist soldier. Have you gone completely mad? Or is this some type of joke?"

Coleman was compromised. They were not 100% sure of the information they had, but 10% sure in this situation was enough to scare them badly. Could it be a trained terrorist had now been working within the heart of the British Defence research operation?

"We have no option; we are unable to prove these pictures are correct, but also unable to prove they are incorrect. Considering the work that is being done at this facility, there can be absolutely no room for even a one in a million chance of any links to, shall we say, 'questionable' organisations.

We have a duty to investigate these circumstances and will now do so. If we find anything that in any way leads us to believe that you have any involvement with such people, you will be detained.

Therefore, your work here is now over; your job has been terminated. You are bound by the Official Secrets Act for the rest of your life, and cannot discuss anything to do with your work here, or anywhere else."

There was no opportunity to discuss this further; they left, with Wilson following like a dog. The two security men came back into the room, and requested that Coleman followed them.

It was not very pleasant being evicted from your house in such a way, even if they did own it, and it was part of the job. The two guards were helpful and kind to him. He knew them well by now. They were as confused as he was, but they had no choice either.

He was helped to collect his personal belongings from the house, but refused entry back to the lab. Anything left here would be checked and returned to him in due course. He had his pay-as-you-go mobile, but the laptop had been taken away from him. No doubt they would check this very thoroughly.

No trace would ever be found of any messages to Ella, or emails sent. The software program he had purchased would eliminate the data to US defence standards. Not even forensics could recover any data from this hard drive.

Four hours after the meeting he was back in Cambridge.

From that day on, every position Coleman would apply for would result in failure. He even applied for a lab technician's job, to prove the point. Somehow, his record was being checked, and blocked from any research or scientific job anywhere in the European Union.

The Europe-wide terror laws now allowed the sharing of information. He had been black-listed.

Coleman vowed revenge, and vowed to help his true friends in their now so understandable fight against the West.

7. The Farm

About half a mile to the south of the BBR complex was Hilltop farm. It had only taken Coleman about 20 minutes to get here from his rented flat in Peterborough. The farm was so named because the farmhouse occupied the top of a small hill and was surrounded by a massive field.

Coleman sat in the lounge, close to the window overlooking a fantastic view of fields and crops growing in the summer sun. He could see very clearly the BBR complex, and the A1 carrying numerous people on journeys to everywhere.

The farmland covers over 2000 acres and extended down to the edge of the A1 and the road leading to BBR. On the other side of this road, land belonging to the farm extends to encircle the BBR complex. It was easy to imagine that, at some time in the past, the land BBR had been constructed on was in fact part of the original farm. To the south the farmland extends to the borders of the A14 trunk road.

"Now then, Mr Cartwright," Alan Marshall began. "I understand that you need access to my land to carry out some sort of drilling operation. Perhaps you can explain this a little more for me?"

"Yes, it's quite simple really, we have been contracted to install a cable under the A1 trunk road, at a point 400 yards to the north of the junction of the A1 with the Woolley Road. We intend to do this using horizontal drilling, so that any disruption to the traffic is avoided."

Marshall was an arable farmer and luckily had not suffered the devastation brought about by foot and mouth during 2000. However, as with most farmers like Marshall, the assistance from Brussels that had been planned into the long-term finances of the farm was drying up, beaten away by endless bureaucrats. As Europe now moved closer together, the unfair subsidies enjoyed by farmers throughout the union were now being reduced. This burden on Brussels' finances had to be stopped and made to represent the needs of the community as a whole and not just the privileged few.

The effect of the entry into the Community of the new members, many of whom were ex-Soviet or other communist states, was taking funds from even the newly trimmed agricultural support budget.

Mountains of food were being produced unnecessarily and stored at further cost. This too had to stop and farmers all over Europe were now missing the money they were all so used to. Regardless of the continued French blockades and protests, in the past so effective, these changes were now a reality.

The letter informing him that access to his land was required by the Highways Agency was not unusual. Three years ago the new A1M was built, stretching from Brampton to Peterborough, removing a huge bottleneck and traffic disaster area. For 2 years he had put up with the contractors all over his land, and given in to the compulsory purchase order stealing a 100-yard wide strip along side the A1 almost 1/2 a mile long.

He was not alone; land along the west side of the old A1 road had been purchased by compulsory order. This included a Little Chef, a complete hotel, some very fine woodland and even the removal of a war memorial dedicated to the brave young America fliers of World War II. All were demolished to make way for the new four-lane motorway. The memorial was relocated and can still be seen today.

It took over 28 months to complete the road, on what was one of the busiest stretches in the country. The northbound A1 met the northbound A14. It was complete and total chaos for the period of the work; traffic would regularly queue for 10 miles.

The speed limit was reduced to 50 mph for the extent of the works, and no one paid any attention. The Police were forced to install cameras to enforce the reduced limits. This just added to the delays.

The construction removed the old northbound carriageway and built out to the west. The new road occupied land about 100 yards to the west of the old northbound carriageway. A huge part of the top of a hill was removed to provide a more gentle slope northwards, down towards Sawtry.

The southbound carriageway of the original A1 was kept and turned into a B road that ran parallel to the new motorway. This provided a route for local traffic and farm vehicles. Also a route for those that were not happy using a motorway. It was still possible now, after the road was complete, to travel from Brampton to Peterborough without having to use the new motorway, and keeping almost to the same route.

At Alconbury, the side road moved away and then over the top of the A14 falling down back to the A1 near the south side of Alconbury village. The overhead roundabout provided for access from the A1 and Alconbury, was now used by all employees of BBR. The central reservation, where southbound workers crossed over the A1 had been closed. To get onto the southbound A1 or back to Huntingdon, everyone had to travel north a short distance, and then use this new junction. It was not convenient but it was much more safe.

This junction is where the A1M formally started; past this point was motorway. The contractors had left a lay-by intact, about 300 yards south of the junction on the northbound side. It quickly was populated by a mobile catering trailer, offering food, 'the last before the motorway'. Not that anyone would fade away from hunger before reaching Peterborough, but it was a great sales pitch.

So after the building of the new road, the letter did not seem unusual to Alan Marshall. He was experienced in negotiating and dealing with such things.

"We are writing to inform you that we shall be needing access to your land adjacent to the A1M motorway for a period of 4 days commencing Friday 9th July and finishing at the latest on Wednesday 14th July."

It was next bit Alan liked most of all:

"As the reason for this request is the provision of a private TV cable under the road, you will be entitled to compensation at the normal rate of £6,000 for the 4-day period."

Coleman had to appear completely cool and normal. He expected Marshall to try to up the figure that was agreed, and he would do so if needed. Everything had been put in place to allow Marshall to check and recheck his company's credentials. If he called the number on the visiting card, he would be answered.

"Mr Cartwright, I presume you are the contractor's representative rather than the cable company's?"

"Yes," said Coleman, "why?"

"I agree to the fee of £6000 for the use of the land, and inconvenience. This I would imagine is paid from your budget for the job being completed. I want this payment in cash, and with no record."

"I can arrange that, if it is what you want. We will show you allowing us access as a favour, and hide the payment as wages and costs in our budget."

"Then we have a deal, Mr Cartwright," Marshall replied rubbing his hands together.

From his briefcase Coleman took the right of access agreement for Marshall to sign. It showed already that no fee would be paid, a hunch that had paid off. He gave Marshall an envelope containing £6000 in cash. The two men shook hands, and Coleman stood to leave.

"I can see you are used to working with farmers and land owners, Mr Cartwright!"

Work was due to start on Saturday. Coleman, on behalf of the 'contractors' had already been on the telephone to Marshall advising him. The first of several vehicles would arrive Friday morning. The setting up and positioning of them both was critical to the operation.

The payment of £6000 for the inconvenience of having four vehicles on his land was a real bonus for Marshal. It was only a drop in the ocean compared to what the farm was set to lose, but this was money he could pay himself, and avoid putting through his books.

Blinded by the thought of a few weeks' holiday with his family, free of charge and some left over to clear the mounting personal debts, Marshall had fallen into the trap. He could not complain or interfere at all in Coleman's activities. Not that Marshall would want to after over 2 years of road building.

It is far cheaper to drill a horizontal hole under a road and pass a pipe through it than to dig up the road surface, install the pipe and make good. Technology for horizontal drilling has been developed over the past 20 years and has now reached an advanced stage.

Many road repair contracts involve the contractor renting the road from the Government for the period of time it takes to carry out the work. This cost is then written into the agreed price and recovered. If, however, the contractor overruns in time, he is then penalised automatically for being late. For this reason alone, whenever possible cables and pipes are passed under the road using this technology.

Most people would have heard of a 'mole' used by British Gas to install a gas pipe to your house, or BT to put a phone line in. This small device is powered by compressed air and vibrates very fast. It is pushed along under the ground and is steered remotely from above.

The technology to drill long distances horizontally is not dissimilar, but uses conventional drilling heads not compressed air.

A hole is normally dug big enough to accommodate the drilling gear, and deep enough to get under the road. A similar hole is dug on the opposite side, and you just drill a hole right through.

In agreement with Marshall the preparation work had been done in advance on Wednesday and Thursday. Coleman had sent the four men with the JCB to the side of the A1, onto Marshall's land.

A hole was dug on the west side of the road, very close to the roadside, just within the hawthorn hedging. It was about 12 feet across and about 10 feet deep; more like the entrance to a tunnel than just a hole in the ground. The ground sloped down west to east up to the face at the far end of the hole. The drilling vehicle would back slowly down the ramp to a position up against the face, nearest the road, where it could start to drill.

Coleman had deliberately dug this hole, but had no intentions of using it, other than to park the second drilling rig. He did not intend to drill under the A1 as the farmer understood. The second rig was just to make any interested party believe that he was actually drilling under the A1. His ambitions were about 100 yards more to the south, and a little deeper, in more ways than one.

To accommodate the second and most important drilling rig a second such hole had been dug, this time not as deep, the angle required was less. It was also not so obvious.

Ella had returned to Palestine after the week together in Boscombe down. Through her normal channels she arranged to visit Libya. Three weeks after her return she had met with the leader in the desert and discussed what Coleman had told her. Or rather not told her. She had faith in him, and so too had the leader. They agreed to Coleman's requests. She had been true to her word.

Ella was now aware of the fact that Coleman had been removed from his position. He had insisted this would not affect his plans in any way. In fact, it had made it a little easier, as he needed to resign and leave Boscombe Down anyway. There was now a timescale of around 3–4 months within which the plan could be realised.

By email, Coleman was advised of a deposit being made in a new account that had been opened in the name of Contract Horizontal Drilling Ltd. The Company documents and account cheque books were left for him in a deposit box, used by Coleman continually for dead drops.

For 4 weeks he had rented a piece of deserted farmland in Essex, just outside Colchester. Together with his four new comrades, recently arrived, they practised and trained using the new drilling rigs. Each rig was fully functional and had cost £125,000 each, second-hand. Fitted to the back of a Mercedes 7.5 ton truck, they looked every bit the part.

They modified the trucks by adding a compressor to the back of each and a vacuum pump. They only needed one truck to drill the intended hole. The second was a back up, but also to be used as a dummy driller working under the A1.

At the end of the 4 weeks, each man knew his job, and each man could do every other job involved, including Coleman.

He knew that they would have continued with his research at the lab following his departure. He had written up some of the process that had been used, and some of it was not yet finalised. They were clever enough at the facility to fully understand his work, and where he had achieved the first results.

It would have been at least 2 months before they could replicate his results and give BBR any reasonable quantity of the new anthrax. The testing timetable that was being agreed would not allow a changeover for a further month. This meant that, during the next 2 weeks, BBR should have changed the testing product.

Carol had confirmed that the tests were to change and that a new batch of anthrax had arrived. Some of their routines had been changed. They had also been told that what they had been given was more sophisticated. Changes were also made to their personal protection in the lab. This was the news that Coleman had waited for. He now knew the anthrax/cold virus was being worked on for an anti-vaccine.

8. Carol at Work

Carol was on the 08 30 bus into work, departing from the bus station in Huntingdon town. The bus was a normal Eastern Counties bus, to all intents and purposes a local bus on its normal route. In fact it was the staff bus for BBR and security on the bus was very high. No pass, no access, three security guards on each bus. One at the front, one at the back and one to check everyone's identity.

Concern as to where the animal rights people might strike next would never go away.

She was responsible for the care and welfare of the rats in project 765. She had to look after these animals, make sure they were fed, watered and as happy as they could be, whilst being infected with a virus, a cold virus she was told.

The laboratory life for the rats, whilst they were being tested upon, was 3 weeks. On every Saturday some were changed. Carol hated Saturday, and today was Saturday.

The entrance for project 765 was separate. She had to walk a further 300 yards from the main gate, and it was secure at all times. Passing her ID card through the reader, she gained access to the front foyer. As the door closed behind her, she heard the familiar hiss as the seal was made and the air sucked out. There were still further security checks required.

"Mornin' Carol," the security guard said and grinned.

George had been with the company for 10 years. They employed and vetted their own security personnel and would not contract out the security work. It would be far easier to infiltrate a private security firm than it would their own, particularly when they were being vetted by the MoD in advance of any employment offer.

Considering he was a security guard, there was little to show this on his desk. He had a radio and telephones, but had only one CCTV screen, which displayed a picture of the outside of the building so that he could see who was approaching the door.

This was deliberate; CCTV pictures could be copied, and the possibility of this happening was a risk. Without the pictures in the first place, the risk was eliminated.

There was nothing to monitor, all staff were checked in and out, they could only pass through doors with their ID cards, and the laboratory was 30 ft underground. What was there to keep a check on?

Again using her ID card, she gained access to the stairwell that took her down the 30 ft to the basement.

It was obvious inside this area that money had been spent on the refit. Everything was new and state of the art. The walls were clean and painted with a paint that provided a very shiny surface. The floor was moulded into the walls; there were no skirting boards or any other architectural timber on the wall. It was more like the operating theatre in a hospital.

Swiping her card again, Carol walked into the reception room. This was only about 6 ft square and, as she shut the door behind her, it too sealed as the front door had done. The door in front was locked, and she knew it. To the left were two lights mounted into a moulded plastic panel, recessed in the wall, exactly level with the surface. No cracks or joins. The light showed red, meaning the door was locked. She could now hear the blowing noise of the air being replaced in the room; after only 20 seconds the light went green and she could get through the door.

Carol had to dress before going into the laboratory areas and walked to the ladies' changing room. 'Shower in shower out' read the large poster on the wall just visible from the shower Carol now occupied. Part of the job she was told: a clean environment. It would have been a dream for any woman to have a shower like this one at home. Beautifully tiled, large, complete with a seat. The shower was powerful, unlike most domestic ones. This routine did not bother her too much, as it saved her money, using their power and hot water to keep clean, not her precious resources at home.

Having finished her shower, she put on the disposable underwear provided and climbed into her lab suit. A one-piece waterproof and dust proof overall. A little sweaty; it was tightly sealed around the neck, wrists and ankles by wide, flat elastic. These clothes would be worn once and then burnt.

The towel was thrown into a chute marked 'waste for incineration'. Pushing her head cover on and her mask into place, she was now ready for Saturday morning.

"Hi Carol!" came the welcome from John; he was the night shift, now able to go home as Carol was on duty. "They are all ready to go and the new batch is in the conditioning room." John was referring to the rats.

"How many today, John?" she enquired.

"You're lucky, they are only replacing 100, they need to see how much longer they can last without help." He left quickly, not wishing to hang around; he hated Saturdays too.

"Only 100, that will not take long." She smiled to herself.

In the centre of the room was a large table about 20 ft long and 10 ft wide. It was covered with cages, all the same height and size. This is where the rats lived during their stay with BBR. These were ordinary rats, nothing special, but they were bred for lab use and have never known any other type of life. Not having ever known freedom, they did not miss it.

To the side of the small pens containing the rats were a stack of what could have been bread trays. These had lids and were clearly marked with signs and letters indicating BIOHAZARD.

"Let's get this done," she thought, "then I can have some coffee."

She took the first tray, picked it up and placed it on the top of the pens, just to the right of the first cage holding ten rats. They were large pens containing ten smaller pens. Each rat had its own area. They were well looked after and many domestic pets would have enjoyed the attention compared to being neglected at home. Apart from the fact they were being used to test anthrax and its vaccine, they had a good, comfortable life.

Opening the first of the pens and then a smaller pen, she reached in and removed the rat. It had no fight in it as this was now in the final stages of anthrax infection. She liked them, they were cute, and she always had a little time to make a fuss of them. She hated this job, but it needed to be done.

Stroking its little head slightly, she pushed it between her first two fingers on her right hand, Holding its body firmly with her left hand, squeezed the two fingers tightly together, she pulled sharply and twisted.

The rat was dead instantly and painlessly. Then the next, and the next, each one moved to the bread tray ready for final cremation in the incinerator.

This was far quicker and more humane that killing each rat with an injection. It was also a lot cheaper. To learn the technique was not difficult; coming to terms with using it was. She hated it but the extra she was now paid as part of Project 765 was worth it.

Anyone who worked at Project 765 was a volunteer. No one had been forced to work there, although a 25% increase in pay and better conditions including free health care did force a few to volunteer.

They were informed it was a contract for the MoD and all had to sign the Official Secrets Act. They were given a lecture on what this meant, and the restrictions it imposed upon them having signed it. It was a condition of the new jobs; you had to sign to work there. The same lecture gave information about what happens if you breach the regulations.

For the first time, she could afford to pay everyone and buy herself and Sammy some clothes. Clothes that made her feel good about herself and her new love in Michael. She now had a TV and a video; at last Sammy could watch the things other kids watched: Bob the builder and Thomas.

Coleman had been on site adjacent to the A1 for 4 hours now. He knew Carol started work at 9 o'clock and they had been drilling since 5 am.

The reconstruction of the A1 and the changes made by the police and local authorities to protect BBR had also forced upon Hill Top farm a new access road. It used to stretch from the side of the A1 at almost 90 degrees direct to the house. This was a farce anyway on a major road: tractors turning directly 90 degrees of the carriageway, no slip road. Many an early morning sales rep had a rapid awakening at this junction.

A new concrete road was installed just past BBR on the Wolley road, and came parallel to the A1. This gave Coleman a good surface to get the two Mercedes trucks in, plus support vehicles. It was summer and the ground was dry, so there was little risk of any wheels becoming stuck. They only needed to get them in; Coleman would not be waiting to remove them.

Two drilling trucks were on site, one facing as though it was drilling under the road, a feint in case the farmer came by. The second rig was in place and now drilling almost parallel to the carriageway. Entering the soil just below ground level, not such a deep hole this time, and inclined at about 10 degrees, the drill had now covered almost 500 yards and was near to the target.

Project 765 occupied a basement some 30 feet below ground level. It was a converted animal accommodation room and capable of being isolated. The air-conditioning kept a constant negative pressure of 5 lb. This ensured everything stayed in and did not leak out. This was very important to the project; there could be no risk of the anthrax being able to escape, however insignificant. If there were a leak, BBR was finished and HM Government would need to start explaining very fast to the rest of the world what was going on here.

With the new rats installed in their pens, Carol's next job was give them the normal dose of virus. This was contained in a locked steel cupboard set into the wall and could only be accessed between 10.00 am and 10.30 am, everyday. The safe was alarmed, and a timer disabled the lock. If the flask went missing at 10.30, the alarm was automatic. She had 30 minutes to carry out the work; it only took 10 minutes so there was no problem.

The drilling bit passed through a plastic pipe about 5 inches across. As it progressed through the ground, it pulled the pipe with it. There was now 495 yards of pipe in the ground. By surface estimates, the distance was 510 yards, allowing for the slope.

At exactly 10.00 am Carol opened the safe and removed the flask containing the virus. She had no idea what it was other than it buggered rats big time. In its place she put a full bottle of Diet Coke. She closed the door.

The flask was a similar size to a Coke bottle except it was steel on the inside with a carbon fibre coating. This one had rubber bands around the outside in case it was dropped. At one end a thermos like cup lid could be unscrewed to reveal another seal, and access to a milky fluid within was only possible using a hypodermic.

She was aware now of a strange noise, a buzzing grinding noise that was getting louder.

Coleman knew he had to complete the job very quickly before the security systems could detect anything. He assumed that the way he was to attack the laboratory would not have been considered when they installed the alarm systems. He still had to get it right first time.

The drilling rig was contained on the rear of the vehicle; behind this Coleman had installed a compressor and a vacuum pump to be used with the drilling operation.

Most large supermarkets or banks now use a system to send paperwork around the building. Small bottle-shaped containers are pushed around a pipe system by compressed air and vacuum. The money can be put in a bottle and pushed to the cash office completely securely. This was how Coleman would get the anthrax.

Although she was expecting it, the drill still made her jump when it came through on the north wall of the lab. It pushed through about 6 inches revealing a blue pipe behind it. The cutters stopped rotating, retracted and were gone like a wild animal. It was quiet, the noise was gone and the dust was settling. A few seconds later a whistling noise started and the blue pipe was shaking, moving more and more. Eventually, a plastic shape came through the pipe and shot about 6 feet across the floor. The whistle stopped momentarily and changed to a whine.

Opening the carrier, she inserted the cold virus flask into it, and closed the top, then pushed the whole thing very hard into the pipe. Immediately it was pulled from her hand and sucked along the pipe and gone. The whine became quieter.

Coleman had told Carol that, once the flask had been sent through, he would wait for her after work. She should be able to get out as usual as no one would miss the flask until the next day. The hole in the wall could be covered for a short time; enough to make good her escape.

The whistle started again. "Something else is coming?" she thought to herself, "what can that be?" The plan with Michael was that, once the flask was gone, he would remove the pipe. But now it was returning. The whistling continued and with a pop it stopped and another bottle lay on the floor.

Carol moved over to open it, confused, but thought it might be something else from Michael. It was the same type of bottle as the first and she could see something inside. Kneeling down, she picked it up and opened it. She heard a slight hiss coughed and died where she knelt. The cyanide gas killed her and all of the rats in less than 5 seconds, far quicker than her fingers could have done it.

A claxon started sounding at Project 765. The plant security personnel and also plain clothes MoD police were now converging upon the whole building. Coleman had overlooked something. Was there a malfunction or was there something wrong? Had they detected that he had stolen the flask already?

9. Response to BBR

The Cambridgeshire Police were aware that there was a MoD interest at BBR and they had operational plans included in their standing orders to deal with a security breach at the Project 765.

They had not been told about the research that was being carried out, nor of the nature of the chemical threats that it involved. Part of the standing order was that, in the event of such a breach, they would then have authority to open top secret MoD papers held in the safe at Police HQ in Hinchingbrooke Park. Only the Chief Constable had the authority to open these papers, and he alone would read them before briefing his staff.

The Chief Constable had an identical copy of the information that was carried in his briefcase at all times day and night. The standing orders laid down a response plan to the alarm being activated at the Project 765 building; they would not respond to any other alarm at the BBR complex, only this one.

If the alarm went off, it would be one of two things, either a malfunction of the environment control system, or a security breach. No one knew the truth about what was going on at BBR, except perhaps 30 people, in the whole country.

In the event of a malfunction the building was leakproof, even up to 1.25 atmospheres. This was not such a serious problem and would be identified within 5 minutes of the alarm being sounded. Once the problem had been found, a call would be made to Police HQ to stop the response vehicles.

An alarm for any other reason had to mean that security had been breached and there was a threat of chemicals being removed or released.

All the police knew was that a military research chemical was on the site and that was all. They had no idea of its strength, its ability to kill, or its attraction to any would be terrorist or organised terrorist group.

The scenario had been practised many times, and the few involved in the response were well trained. They were only told that it was a response to a terrorist threat and that orders would be issued *en route*.

The Cambridgeshire Constabulary was lucky and had a helicopter at their disposal. It was based at RAF Wittering some 3 miles east of Huntingdon. This was a central location within the county and within reach of most places within 15 minutes' flying time.

The crews operated a three-shift system changing at 2 pm, 10 pm and 6 am.

They were on 24 hour standby to launch, which took 15 minutes, provided the aircraft had been on the ground for at least 1 hour.

A relaunch meant a longer wait, as safety and maintenance checks were necessary, plus the aircraft would need to be re-fuelled and if necessary the engines washed.

Depending on the number of hours of flying time recorded, and the number of times the engines were started, it was possible the turbines would need to be washed. This sounds a strange requirement, but the volume of air consumed through a gas turbine engine is massive. Small particles of dirt stick to the compressor blades. This reduces the efficiency of the engine, increases fuel consumption, and reduces the engine's life. Using some very clever detergents, they just wash the dirt away.

The helicopter was equipped with long-range TV cameras, infra-red cameras and a huge search light. From the air, the officers could follow any vehicle with ease and direct resources onto the vehicle to stop it. It could video an incident, collecting valuable information and evidence.

There were also two armed response vehicles on constant patrol in the county. one car in the north, and one in the south. Both were Volvo V70 estate cars, the T5 engine version, capable of over 140 mph in the right hands, covered in the normal high visibility markings.

The drivers were Class 1 police drivers or above. Above, meant they were qualified police driving instructors. They had served their time on traffic and progressed through a rigorous firearms training course to become qualified firearms experts. Again, most of them were at instructor level.

Their daily uniform included the now common black flack jackets. These, however, had cavelar plates inserted in the front and back for protection; they were different from the familiar jackets worn by 'normal' police. Their jackets were designed to defend against knife attack, not to stop bullets, as were the ARV personnel wore.

The ARV could be called into deal with any incident where firearms were being used, or just suspected.

The people of St Neots were very surprised to see the ARV in use one Saturday in the summer of 2001, with officers brandishing sub-machine guns. A passing pedestrian was shot at and hit in the neck by an air rifle pellet. The police response was the same for this as if she had been shot with a bullet, and understandably so.

They wear side arms all of the time, and in a locked steel case in the back of the car there is a variety of weapons available to them: pump action shot guns, rifles and the more common Koch and Heckler sub-machine gun.

Cambridgeshire is a very large county and covers an area from north of Peterborough to Wyboston in the south and across almost to Newmarket in the east.

Two areas were designated for the ARVs to patrol: one from the Peterborough area to the Wisbech area and 5 miles either side of this route; the second from the county boundary on the A14 near Newmarket to the Black Cat roundabout on the A1 at Tempsford, also taking 5 miles to the north of this route.

The alarm sounding at Project 765 triggered several things and put a well-planned response into action. The site's security personnel immediately sealed the whole complex. The doors to the 765 building were all locked down remotely by the security control room.

On the ground, security men were now moving to positions at points all around the building, and to pre-arranged checking points on the internal roads and pathways. Staff at BBR had seen this before when there had been security drills. They knew that, from the time the alarm sounded, no one would be allowed in, or out, of the complex, and they would be stopped and checked many times.

At Police HQ in Hinchingbrooke Park the alarm sounded at the same time as it did in BBR. The duty inspector quietly, without any hesitation, reacted.

"All Units this is a priority call, Code 765, I repeat, priority call code 765, please respond and acknowledge."

"Contact the Chief, get him in here, everyone else, you know the drill, but this time it is for real."

The radio now sprang to life and call signs from various people started to acknowledge the orders given.

The crew of the Northern ARV were on a refreshment break, eating in the canteen of Wisbech Police Station when the code 765 call was put out on the radio. Standing orders for the ARV vehicles included the response to the code 765 call, and strict instructions as to how officers would deal with such a call.

They knew immediately what this meant and what to do. Without hesitation, both officers left their meals and ran to the car in the main car park at the rear of the station. One moved quickly into the driving seat, and the second on this occasion got into the nearside rear passenger seat.

"Get your lads to clear the way through to Peterborough, if you have any cars that way, Bill," called Alan as they ran past the front desk of the station.

"Alpha Victor 1 responding, position 14 miles east of Peterborough, ETA 765 15 minutes."

Too long, thought the inspector immediately. Alpha Victor meant armed vehicle, and it was 15 minutes away, by now moving very fast towards the A47, and would skirt Peterborough on the bypass, heading south on the new A1M.

Alan sat in the driver's seat of the Volvo and, with remarkable calm, started the engine and pulled away in perfect control. No big wheel spins or dramatics. The car pulled out into the traffic, heading for the A47 bypass. Hitting a bank of switches on the top part of the dashboard, he lit up just about every flashing lamp and warning lamp available to him. The sound of the siren was very clear, and the turbine-like engine pushed them on, very fast, through the traffic.

Police vehicles ahead of the ARV were now trying to clear junctions and reduce delays, allowing the safe passage of the ARV along the A47 towards Peterborough. The first local patrol car had stopped traffic on the A47 bypass roundabout, allowing the ARV to move easily on towards Peterborough.

On the back seat, weapons were being taken out of the steel locker secured just behind in the boot space. Once these were all checked, loaded and safe, Phil would re join his partner in the front. At some time on the journey the car would make a rapid stop, possibly at a junction or roundabout. Phil would jump out of the back and into the front.

A similar traffic Volvo was waiting at the roundabout at the junction of the A47 and the A15 to the east of Peterborough. It would then assist the ARV to move south towards Brampton.

"Hotel 4 we are 10 minutes from launch and will be on target in 15 minutes."

This was the helicopter and they were ready to go as planned. The BBR alarm also sounded at their office, a small building on the north of the runway. They had orders to proceed to BBR and await instructions. Pre launch checks had to be done; there was no jump in and go for the helicopter. These checks were important for the crew and for the safety of the public.

"Alpha Victor 2 please acknowledge," the inspector was impatient. By now they should have responded to the initial call.

"Control Alpha Victor 2, we are westbound on the A14 just passing Cambridge. Traffic is heavy, progress is slow. ETA on target is minimum 10 to 15 minutes."

"Alpha Victor 2 proceed to junction A1 and A428, head north on A1. AV1 will approach, moving south on A1M, acknowledge."

AV2 responded and pushed on through the traffic towards the A1.

Control had the three main response vehicles up and running, the first would not be on target for almost 20 minutes. "Good," he thought to himself. "Where is the Chief?" he called out to the Control room.

The Chief Constable was now in HQ, as luck would have it he was nearby at the time and came directly to his office. He had the papers on his desk and, two senior officers a discrete distance away waited for his instruction.

"Gentlemen, this is very serious, the Project 765 uses weapons grade anthrax to develop vaccines. It is possible this has been compromised, put the standing orders into action, keep me informed, I will be in the control room."

No point in beating about the bush.

"Alpha Victor 1 and 2, all transmissions from now on are secure, please switch to channel 5 and use open channel."

The police had long wanted a secure channel for their radio communications and it had been granted to ARV-type vehicles and for other important use.

In another part of the control room civilian staff had opened a direct line and were in contact with BBR and the MoD. They had ordered the local hospital on to full alert to expect a chemical incident.

Four ambulances were now moving towards a rendezvous point pre-arranged in the rehearsals. They would stand by, awaiting instructions. A similar call had gone out to the Fire Service and two engines were now responding to their own pre-arranged stand-off point.

A & E staff were fighting their way through Saturday traffic and shoppers to get back to their posts. The hospital directors had sealed instructions too, and they also had special boxes in store containing the latest vaccine and serum.

The control room was issuing further instructions to the units responding.

"Alpha Victor 1 and 2, on direct instructions from the Chief Constable you are now authorised to use weapons, I repeat you are authorised to use weapons. You are facing a possible terrorist threat, involving the removal of chemical weapon substances from BBR. You must assume you will be fired upon if you approach any suspect."

This gave the officers official permission to use their weapons. Although by now both crews would have weapons ready to use, they needed authorisation to actually draw and use them.

At the exact same time the police were alerted, a message was flashed by them, this time using secure MoD computer systems, direct to Hereford, home of the 22nd Airborne, the SAS.

The meticulous planning of the MoD had foreseen a possible threat and a direct response had been formulated using the SAS. They had trained to respond to the threat of BBR being breached, although they had never been seen training and the Cambridgeshire Police had no idea of what they could or would do.

"Major, sorry to disturb you Sir, we have just been notified that operation 765 is now active; you are required back on camp immediately."

The duty Sergeant had never had to make this call before, but he knew what it meant.

"Thank you, Sergeant, I will be there in 4 minutes, please ready an aircraft and get the duty team ready to go immediately, the standby team leaves in 20 minutes by road."

Two teams of eight men were tasked with the job of responding to the alarm. Each knew the situation and each had a job to do. The first team would be moved by air to a place near BBR where they could be deployed quickly if needed. The second team would move by road as a back-up for the first and to bring their equipment required to deal with the incident.

Within 1 minute of the alarm sounding, three police units were responding to the call, two of which would be there within 20 minutes. On the other side of the country, nestling in the Brecon Beacons, another helicopter was about to lift off and join the response to the problem at BBR. ETA was 35 minutes.

Coleman had not considered that the environment control of the lab was so good. The hole he had drilled through the wall had allowed the pressure to equalize, in fact it was now positive rather than negative. He had continued to blow air through the pipe, not wanting any cyanide coming his way.

He had planned the escape very well, and had built in a contingency plan. He did not foresee the need to go so quickly. The layby just before the start of the A1M was 300 yards further north than where he was drilling. A car was parked here, a normal car, not a fast flashy get-away car. It was a red Ford Mondeo. Coleman had not stolen it; he had purchased it legally, an average car that could be lost amongst the many others on the road that day.

Parked on the new road, built to access the farm when the changes were made by the building of the new motorway, was a Land Rover Discovery. Coleman chose this for two reasons. Firstly, it looked like a farmer's vehicle and would not seem out of place, it also looked like a contractor's vehicle and fitted in with the image of the drilling being carried out.

This was the back-up vehicle. If escape were not possible using the Mondeo, for some reason, he would use the Discovery, and could, if needed, drive across land.

The noise of the alarms surprised Coleman; he could not understand how they had found out so quickly. He was not going to wait though. He had assumed no one would be aware of the theft until a shift change. This gave him several hours, or so he thought; now he had been compromised and needed to act.

Taking the flask of anthrax he and two of the others moved up the side of the field, and crossed over into the layby. Coleman had created a small gap in the hawthorn hedge a few nights previously. Their car started straight away and they pulled out normally into the traffic and headed up the A1M.

The two others who were with Coleman, walked to the Discovery, got in and sat and waited. They had strict instructions to follow. If they drove off immediately after the alarm sounded, it would seem obvious they were running away. Coleman did not want undue attention drawn to the Discovery and instructed them to wait for 10 minutes before moving off.

It must have seemed like a lifetime sitting watching the growing drama within BBR. Eventually, calmly, they drove off along the farm road towards the Woolley road. When they got to the junction and realised if they turned left, they had to pass BBR's main gate and security point, they panicked and they went right, a big mistake.

George knew that each room in the project building was airtight and sealed. If there was a leak, he knew he was safe, even in the next room.

However, it was his job to investigate what was wrong. The control panels for the environment control system were behind his desk, and looking at them, they showed normal in all rooms, except one, the lab.

This panel was showing positive pressure, not just equal pressure. If the system failed, he knew that pressure would equalize, to go positive meant something was blowing air into the room, and not sucking air out.

He disabled the system for the lab, just to see what happened. If it had malfunctioned and was blowing air instead of sucking air, then the increase in pressure would die away. The pressure moved up further.

"George here, I have positive pressure in the lab, all other rooms are 100% correct. Pressure source is not our systems, I am going to investigate."

The security control room responded,

"George, we have the MoD outside and more of our guys are on the way, the police are moving, you are now locked in. Please confirm exact problem soonest."

BBR had provided the guards at Project 765 with an NBC suit, specially made for the job, and not standard issue as used by the armed forces. He was used to wearing it, as frequent drills were carried out for just such a problem.

It took him about 1 minute to get into the suit, he had practised this many times and was very good at it. He had never considered that it might be necessary for him to wear this for anything other than a drill. He made his way through the various doors and air locks to the lab. Even though there was a major security emergency in progress, he still had to pass through each door in the normal way.

Stopping for breath just outside, George leaned against the door and stared through into the lab. From the glass panel in the door, he could see the hole in the wall, and the 6 inches of pipe coming through. The room was full of airborne dust, blown through by the drilling and compressor sitting at the back of the drilling rig.

"There's a fucking hole in the wall, how the hell did that get there, we are 30 ft underground." He yelled down his mike.

"Please confirm, there is a hole in the wall."

"Yes, someone has drilled a fucking hole through the wall, Carol is on the floor, and there is no movement at all from the rats."

"Police HQ, this is security control at BBR, we confirm that we have a situation red, the building has been entered by force. It is unknown at this time what, if anything, has been removed or left behind. We will advise."

The BBR security control forwarded this information to the police and swung the big CCTV cameras to the north to look at the fencing behind 765. The fence was intact and there was no sign of any holes in the ground. All they could see out of the ordinary were the drilling rigs working under the A1 and a green Landrover Discovery.

George was safe from gas and chemical agents inside his suit; he released the door with his ID card and waited for the door to unlock. With a click it was free and he moved quickly to Carol. She was still kneeling over the deadly bottle, but had slumped slightly forward stuck against the leg of the big table.

"Carol..., Carol, are you OK, can you hear me Carol?"

Moving her back and onto her side, he could see her face mask had a brown area of stain in the middle, caused by her momentarily vomiting bile from her stomach in the split second it took for her to die. Even to George it was obvious she was dead. George could not locate a pulse. He tried, but through the suit even if she were alive, he would have had difficulty feeling anything. She was dead, killed by the one person she loved.

The expression on her face had not changed, complete surprise; her eyes were open staring into oblivion. George gently moved his had over her face and closed them. . He removed her mask, wiping the mess from her mouth, and laid her gently onto the floor, straightening her legs from beneath her.

Looking around the room, George reported to control that all of the rats were dead. Something had gone very wrong in the lab that morning. He examined the pipe sticking out of the wall, and through his suit could feel the gentle force of the air being blown through from the surface.

Opposite him in the wall was the safe where the anthrax was stored. It was closed and undamaged. The green lights at the side on the left showed him that all was well. Had the contents been missing, an alarm would sound automatically. The lights would be red.

"The virus safe seems secure," called George over the radio. "Green lights and no sign of forced entry. No alarm, what do you want me to do?"

"Standby, George, we need to discuss with the MoD police."

Less than 1 minute later, the security control responded.

"George, MoD is going to release the lock on the safe, open it and confirm contents please. Stand back while it is opened, to be safe."

George moved away and through the lab door, allowing it to seal once again behind him. Through the small window, he watched as the green lights set in the wall next to the safe turned red and flashed.

"Safe is now unlocked, George, please take a look."

Slowly he moved back into the lab and up to the safe door. He had no idea of what might lie behind. It could be what was expected, it could be a bomb.

He opened the door about half an inch and using a flashlight George examined the gap to see if there were any foreign wires or contacts that had been put in place. There was nothing to be seen. Slowly he opened the door and looked inside.

"The safe contains a bottle of Diet Coke, nothing else."

"Please confirm, George, you're saying a bottle of Coke?"

"Correct, only a bottle of Coke."

"What will happen to Sammy?" he thought, leaving the room as it was, shutting the door and walking back through the various sealed areas to his desk.

He informed control of what he had seen, sitting at his desk, still in his NBC suit and wept for his friend, Carol.

Alpha Victor 1 had now arrived at the roundabout junction of the A15 and A47. The traffic car had the road blocked to allow the ARV to pass uninterrupted, As soon as it had cleared the junction, they followed.

A police driver is one of the most professional drivers anyone can watch, and they become a part of the machine, merging completely as one. The driver is left to his own, it is very rare his co-driver will interfere. At every point the driver is evaluating the safest way, the quickest way to deal with, and overcome, traffic *en route*.

The two cars were now speeding along the A15 towards the junction with the A1, to turn south towards BBR. The ARV had the lead and was holding a position to the right side of the outer lane. The traffic car was in the same lane, but to the left side. The combined width increased the visibility of the fast moving cars to traffic in front.

Most people when seeing the police in their mirrors will hit the brakes and slow down, even if they cannot pull in out of the way. This is a problem that the drivers are taught to deal with. There is no anger or frustration, just cool, calm, deliberate actions, waiting for the road to clear, and pushing on.

From 2 miles out, the helicopter already had the TV camera on full zoom, pointing at BBR. It had the information about the hole in the wall, and the drilling rigs outside. The police had already confirmed that no drilling was being done there, and that these rigs were suspect.

The green Discovery had also been seen leaving, by the CCTV cameras, and Hotel 1 was now moving towards the direction it was reported leaving.

AV2 was northbound on the A1 from St Neots. It had cleared the roundabout at Buckden and was speeding north. The entrance to BBR was on the northbound carriageway. AV1 would have to U-turn at the Brampton Hut roundabout. Patrol cars were already in place to stop the traffic.

"AV2 this is Hotel 1, we have target vehicle, green Disco' moving west from BBR along unclassified road towards Woolley."

AV2 was now turning from the A1 into Woolley road. The driver had topped 125 miles per hour on the way, and triggered just about every speed camera. The car sped along past the main gate of BBR and was now moving faster and easier than the Discovery ever could.

"AV2 you are about half mile behind target vehicle and closing, he is still heading into Woolley, road is clear."

Woolley is a small hamlet of about ten houses, very smart and expensive. They were unused to a lot of traffic and this was going to surprise them greatly. There were two ways out of the village, one that was almost straight on. Provided no one was in the way, there was no problem. The other would take the Discovery on more small single track roads through Barham towards Molesworth, the USAF base.

AV1 was now southbound on the A1, still in tandem with the normal traffic car, this time occupying the two outer lanes of the 4-lane carriageway. Police HQ had now displayed a message on the overhead road signs: 'Move over to the left emergency'.

Both cars were travelling at well over 120 mph and were about 4 minutes from the Brampton Hut roundabout.

By now AV2 was within sight of the Discovery and the second officer Kevin had made his weapons available. He put the pump action shotgun on the floor to his left, resting up towards the door. His sub machine gun was now slung over him across his chest from right to left. On the floor to his right was a second sub-machine gun for the driver to grab as they stopped, if they stopped.

Kevin would go out first, using the door as cover. It would not stop a round, but it made him a more difficult target to any shooter. He would provide cover for his mate, whilst he stopped the car safely and slung his own weapons.

"AV1 and AV2 this is control, we now have confirmation that dangerous chemicals have been removed from BBR by unknown persons. Assume suspects armed and dangerous. You are authorised to use weapons, weapons are now free. Normal rules of engagement apply."

"Control, this is AV2, please confirm last message, we are free to fire if necessary."

"Affirmative, AV2, Chief is with us in control room, you have authority to fire."

"OK, we have covered our arse, let's stop these people and see what's up."

Kevin hit a bank of switches added onto the dashboard, the car lit up once again with blue and red flashing lights. The headlamps came on alternating left and right, and the horns started blurting out the familiar siren sound. The PA system fitted to the car was seriously loud, designed to be used to advise people to evacuate or stay indoors.

"Pull over and stop, we are armed police officers, pull over and stop." No response at all from the Discovery, it sped on along the narrow lane.

From the air, Hotel 1 could see that they intended to try to stop the car, and had lit up every light possible to get the attention of the Discovery driver. The cars were marked on the roof with their call sign. This enabled air support units to identify the ground units involved.

The Discovery did not stop; it had seen them because the passenger looked back. He also leaned over the front seat and grabbed something from the rear.

Speeding on along a very narrow road they were exceeding 75 miles per hour. Not fast particularly until you consider the width of the road.

AV2 knew the road ahead was clear, the helicopter was telling him. The Discovery had no idea.

They were less than 50 yards behind when the Arab fired. A burst of rounds came through the rear windscreen of the Discovery, smashing it to pieces and throwing glass onto the chasing police car. The rounds hit the lights on the top of the car destroying them.

"Fuck, drop back," Kevin yelled, "Drop back."

"Control, AV2, we have been fired on, by male occupant of the Discovery, small sub machine gun, request immediate back-up."

"Control, this is Hotel 1, target vehicle is moving south towards Woolley and heading to the A14. Speed is too high to make the turn to Barham, they have to go straight on. Divert AV1 onto A14. Close down A14 both directions."

"AV2 confirmed, AV1 *en route*, diverting onto A14, will approach you from east. A14 now closed westbound at Brampton Hut, and eastbound at Thrapston. You have the full road; try to keep them on it."

They kept a distance of about 70 yards, still in contact. The helicopter above was advising road conditions and position. AV2 had advance warning of turns and bends and other obstructions. The co-pilot was talking a commentary just as if they were running a motor rally circuit. Both AV1 and the control room were listening.

The Arab fired again but, because of the bends and distance between them, the rounds went astray. They thundered into Woolley and the Discovery took the natural route, straight on. To go right towards Molesworth meant slowing down, and that was too big a risk.

"Don't push him, let him lead us, he has to go either onto the A14 or through to Easton."

"Control, AV2, please block the road from A14 through to Easton," Kevin requested.

"AV2, this is already done, there is a 40 ft trailer across road. He has to head either west or east along A14."

The helicopter now informed them that the Discovery was nearing the junction with the A14. They wanted him to go west as it gave them more room. About 300 yards short of the junction with the A14 the Discovery suddenly braked very hard, and more rounds came crashing towards the police car, churning up the dirt on the bank at the side of the road.

Turning hard right, it moved onto a dirt track heading west across a field, and on towards the farmhouse at the top of the hill. The police vehicle was unable to follow on this terrain and slowed to a stop at the track entrance.

"AV2, continue south turn right onto A14, we will guide you back in on the target."

The helicopter had now gained height to get a clearer view of the options open to the Discovery.

The Arabs sped on across the field using this track. They realised they had shaken the police car, but also knew the helicopter was still following them. The track joined the road leading from Barham to Spaldwick. If they turned right, the police could be chasing them through country lanes for the rest of the day. If they turned left, they had to go onto the A14.

The aircrew realised this and moved, positioning the helicopter on the right side and closing making it obvious they were there. They were trying to force the Discovery to move left and on to the A14.

The Arab tried to fire at them but they were moving left to right all of the time, deliberately making a shot difficult. The sound and sight of the helicopter so low was frightening.

The natural reaction would be to turn away from them and they did, heading towards the A14.

The Discovery was a V8, not the Tdi that most people would buy. With fuel consumption in the mid-teens, it was not as popular. It sped down the road, heading onto the A14 heading west.

AV2 was waiting on the dual carriageway for them to join the road; as the Discovery started down the sliproad, they saw the police car and stopped. They had clear line of sight between them and the police and they used it.

A rapid burst of automatic fire tore up the ground in front of the car, Kevin opened the door and rolled out and ran for the side of the bridge.

"Get out of sight," he yelled, "pull the car back."

More rounds hit the car on the front nearside and the rest hit the tarmac. This time in response there were four sets of two shots, controlled rapid fire from Kevin's Koch and Heckler. Both offside windows disappeared and the passenger with the gun fell forward and screamed.

The Discovery driver immediately drove off, and onto the A14.

"Kev, come on let's go, get in the bloody car."

The road was blocked to the east of Thrapston, this gave them about 10 miles of free road.

The police knew that, but the Discovery did not. All exits from the road were now blocked using large vehicles commandeered from the traffic on the road by the police.

The big V8 accelerated away remarkably fast, but not fast enough for the T5. AV2 had joined the road further back and was now at full speed on the tail of the Discovery.

"Close up see if we can get past," suggested Kevin, "I am sure I hit the passenger."

"Control, we have exchanged fire with vehicle, passenger may be injured, and we are now trying to stop them."

The big Volvo responded and increased speed, closing the gap between them. The driver was moving from the outside to the inside lane making a shot harder.

" We are moving up on target, closing now to attempt overtake, 50 yards," Kevin was now giving a full commentary to the control room.

It was harder, but it still came, another short burst, this time without the glass, punching holes across the bonnet, three of them, and a fourth came through the top right corner of the windscreen, leaving a crazy-paving effect. The driver could still see OK, and dropped back once more.

"We have been fired on again, ETA AV1 please."

"They're behind us Kevin."

In the rear view mirror, the driver could see, and now so could Kevin, the blue and red flashes of AV1 travelling at almost 140 mph on a clear road. They fell in along side AV2, and examined the outside of the car.

"You two OK?" They responded with the thumbs-up sign.

Half a mile to east of Thrapston, a military helicopter had just landed on the carriageway, eight men in full camouflage gear jumped out and ran to both sides of the west-bound carriageway. No hesitation.

They deployed in four pairs, two pairs either side of the carriageway, 400 yards apart. The forward two pairs both had disposable type 66 shoulder launched anti armour rockets. These were carried by the lead man with his back-up behind. The back-ups had standard issue sub machine guns.

The 66 is literally a disposable weapon, break it open into firing position, point, fire and throw the remains away. It was a fearsome weapon that had proved itself time again in conflicts as far apart as the Falklands and the Middle East.

The first forward pair crouched in the central reservation, and the second were about 50 yards back on the verge. They were not totally visible, but you could see them if you knew where to look.

The other two pairs were farther back, both pairs nursing a minimy machine gun, belt fed.

"AV2, control, position please?"

"We have just cleared junction with B663 Keyston, ETA Thrapston roundabout less than 2 minutes," Kevin responded.

"AV1 and 2, drop back slowly, not obviously, to 1000 yards, then stop and await instructions. Secure the road, no vehicle is to pass either way."

Strange, Kevin thought to himself.

"Control, confirm last transmission."

"AV1 and 2, drop back to 1000 yards and stop, military will take over from here."

Both cars slowed and increased the distance from the Discovery, They could see about 1 mile in front almost into Northamptonshire. The Discovery continued, seemingly unconcerned that the police cars had dropped away.

In front was a long slow hill down towards the left, then the road rose back up again to the horizon. 2 miles ahead was the junction of the A14 and A605 to Peterborough. A mass of blue lights could be seen just past the brow of the hill in the distance. There were several police vehicles, ambulances and two fire engines, one of which was from RAF Molesworth, a foam-spraying engine from the airfield.

The dark shadow of the helicopter sitting in the field, just to the north, was a big surprise to the police drivers. Its rotor was still moving.

The Discovery sped on, it too must have been able to see the lights. Where he was intending to go was anyone's guess.

It was now around 30 minutes from the time the alarm had first been raised at BBR.

Half-way down the hill Kevin saw a flash and a puff of smoke from the left verge. A second later the Discovery exploded and left the road. The force lifted it about 10 feet in the air and crashed it onto its roof, sliding along the road surface, on fire. It stopped midway between the two pairs of soldiers.

The driver had not seen the soldiers until the last minute, he knew that he was dead, and let go of the wheel, clasping his hands together he had prayed.

Instantly, six of the eight appeared, moving forward to the vehicle. They advanced in pairs, the lead man would run forward, drop down to a squat whilst his partner ran passed him and on further, only moving 10 feet at a time, slowly, deliberately.

All had their weapons raised and ready to fire. The remaining two stayed put on the central reservation. Although the vehicle had been hit, and hard, it was possible for resistance to continue. They had another 66 lined up continually on the wrecked Discovery.

They reached the vehicle as close in as they could. It was burning fiercely now. Although it must have been obvious that the two Arabs were dead, they had to check.

Moving away just as quickly as they came, still conscious of threat and covering each other's back, they re-assembled 100 yards west of the wreck.

"Fuck me!"

As Kevin sat trying to take in what he had just seen, a dark helicopter flew in from the north, landed, collected eight people, and left.

The instant they were gone, a convoy of flashing lights began to move forward from the far side of the hill towards the wrecked Discovery.

"AV1 and 2, secure the road no one is to pass, assume hostile until stood down, control out."

10. Coleman Escape

Passing through the gap in the hawthorn hedge, Coleman walked calmly towards the Ford Mondeo pulling up the zipper on his trousers. The two Arab men were deliberately a short distance behind.

He opened the boot of the car and carefully placed the dark flask containing the anthrax into the boot. Using an old blanket, he wrapped it up and then wedged it into the wheel well.

Looking around him casually, he could see nothing out of the ordinary. Apart from the wailing of the claxon at BBR, it was a normal Saturday morning on the A1. Just as casually he walked around the car, and got in.

Coleman drove and the two Arabs had got into the back seat of the car, sitting normally and casually. Considering they had somehow triggered the alarm at Project 765, they were all remarkably self-controlled.

Not wanting to draw any attention to themselves, Coleman waited a few minutes before starting the car; moving off, pulling out into the Saturday morning traffic, heading north on the A1.

He knew that it was entirely possible he was being watched, or even followed. Coleman had already considered that his plan may have been compromised, or perhaps the local police may have been lucky in noticing his car. It was unlikely, but his instinct taught him to expect and plan for the worst.

The only other vehicle in the layby was a 40 ft artic' lorry. It had the curtains drawn, the driver obviously still asleep. This concerned Coleman a little and as he drove he was pondering the point. There could be someone inside watching them from behind the curtains. He eventually dismissed this thought, knowing he would be approached very quickly if they were watching him from the lorry. His deadly bounty would be wanted back very badly.

He travelled north on the A1 at 70 mph, no faster, and with great care, not wanting to draw attention to himself. In fact at 70mph he was possibly doing just that. Everyone else was speeding past him as if the limit was to, all intents and purposes, a minimum speed.

His idea was to put a feint or a decoy route before heading off in the direction of his intended destination. The road was reasonably busy, people making their way along through their own lives, oblivious of the deadly cargo being carried so near to them.

Coleman had studied this stretch of road in minute detail. He knew where every camera was, and possible point of compromise, where the police could join the road and follow him. In his mind, as he passed each way-point, he made a mental check against each location.

He continued north, passed Sawtry on the left, then Stilton, the original home of the famous cheese, under what used to be Norman Cross and then he turned off the motorway at the junction for Peterborough. He had his flat in Peterborough and it was a comforting thought to divert off and get home to familiar surroundings. But he could not, for now. He turned left towards Oundle and entered the new Services that were completed under a year ago.

Acting as though nothing was wrong, he drew up next to a fuel pump, got out and started to fill up the car. This was deliberate and he took his time, to be sure the garage's CCTV recorded the car.

Most garage forecourts will no longer release the pumps until the index number of your car has been recorded. This is then checked automatically against data from Swansea DVLA.

If the police were treating his car as suspicious, then they would not expect him to stop for gas. Another feint; again, in the hope it would confuse any follow-up attempt.

As they left the garage, Coleman moved back towards the A1. He travelled completely around the roundabout and re joined the motorway on the southbound carriageway.

From the slip road leading onto the motorway Coleman could see the overhead road signs. They were now displaying a warning to pull over and allow emergency vehicles to pass. A few moments later two police cars flashed passed him, down the slip road travelling south towards the alarm at BBS.

After only one and half miles, he left the road again, following the signs for Stilton, up past the strange round hotel building and then joined the B road that paralleled the A1M and continued south. The design of this junction is such that he had to cross the motorway twice, firstly east to west and then west to east. Both times they had a clear view of the traffic, no more police cars!

This was the part of the road that was retained when the new motorway was built, to allow non-motorway traffic access north and south. It was the original southbound carriageway and had now been converted to a two-way road.

He continued down his route, passing Sawtry again and south past the newly located memorial to the American pilots. On over the junction at the head of the A14, he drove in and parked his car at the McDonalds restaurant just outside the USAF Alconbury.

The base is no longer active; the aircraft have long since gone. There are a few Americans looking after the base, the understanding of the local community is that they are housekeeping the base just in case it is needed for some future defence of the west.

Just how quickly they could re-commission the base is questionable. Parts of the runway have been rented out to various storage businesses, including a fleet car supplier and a containerised storage company. It would take at least a week to clear the runway.

During the second half of 2003 the Government announced that a deep review of the airports surrounding London had been completed and the recommendations were that new capacity had to be provided for the growing demand in air travel.

This immediately rang alarm bells within 30 miles of any of the major London airports.

Stansted had been put forward as the best place to build a new runway. This renewed the huge row with the local residents. Gatwick was proposed; although legislation set in place many years ago prevented the building of the second Gatwick runway for some time forward. Heathrow was already building as fast as it could.

New capacity was required and, in order to meet this demand, the Government now proposed that Rugby Airport be developed and that Alconbury USAF base be developed for commercial use. A second runway for Luton was ruled out completely.

Out of all of the suggested solutions, without a doubt, the development of Alconbury was by far the most sensible, and economic.

The base existed; there were two good long runways and taxi-ways available, suitable to despatch and receive a 747 without any issue. The base had only been closed a few years, which meant that local residents were used to the noise of military aircraft taking off.

Judging by the amount of complaints and protests you would thought that Alconbury never existed before. The strict regulations governing engine noise from commercial airliners provide much lower levels of noise pollution than military jets on afterburner. If the residents had put up with the USAF for all of the years they were in residence, then a 737 would be nothing.

The completion of the new road to the west of the site gave instant access to the motorway network. All that would be needed was the slip road to be built for rapid access. To the east side of the site was the main north–south rail route, a fast, good-quality route direct to London. Simplicity itself to spur and build a new station.

In terms of employment alone, the project would provide over 12,000 jobs. Revenue for the town and the county would be enormous.

But it was not to be. The final decision was made to demolish dozens of Grade 1 listed buildings, eat up further acres of the Essex countryside and build the second runway at Stansted. If ever a decision has been a folly, then this one has to be the one.

Even after building the new A120 from the M11 to Braintree and covering more land in tarmac, they decide to take more, and do the same for the new runway, whilst 40 miles to the north, the facility exists, dormant, covered in containers.

The idea of the detour that Coleman had made was to give the motorway cameras a chance to film his car moving north, and then into Peterborough. He had studied their locations, and the CCTV cameras would have filmed him as he moved north from BBR and turned off from the northbound carriageway. The garage cameras would have recorded his visit for fuel and possibly logged them with the DVLA, then the road cameras would have caught him moving around the roundabout.

From this point, he would have been out of camera shot and unseen, moving back onto the southbound side. The next CCTV camera was just south of Stilton, and by this time Coleman had come off of the motorway and joined the B road to the south. This road had no cameras.

Any eagle-eyed policeman trying to trace cars moving away from the layby near BBS would have to assume that the Mondeo drove into Peterborough, considering it unlikely to have retraced its journey south. Hopefully, his new route to the south would have been undetected. Any follow up would have then been centred on the Peterborough area.

Parking the car next to a small blue Citroën van, Coleman and his two friends made sure nothing was on view inside the car, locked it and walked into the restaurant.

This McDonalds is one of the most famous locations in the UK. The building is in the shape of a flying saucer. It was built as a burger restaurant in the early 1980s. The original owners used what were then state-of-the-art computers at each table to order the food. The aim was to provide a gimmicky venue for the thousands of USAF families based at Alconbury. The software failed, the idea being a little before its time and the ability of the programming. The restaurant quickly followed.

After about 2 years of being empty, it was bought by McDonalds and has been thriving ever since.

From the outside it does look like every kid's idea of a flying saucer, complete with a tunnel as an entrance. What does spoil the effect somewhat is the double glazing and conservatory sales area right next door.

They ordered their food and found a table at the side of the restaurant and sat down. None of them was able to eat it. Their mouths were too dry, and they all were still riding adrenalin highs. The fright of the alarm sounding so quickly and unexpectedly, and the rapid exit had them all very hyper. Although they had all had some time in the car to relax, they had not been able to.

"Slow down, and take it easy, we must act normally. Speak English, I do not want to draw attention to us."

Trying to appear normal, the three spent some time talking and trying to eat what felt to them like cardboard hamburgers. They drank more coffee, taking advantage of the free top up offer.

Coleman relaxed and, in his mind, started to analyse just how the alarm was triggered so quickly. He had covered every point, or so he thought. The training and the discipline his Arab friends had taught him had been used to the best of his ability. But he had missed something.

Why did the alarm trigger so quickly. Did Carol betray him before she died? Did she die? Was he set up? If so, why are they not chasing him?

"Not possible," he thought; the cyanide would act within seconds, and he knew that it was very quick. He knew that Carol was not expecting a second delivery and would be curious. It was her nature. Slowly he started to understand what he had missed. The pressure in the room was monitored and the changes when he drilled a hole in the wall caused the rooms pressure to change and set off the alarm.

Angry with himself, Coleman checked his next moves again in his mind; he could not afford another problem.

"Was everything OK, sir? Can I get you some more coffee?"

They were very free with the coffee here, that's for sure. Coleman refused politely and gestured to his comrades.

They used the toilets, washed their hands and faces, pulled themselves back together and eventually made their way outside, back to the car.

Opening the boot of the Mondeo, Coleman removed the blanket containing the flask, and put it in his sports bag that had been left in the boot the previous day, carefully zipping up the top to make sure no one could see inside.

The rear of the blue van was now open, and the sports bag was put in-between two other large canvas bags. Both were sports bags: one was a large Reebok leather effect bag, and the other a green jaguar holdall.

To the right of these bags was a full-sized golf bag, complete with wheels and cover. Wedged firmly between the two bags, the deadly cargo in Coleman's bag seemed quite safe. The younger of the two Arabs now climbed into the back and sat down, Coleman and the other Arab, Shaviv, sat in front. Shaviv was driving.

They drove out of the car park and headed slowly east towards Huntingdon. Without them seeing, less than 10 seconds later, a dark saloon car moved quietly away and followed them.

It was not his intention to return to his rented flat. They needed to lay low for a few days. The authorities would quickly realise that he could be involved in the theft of the anthrax. Even Wilson could have figured out that he knew when and where the anthrax would be moved.

Coleman needed to stay local as his aims required this, but out of view for a couple of weeks.

They moved past the main entrance to USAF Alconbury, past the odd scene of the fighter aircraft flying out of the ground, directly opposite a church. Past the little bit of America you can see on the left, the housing used by the USAF personnel, a little township built in American style. They passed by the old house once occupied by John Major when he was Prime Minister, still protected by a very sophisticated alarm system.

Coleman felt something was wrong, Shaviv was too quiet, he seemed to be spending more time looking behind him, than in front.

"I think we may have a tail," Shaviv said quietly, "there is a dark-coloured car following us behind."

"You're being stupid Shaviv, it's just an innocent car, nothing to worry about."

"No, it is not, the car came out of McDonalds. They are hanging back, shadowing us, matching our speed. A normal British driver would be up my arse by now."

Coleman did not make it obvious he was looking, but turned to talk to the passenger in the back. They were now approaching the outskirts of Huntingdon and a large roundabout.

"Slow down to see if he will pass, turn right and take the dual carriageway back towards the A14. He can pass on this road."

Indicating right, Shaviv turned around the roundabout and drove towards the A14. This was a busy link road and traffic was often queued. He drove very slowly, annoyingly slowly, and hoped the car would pass. It did.

As they reached the roundabout, there was a small queue of traffic, five or six cars in each lane. They were one car behind the saloon which was still on the offside, but they were on the inside lane. Coleman could see the occupants, neither of them turned and looked. Maybe they were being too cautious.

The detour was a pain; Shaviv drove completely around the roundabout and back in towards Huntingdon. The dark car moved away and did not follow them.

It was now late morning and they had to get to safety and out of sight. Coleman had his flat in Peterborough; he still had a flat in

Cambridge, both of which were known to the authorities and would have been watched possibly.

Coleman had decided the best place to go was a Travelodge-type of hotel; it was less likely that anyone would know they were there. The good thing about these places is they ask very few questions and it is, more often than not, unoccupied by staff. He had booked rooms at this lodge many times over the past weeks. The staff knew him now. The Travelodge on the eastbound side of the A14 was near to St Ives. Coleman had been there for the last 3 days with the two Arabs.

Once back on their original route, they drove through the centre of Huntingdon, around the ring road, travelling on the back roads towards St Ives. Coleman deliberately again did not take the most direct route. At St Ives he drove around the town and then joined the A14 there. A few more miles east of St Ives was the Travelodge.

Coleman took the anthrax, and Shaviv and his mate removed all of the other bags from the van. They took them carefully through into the hotel and placed them in Coleman's room. He insisted that he wanted to be in constant control of them and have them in view at all times. After all, they did contain the stolen anthrax and their weapons.

Once safe in their rooms, they relaxed a little. Shaviv took out one of the guns and started to check it, and load it. They quietly went over what had happened and where their other two friends might be. It was intended not to have any communications between their two original vehicles, or any personal communications other than mobile telephones. The mobile that the others had was diverting to voice mail. It was turned off.

Coleman put on the television to see the news; he wanted to know if the problems at BBR were being reported and just what they would say had been stolen. The news presenter discussed the alarm and emergency at the BBR complex with his defence correspondent. Then the news showed pictures of a badly burnt out Discovery that had been chased from the scene and had blown up mysteriously.

The programme put forward the idea that this was some form of terrorist activity or animal rights activity that had gone wrong. They were convinced this was a foiled terrorist attack.

"They had no explosives in the car, they had been killed by the police or the army," he thought, a demonstration of how seriously they take this situation.

"They are both dead," Coleman announced to the others, "This leaves just us to finish the work we have been given. We will go, on we must not fail, we will not fail."

The dark saloon car that had followed them from the McDonalds in Alconbury now pulled into the car park and stopped across the back of the van forming a T-shape. One of the men got out and looked around the van. The second sat still surveying the area for people that might compromise them. Across his lap lay a sub machine gun, a Koch and Heckler.

He looked underneath the van and then into the back through the small glass windows. It appeared it was empty, but it did not satisfy him.

Using a thin flat piece of steel he quickly slotted it down between the window and top of the door, releasing the lock, and slid inside. The car parked at the back hid most of this from any onlookers, and avoided any interference.

"It's clean, they are inside, let's go."

"Nothing at all, not a trace?"

"Nothing, they have it inside, they have not had time to pass it onto anyone."

They drove off in the car and parked in the car park reserved for customers of the Little Chef. If anyone did happen to look outside, they did not need to see the car too quickly.

They left the machine gun hidden and took only their side arms. Walking as normally as possible, they moved to the front of the Lodge and waited for someone to leave. Passing through the door, they then moved slowly up and down each corridor, listening for people talking. Someone would be talking Arabic. There were very few cars in the car park so there were not many guests at this time.

Coleman had three rooms, all next to each other on the first floor to the right of the stairs. His room was the last, farthest from the stairs; the other two had a room each, next to him. It could have been instinct or luck but he knew something was wrong, his guts were telling him.

It did not take them long to locate a room where the television was working. It did take a while for them to hear Arabic spoken lightly within. They knew that there were three of them, and it was logical that they would have room each and not be sharing together. This would look odd even nowadays.

They took the room to the right first and forced the lock open. Sliding inside the door they drew their side arms and went in.

"Quiet, turn off the television," he commanded.

"What is wrong Michael?" asked Shaviv.

"I don't know, can you feel it, can you feel danger?"

Listening they heard the door being tried in the room next door, it was Shaviv's room, and he had not yet been back in there today. The sounds increased, the door had been forced or the lock picked.

"Someone is in your room, quickly get the bags together, Shaviv, climb out of the window and drop to the floor, take the bags to the car."

Coleman's heart was now pounding like a steam train. They were on the second floor of the Lodge and Shaviv had to drop about 15 feet to the ground. Without hesitation, he dropped out of the window and landed like a cat and rolled to one side. The bags were dropped to him quickly.

"Now go, join him, and get to the van, I will come very soon."

The second Arab left in the same way and Coleman shut the window behind. Together, they gathered up the three bags and raced to the van. The driver's door was still open, but that was a benefit this time. Pulling open the back doors, they stowed their deadly cargo in the back.

"They have been in the van; they are looking for the virus. How did they know, who are they, secret British police?"

"Shaviv, there is the car that followed us, you were right."

"Get in the van and start it; I will deal with their car."

Closing the rear doors, he walked towards the Little Chef and the car that had followed them. It was a dark Vauxhall; he knew it was the one that they had seen earlier. Using his knife he pierced the tyres of both nearside wheels, away from the gaze of anyone in the restaurant.

Returning to the van, he opened the rear doors, jumped in and waited.

Coleman knew they would check his room next; he had to stop them whoever they were. There was no way he would allow them to stop him, they would have to kill him first.

The room was typical of the Travelodge. These hotels are prefabricated using a cell structure and can be made any size like a Lego house, and then the builders build around the timber frame.

Just inside the door to the left is a wardrobe with sliding doors, and then an area to store cases, and make tea on the shelf above. Had they not been disturbed, the tea would have been ready now. A little further on the right, the door to the bathroom was ajar.

Coleman hid inside the wardrobe and closed the door almost shut. When they came in, the room door would hide the wardrobe, until they closed it. It would then be natural to be more concerned at the bathroom door being slightly open. If Coleman was coming in the room, he would focus on the bathroom first and clear this room; so he hoped.

He had to force himself to breathe slowly and control his reactions. The door was tried, it was locked. He could hear what sounded like thin keys banging together; Coleman knew that, whoever they were, they were picking the lock.

The door opened, it did indeed hide the wardrobe. Two men moved forward slowly and deliberately and just as Coleman predicted were looking toward the bathroom door. They moved forward, one had his back on the wall to right, whilst the other moved into the bathroom door.

Slowly, Coleman started to move the wardrobe door back, just enough to enable him to slide out, still hidden by the room door that had been left half open.

Without a sound he pounced on the second man. His back was to the wall, his gun, held in both hands, was pointing down at the floor. Coleman moved so quickly that he had no chance. With one swift action he cut his throat right through and pushed him forward onto his mate.

He turned, horrified at the sight of his friend spurting blood and gurgling in death's arms and momentarily took the weight of his dead friend. As the reality of the situation hit him, he then dropped him just as quickly, but too late. The contents of the boiling kettle hit him in the face.

He dropped his gun, screaming in agony and fell to the floor where Coleman without hesitating sent him to join his friend.

The door to the room was still open slightly, and stuck against the leg of the first dead man. He needed as much time as possible to clear the area before these bodies were discovered. Where could he go now, this was a big problem? They cannot abort their mission and run; they have one of the deadliest creations on earth in their care.

He picked up the first dead man by his shoulders and pulled him along into the bath room, pushing him in a line alongside the bath. The second man was pulled into the bathroom in the same way and left in a similar position, slightly on top of the first. Coleman then closed the bathroom door. It was obvious something bad had happened. Anyone entering the room would see the blood everywhere.

The two firearms would be traceable; perhaps if he left them next to the bodies in the hope it would confuse the police in the follow-up.

Having cleared the obstruction, Coleman left the room and shut the door. Walking as calmly as possible through the reception area, he dropped his keys into the box and rejoined his friends in the van.

"Go, go, let's get out of here," he yelled at Shaviv,

"They are both dead, whoever they were."

Like a man possessed, Shaviv backed the car out of the parking bay and turned to leave, just as a police car raced into the car park.

"Shit, how do they know we are here?" Coleman yelled.

"Someone must have seen us rip the tyres on that car."

"Fools, stupid fools, it was not necessary to do that. Drive!"

Shaviv's speed would have attracted their attention even if they had not had a report about the punctures. The police car now started moving towards them, intending to stop them. They raced out of the car park and onto the eastbound A14. For a small van it was quite fast, and they needed it now.

The police car followed them at a safe distance; this was not a traffic car but a normal patrol car. It was wailing and flashing its lights but the driver would not be a fully trained traffic driver, even less for a pursuit. However, you could bet your life that a pursuit car was already flashing along towards them from some direction.

"We need to get of this road, and into the small side roads," Coleman yelled. "Take the turning on the left."

Turning from the dual carriageway, they had to go left and towards Fen Drayton. Driving as fast as the van could manage, they passed through the village and then back on a course to the A14. The road would take them over the top of the dual carriageway and on towards Hilton.

The police car was still behind and had the advantage of speed on them. Two officers could be seen clearly, one was talking on the radio continually.

It would not be long before back-up would arrive, possibly the helicopter. Plus eventually they would find the bodies in the bathroom. How they knew to come to the Travelodge could not only have been a result of them puncturing tyres but also the two people Coleman had just killed. But who were they? Police, not possible. If they were police officers, they would not have come alone. But they obviously called the police. Perhaps!

"Shoot them, open the door at the back and shoot them," Coleman shouted above the noise of the screaming engine.

The young Arab took the shotgun from the bigger of the two holdalls and opened the rear door of the van, kicking it to one side with his foot. He fired at the police car now about 20 yards behind.

They obviously saw the weapon as the driver hit the brakes and dropped back, his colleague no doubt would have reported the weapon being used.

It was a pump action shotgun firing one round at a time; the first round hit the front of the car, destroying the radiator and headlamps, steam poured from everywhere, but the car continued.

The second shot went a little lower, shredding the offside front tyre; the car lost control immediately, careered to the right, hit the bank, and took off, rolling in the air, landing on its roof.

"Yes, fuck you!!"

"Keep going, keep going, keep driving."

Coleman was worried, it had gone seriously wrong now, and he could see failure in front of him.

The van continued and sped into Hilton, past the pond and the ducks, to a T-junction. Suddenly, Coleman sat up and forward.

"I know where I am, I have been here before, turn left, and drive, I have just decided to bring forward the start of our demonstration."

The road took them out of Hilton and into the outskirts of Papworth, the home of the famous heart hospital. Through Papworth and across the A428, Coleman knew where he was going now.

Five minutes later, they drew up in the car park of the Abbott; he sat for a few moments to compose himself, and then said.

"Act normally and follow my lead, do nothing until I say so. OK?"

As the three walked into the bar, they could see that something was going on. Preparations were well in hand for something.

"Haaallo Derrrrick," said Jimmy, "you and your friends want a drink? What shall it be this time?"

"Yes please," Coleman said, talking in his normal voice, a clear crisp Cambridge university accent, "three large brandies."

He was taken by surprise at the accent and confidence Derek, as he was known to them, was showing. As Jimmy turned to get the glasses for the drinks, Coleman reached into his bag and pulled out the Ouzi machine gun. He pointed it directly at Jimmy's head.

"Silence," Coleman shouted at everyone, "Silence. In 10 seconds I am going to kill this arrogant shit behind the bar, unless you all shut the fuck up."

"Close all the doors and get everyone in here where we can see them. Shaviv, get the other bags in here."

"Things are not always what they seem, Jimmy, I know you all laughed at me behind my back, that is what I wanted, but who's laughing now?"

11. The Party

Any excuse for a party was the norm at the Abbott. This time, however, there was good reason. Paul's wife, Beryl, was about to turn the corner and become 40. Paul had been forbidden to arrange anything, let alone a party, but he took no notice. While she was working, the plan sprang into action and the party was being prepared.

At 11.30 Paul and Tom arrived at the Abbot with the disco in the trailer and started to unload. Jimmy was late and the pub was not yet open. After a little banging on the door, it opened to show Jimmy, half asleep.

Going to the pub a couple of times every week is great for most of us, but the thought of working 7 days a week continually in the pub is not everyone's idea of a good time. So no one can blame Jimmy for sleeping when he gets the chance.

"You're late, as usual," Paul said jokingly.

"Bollocks!" grunted Jimmy, "Coffee?"

"Great, thanks."

He disappeared into the kitchen to make the coffee, turning the lights for pub at the same time.

Setting up the disco was the first job to be done as it involved much humping of equipment and lights. Once this was complete, or at least in one place, the plan was for the others to arrive and start decorating the bar.

Jimmy had already removed the wall exposing the complete pub, open for a good time tonight. The disco, unusually, was being set up at the opposite end of the pub, nearer to the door and toilets. It was hoped this might give some of the guests the chance to hide at the other end of the pub, away from the noise.

119

It also gave Tom a better view of what was going on in the whole pub rather than just on the dance floor. He could stop them all hiding away and get them dancing more easily.

The area where the giant TV set normally stood had been cleared, and the disco would be set up in its place.

Jimmy returned with the coffee and the three sat talking about the evening's plans, football, and nothing in particular. Jimmy's brain was staring to engage and he was now ready for anything.

"When I have set up, I need to copy those CDs of yours, Jimmy."

"No problem," Jimmy replied, "they're behind the bar on the CD player. Just help yourself, to the CDs I mean."

Ant and Jane arrived to lend a hand, and were soon followed by three others, all bearing handfuls of decorations. William had long since returned to University. The village also boasts a couple who make a living from balloons and they too had turned up to add their own expertise to the day.

Regardless of the preparations, the pub would still have to be open at lunchtime; regular customers would have to fight their way around everyone else. Not that they would mind.

Tom had the sound side of the disco up and running and was already playing some quiet music, checking the system for problems. Paul was hanging the lights and plugging them in as fast as he could.

"Jimmy, I am going to use the phone line from the credit card machine to connect the computer to the internet. Let me know if you need it back?"

"OK," came from somewhere deep in the kitchen.

Tom thought that as this might take some time on-line, it was better not to tie up the main telephone line into the pub. Lunchtimes would not normally require the use of the swipe machine, he hoped. It had the added benefit that Jimmy was paying the bill for the call, and Tom could download some other tracks he wanted and check his email for work if necessary.

A huge database of CD information has been created on the internet. This allows anyone with a CD-rom player on their computer to get track and artist information on a CD, provided it is connected into the internet. Its use has now been extended to provide this information when converting a normal audio CD tracks to digital MP3 format.

Once the computer is connected to the internet and the copy program is running, as soon as a CD is loaded into the drive, the computer rushes off to find exactly what CD it is, who produced it, and what tracks are on it. It then, very helpfully, names the tracks as they are recorded.

Jimmy had five CDs that Tom wanted to copy and he would do this whilst they finished off setting up the equipment. Only the portable had a built-in modem, so this was being used to access the internet. It was also Tom's computer that he used for work.

Whilst the tracks were being copied, he could check his email too.

A simple network cable connected the portable to the main disco computer and allowed them to exchange data. So, once the data had been copied from the CDs, it could be transferred easily to the big computer.

The sound quality was very good. Huge amplifiers powered four large speaker cabinets and, as they only worked to less than half of the capacity, there was little or no distortion.

By now, the decorations were near to completion, a big banner across the fire place let the world know that Beryl had reached 40, tables were decorated and the party almost ready.

Paul had finished hanging the disco lights and a huge amount of wire lay in front of the disco, one bad side of the computerised system.

No one was surprised to see Coleman walk in the bar, although it was unusual to see him at lunchtime and with two other people. They looked foreign, possibly Arabs. After the remarks he had made whilst playing pool last time, particularly to Jane, Jimmy was a little 'off' with him to say the least.

Coleman amazed everyone. He spoke this time very precisely in a clear British accent showing his education. Jimmy noticed and stopped for a moment to look at him, then turned to get the brandies.

Time stood still as the gun appeared. It was strange how it seemed so unreal. You constantly see guns of some description on the television but, when it is so close, it does not register properly, that is, if you recognise it at all.

Jimmy turned round with the brandies to see the barrel of the machine gun near his face. He dropped one glass and managed to put the other down on the bar. Instinctively he put his hands in the air.

"Listen, Mate, take the money in the till, you can have it, take it and go, just leave us alone."

"I am afraid it is not as simple as that, my friend, we have a problem and half of the country's police force are now looking for us. You and your party friends now form part of the best bargaining position we have." Coleman spoke as though he was addressing his fellow terrorists, coldly and cleanly.

"Everyone, listen and listen well. If you do what we say, we will not hurt you. If you do anything that we don't like, we will kill you. Sit down on the floor, do not speak, or move."

Coleman then turned his attention to the other two men, both of whom now had their own weapons pointing at the locals, sitting on the floor. He was clearly deep in thought.

Walking back to the bar, he took one of the brandies and drank it, then returned closer to Shaviv.

"We have been forced to bring our plans forward somewhat. This is not a problem, as everything can proceed as we have originally planned. We have the added bonus of the extra people in the pub. Have you brought everything in from the van?"

"Yes, it is all over there. Shall we prepare everything?"

Shaviv motioned across to the table near the door; there was a large green jaguar holdall placed upon it.

"Good," Coleman responded, "yes, bring the virus to me; I will make sure it is safe with me. Take the weapons out of the bags and prepare them. We may need to fight."

Shaviv went over to the table where the bags had been placed. There were the two holdalls and the one that contained the virus. He brought this one to Coleman and handed it to him, very carefully.

"Don't worry, my friend; it is safe in here, until we open it!" Coleman told him.

From the second bag he pulled out what looked like a electrical control panel. It had several banks of lights; above each of the lights was a small switch. Below each of the lights was a push button. Shaviv plugged this into the mains socket and instantly the lights went red, and then changed to green, one at a time.

The sensors that they had placed around the green a few weeks ago should still be in place, but needed to be checked. Shaviv spoke to Coleman and left the pub. He walked the route around the green that they had taken previously and examined each sensor. All were fine, all intact and all 12 of them were still working. He could see the small red indicator come on as he approached each one in turn.

Each sensor was numbered, and each had been placed in order. They had covered the front of the building placing a sensor near the road, then continued around the green and 100 yards down each road. By the time they had finished their work that day, there was an arc of these little sensors around the front of the pub. They had covered each possible approach route, the last one being left 100 yards up the road, leading south towards Gamlingay.

Any movement in front of the infra-red sensor would cause it to transmit. The receiver, placed in the pub now, would light up a certain indicator. They had installed a ring around the front of the pub that could not be breached without him knowing.

Satisfied, Shaviv returned to the pub and continued by removing the weapons from the other bags and checking their contents. Once complete, he went back to Coleman.

"All OK now, everything is working."

"Show me," Coleman insisted.

The two of them seemed a little distracted now, playing with their new toy; the third was craning his neck to see what they were doing, and Paul had noticed he started to move as though to go towards the door.

Coleman turned and fired one shot from his Ouzi and the round buried itself deep into an old oak beam supporting the upstairs of the pub.

"Make no mistake, any of us would kill you and not blink an eye whilst doing so. To us, life is unimportant; what is important is to succeed, and we will succeed today. Stay where you are told, my friend, and do not try anything again."

"For now, you can occupy yourselves and will continue with your preparations for the evening. No one leaves the room unless I know about it. I want every window and door closed and you can close these shutters also. Remember, ask me before you do anything. Now, can I please have another brandy?"

Jimmy handed the remaining glass to Coleman, arm outstretched as far as it would reach. He shrank away very quickly and moved back with the other villagers. They were trying to continue with the preparations, but most of it was done. Nevertheless, Jimmy insisted that they each found something to make this nutcase believe they were still busy.

The sound of the gun being fired did travel, although not very far. The walls of the pub were very thick. George Mallet was at the front of his house tidying the borders around his immaculate garden. The noise startled him; he knew what it was immediately, having spent his national service in the Army. When he saw that the doors and shutters were closed, it made him worry even more.

The pub should be open, it was lunchtime. Instead, the door was closed and the windows all shuttered up. Strange to say the least. George went into the house and told his wife what he had heard, and that the pub was closed. Her advice was good: call the police, let them know.

"I am sure I have just heard a gun shot from the pub in our village, and the pub seems as though it has now closed," George explained to the operator on the end of the 999 services.

He was unaware that she was in some distant part of the UK and had no local knowledge. Slowly, the operator skilfully pulled the information from George that she needed and asked him to stay inside and stay on the phone.

The control room at Huntingdon was fed this information and the quickly convened group of senior officers now controlling the problems at BBR were told of the incident. They were joined by an army representative.

"Coincidence, or do you think this is related, sir," the Sergeant asked the Chief Constable.

The chief did not answer, not because of anything else other than he was deep in thought too. He spoke briefly to the controlling office, who then called in one of the ARV units.

"Alpha Victor 1 we have a report of a shot being fired at the Abbott public house in Abbotsley, near St Neots, please attend."

Having been relieved after the Discovery had been stopped on the A14, the armed response vehicle had been involved in the hunt for the anthrax that was missing from BBR. They were just north of Stilton on the A1 where the CCTV had recorded the Mondeo passing. Coleman was right, and the police were following the possibility that the car that left the layby was involved.

AV 2 was now dealing with the aftermath of the patrol car being shot at and the accident that followed. A police officer was dead and the other was critically ill. They had used the police helicopter to airlift the injured man to Addenbrooke's hospital in Cambridge.

"AV1 responding, log us as *en route* to Abbotsley. ETA 15 minutes."

It would take at least 15 minutes for the car to arrive but the control room needed a quicker response. The day already seemed too long, and it was only just lunchtime. A patrol car from St Neots was nearby and it was agreed that this could be sent to establish the problem, if any, at the pub.

Shaviv was standing at the window to the right-hand side of the door, looking out through the small diamond shape cut into the shutters. He had a bird's eye view of the road through the village. He saw the police car immediately; it was easily noticeable.

"There is a police car coming towards the village, someone may have heard the shot."

"I doubt it very much, stop worrying!" barked Coleman.

He moved away from the window as if he thought the driver could see him from so far away.

"Let me know which way it is going and when it has passed," Coleman replied, calmly.

"It's slowing down, wait. It's turning into the car park, he is going to stop here, what shall we do?"

"Kill him, just kill him!" Coleman said no more worried than he had been 10 minutes ago. "You, turn up the music, loud, Shaviv, when you can see him, shoot him."

Tom obeyed and turned up the music, watching Coleman with one eye and Ant and Jane with the other.

Shaviv moved towards the window again; he was holding his Ouzi in his right hand. He waited and watched.

The police car stopped at the far side of the car park away from any windows. A young officer, moved slowly out of the driver's side, and looked slowly around the car park. There were hardly any cars there, except for Jimmy's camper van and a blue Citroën van. The disco trailer was still parked at the opposite end of the pub.

He walked to the blue van and peered through the windows. He tried the door, which was open and moved inside, sitting on the passenger seat. There was nothing in the car, no papers, no mess, no nothing. The glove box was empty, but surprisingly the keys to the car were in the ignition. He stood, putting the van between him and the side of the pub; then spoke over the radio, checking the van with his control room.

Carefully he walked around the van and edged towards the front of the pub and up to the door.

"This is the police, is there anyone inside?"

All he could hear was the music from the disco, there was not much chance he could make himself heard. He banged on the door, and repeated his question, but there was still no response. Still no answer.

Coleman looked around the room at each person, daring them to make a sound. He waved at Tom to continue the music. The policeman banged on the door again, then stepped back and looked up at the windows above.

"Control, this is PC171, There are people in the building, I can hear music. I cannot get a response from anyone, are you sure that your information is correct? Could this shot have been to do with the music I can hear?"

He turned and walked to move towards the window to the left of the door as he faced the pub. As he did so, he came in sight of the diamond in the shutter, Shaviv fired once.

The bullet hit him on the upper left shoulder passing straight through his protective vest and exited just below his shoulder blade. He went down instantly and stayed down.

"They've shot him, they've shot him, Jesus, they've shot the police man."

The line between the police and George Mallet had been re-established direct with the Cambridgeshire Police HQ. They knew within seconds that their officer was down; he had been shot in cold blood.

"AV1, be advised that we have an officer down, possibly shot, at the Abbott. Eyewitness heard gunshots and saw the officer go down. Approach with caution. Back-up is on the way. We are attempting to contact the Abbott now."

AV1 exited the A1, around the Wyboston roundabout and sped on towards the power station, turning left at the roundabout, raced past Tesco and through Eynesbury towards Abbotsley. Once again, the Volvo was being stretched to its limits, lights flashing and sirens screaming, a warning to traffic to move out of his way.

In the distance, two more wailing sirens could now be heard, a second car from the station at St Neots was *en route* and an ambulance had been sent to the scene for the wounded officer.

Instead of taking the road directly into the village, they turned off and went around the back to approach the pub from the other side. They would not be seen until the last minute. A little local knowledge goes a long way, and this time it was very useful.

The road was not as fast because of a series of double bends, but it was a good choice on the part of the driver.

The telephone ringing on the bar was unheard for a while as the music was so loud. Coleman was the first to hear it.

"Silence!" He held his arm high in the air, "stop the music."

"Well, answer the telephone, it may be a customer!" Coleman gestured to Jimmy who did as he was told and answered.

"Hello, the Abbott public house."

"This is the police, who are you? Can you tell us what is happening?"

Jimmy never got the chance to answer; Coleman grabbed the phone away from him and punched him hard, then moved him away from the bar and pushed him down on the floor.

"Who am I talking to?" the police officer asked.

"My name is Dr Coleman. Who are you?"

"Chief Superintendent Garwood, I am in command of the police control room. What is happening and why have you shot at a police officer?"

"Contact the Ministry of Defence and they will let you know who I am."

This statement made the Superintendent realise that this had something to do with the problem at BBR. It had already been confirmed that the blue van was suspected of being the van involved with the shooting of the other officers earlier.

"I will not discuss this with you; put your Chief Constable on the telephone. I know he must be there, I am familiar with the orders you have for this very situation. I will talk with him and him only.

The line went dead for a moment and then another voice came on the line.

"This is the Chief Constable, Dr Coleman, can you please tell me what is going on?"

"Listen to me, and listen very carefully, my friend." Again, Coleman was able to keep his calm.

"We have, in the name of our glorious leader, stolen something that you and your Government will never even admit actually exists.

It would cause your Government so many problems if the world were to know it had been developed. So let us be clear on some simple facts."

Coleman went on:

"Firstly, I now have the means to infect most of the people within 30 miles of this building. You do not know the potential of the virus we have stolen. Your precious ministry will have kept that part very secret from you.

Within 2 days, most people would contract an illness and die. Within that time they would infect others, who in turn would infect others, and so on."

"Secondly, and more important to your leaders, it would expose the United Kingdom as the creators of an Armageddon virus, better than the plague if it was to be released. The standing of your so-called great nation would be reduced to that of our brothers in Palestine, to the level of dogs."

By now, what Coleman was saying had sunk in to the people supposed to be planning a party. They were stuck in the pub with a madman who had the means to kill half the country.

"We will establish some ground rules Chief Constable, and you will obey me, do I make myself clear?" He did not wait for the answer, just continued.

"There will be no vehicles allowed within 1 mile of this building. There will be no aircraft within 5 miles of the building. I want a complete, absolute, news blackout on this matter, nothing at all must be publicised. At least not until I instruct it. Please acknowledge you understand"

", Yes we can hear you. We want to recover the officer you have shot, can we pick his body up? He may still be alive." The Chief pushed Coleman a little.

"I know you can hear me, did you understand?"

"Yes we understand, no cars within 1 mile, no aircraft within 5miles and no press. Can we recover the shot policeman? We need to establish some trust between us, Dr Coleman."

"So we can start to trust each other, I will allow one car to stop, pick up the body and go. You have 5 minutes from now, after this time, the restrictions I have outlined will apply. The police car must leave towards St Neots. I want to see it leave. Everyone must leave who arrives in the vehicle; you will inform me when they will arrive. Any other vehicle will be shot at. This is the only concession I will give you. Do you understand?"

"Yes, we understand."

"If anyone who gets out of the car even appears to move towards the building they will be shot too. Do I make myself clear?"

"Yes, very clear."

"Good, then you have 5 minutes from now."

"Thank…" The phone went dead.

AV 1 was now standing off outside the village waiting for the control room to issue instructions.

"AV1 – proceed to village, do not take any risks, and do not approach the public house. Recover the injured PC and get out. Confirm please?"

"Confirmed, we are moving now."

"Hotel 1 will meet you for medivac on the car park at Ernulf School."

The phone rang again in the bar to inform Coleman that the car was about to arrive.

A single light on Coleman's radio receiver started to blink and a beeping noise was heard. The infra-red sensor had been tripped by the police car. Coleman knew the car was coming from the west side of the pub and had approached from the south. Then a second light came on.

"Good, " he thought, " they are working well."

The Volvo now moved slowly around the corner, not wishing to cause alarm, passing the pub, within 10 feet of the door. The officer was lying on his side; the shot had thrown him across the road.

He was not moving and a pool of blood ran from him and down the slope of the road away from the pub.

Both officers had their weapons across the seats next to them, one drove and one sat in the back. They pulled the car between the pub and the dying officer to shield them whilst they pulled him in.

Phil was in the back and, as soon as he felt it safe, he opened the door, and crouched down behind the body of the car. The wounded Pc was now protected by the Volvo.

He lifted his head and shoulders up, resting them on the edge of the back seat, then, climbed almost over him and back into the car.

It was not the best way to get him out of danger, but they had no option. Phil began to pull him into the car and onto the seat, lying down. He was unconscious and obviously in shock. He was almost dead. Kevin immediately pushed large wads of medical dressings onto the wound, stopping some of the bleeding.

"Go, go, get the fuck out of here, move it, this guy's nearly dead."

Without even bothering to look round at the pub, or even shut the rear door properly, the police car moved off, turned left and sped as fast as it could out of the village. Lit like a fairground ride, the car went through 100 mph before it left the village. The long straight road, for once, was now useful in helping to save a life.

Braking down from 120 mph round the double bends, and then on towards Ernulf school, Kevin was crouching down in the footwell behind the front passenger seat, which had been pulled forward. Whilst holding wads of dressings up behind his back and pushing them on to the entry wound in his chest, Kevin used his own body weight to hold the PC on the seat and stop him moving as the car raced on.

From his left side, Kevin saw the police helicopter drop down alongside them, follow for a few yards, and then move off in front to descend into the car park.

As AV1 arrived, they were already down, and the doors were open, waiting. Two paramedics ran forward, gently this time pulled the officer from the car and onto a stretcher. Within seconds he was gone, airborne, on the way to Addenbrooke's.

"AV1 clear, control." Kevin let HQ know he was available again.

"AV1, please wait at the school, clear all civilians, and secure the area. Stand by for further instructions. Arrival of helicopter imminent."

Around 4 hours had passed following the alarm at BBR. Four unmarked Range Rovers with police escort had just passed

Wellingborough on the A14 heading east. The road was still closed to traffic but a way through had been made for the convoy.

The dark helicopter that was seen on the A14 now was airborne again heading for the car park at Ernulf School.

"Now my friends, continue with your preparations. Don't worry about your policeman; he is not dead. He will be OK, if we had wanted to kill him, we would have. They need to understand we are serious."

The other two Arabs were now messing about again with their bags at the far end of the pub, away from the gaze of the others. The flask was still packed away and safe on the corner table within reach of Coleman at all times. In the corner lay the golf bag, but now empty. On the table next to several hand guns and boxes of ammunition was a large grey green object, rather like the bazookas used in old war films.

"If you are busy, your minds are occupied. Remember do not do anything stupid or foolish. Let's have some more music."

Tom turned the music back up and was busy with Paul finishing the set-up of the equipment. Both computers were now running and the lights were up and connected.

With a little click, the CD drive sprang open on the portable computer. It had finished copying the CD that Jimmy had given to Tom.

"It's still connected to the internet, and they don't know!" he thought.

When in the office and on-line most of the time, Tom communicates with others using a very simple program provided by Microsoft MS Messenger. You list your contacts in the program, and if they are on-line, it shows up. Neil's icon was showing him as 'on-line'.

With the music running and Coleman's attention elsewhere, Tom's rapid tapping of the keys went unnoticed.

"Neil, need urgent help, in pub in Abbotsley, man has gun, call police. Very serious, no joke."

"Yeh right, SWAT Teams busy, I'll send the wife."

"Call police, they will confirm, I am serious."

Tom minimised the program and started to look busy with Paul. Coleman turned to Jimmy and asked for some more drinks.

"We need coffee, get some coffee. Shaviv go with him, make sure he behaves."

In the corner of the portable computer screen the MSM icon was flashing, Neil was responding. Tom opened the program and Neil was back.

"You OK? Have spoken to police. There is a car on the way to me with an officer to act as a link to their HQ. They can talk to you through me. Are you using your portable?"

"Yes, why?"

"Turn on the camera!"

Many portable computers have a small camera built into them, originally for video conferencing. This had never really taken off, but they worked and were used more for fun than anything else.

"Only connected at 44 k, too slow!"

"Turn it on, take snapshots every 15 seconds"

The camera was able to record a picture and then, using MSM, transmit it to the other person in the conversation, in this case Neil and soon the police.

A few more taps on the keyboard and the camera was active. Tom simply had to turn it over to point forwards.

The camera was now taking a picture every 15 seconds and sending it to Neil. He in turn was forwarding it, much faster to the Police HQ. They were able to see a little of what was going on, the layout of the pub and the terrorists, without anyone knowing.

Coleman was deep in thought, considering his situation. He had stolen a biological weapon, the like of which the world had never seen before. His friends in the desert would sacrifice hundreds of men to get their hands on it. The British authorities would never let him escape, as they could not risk the virus being even talked about, let alone used. Then there were also the people who attacked him at the Lodge. Who were they? British police, army? This is what puzzled Coleman.

Only the MoD, himself and a few BBR staff knew of the virus. Most of them did not know full details. If they were not police or army, who were they, who were they working for? How did they know he had the virus?

The telephone ringing brought Coleman back to life with a start. He grabbed for the handset.

"Stop the music, stop it now!" he yelled.

"This is Coleman."

"Mr Coleman, this is the Chief Constable. My name is Foster. I think we need to talk about your situation. We are aware that you have taken something from the BBR complex, and we are now aware that you know exactly what it is and its capabilities."

"Yes, that is correct. I was asked to develop it, on behalf of your Government, secretly. Alas, I was only to be tossed aside because of my beliefs."

"So, is that what this is about, you lost your job, and you're angry?"

"Don't insult me, Chief Constable; the job was a means to an end. I was surprised I lasted as long as I did. Our aims are far deeper and farther reaching than a simple job."

"What you have with you is very dangerous, both to yourself and many others around you. We wish to move people out of the village for safety reasons. Is that alright with you?"

"No! it is not alright." Coleman suddenly became angry.

"We have laid down the rules and you have agreed to them. No vehicles at all, within 1 mile of the pub. No aircraft to approach within 5 miles. We are watching and can detect movement within 500 yards of the building. We have been planning this day for a long time now, my friend. Be very sure Mr Foster, we know what we are doing, and as you know will not hesitate to kill.

No one is to be moved out of the village. When we die, they will all die with us. Mr Foster, let us not play games with each other, we are both intelligent men.

I suggest that you convene a meeting to include a Dr Wilson, who works at Boscombe Down research facility, and the Government Minister to whom he is responsible.

They will explain exactly what it is I have stolen from them; they can also let you know exactly what the effect of my releasing this substance would be, not only in terms of dead British people, but the impact on the rest of the world.

Take this meeting quickly, my friend, and then call me to discuss our terms for returning this precious gift you have provided for our cause.

If you break our rules, we will not hesitate to act. Our lives are now finished.

Your predicament is very grave; I will wait to hear from you."

The line went dead.

"Shut that place down. No one in, no one out, road blocks on all possible access road. Get on the phones, call everyone in the village. Tell them to stay indoors, there is a police emergency. No other information. Get hold of BT and have them assist.

I want all the information we have on the village, its surrounding land, ownership, ditches, streams, rivers, get on to the Environment Agency. I want information, and I need it now. Find the latest Ordnance survey maps.

Stop all over-flying, contact Stansted, clear all aircraft from the area. We do not want to spook this bloody man; well! Move."

12. The Meeting

Foster had no time to hesitate or sit and think about this situation. He was a time-served officer, worked up through the ranks from a simple constable. He knew what he was doing.

"Contact the MoD, I want to talk with this Wilson man, and now. I will be in my office."

Foster walked from the control room and upstairs to his office. Inside the quietness of his own space he poured some strong coffee, threw in three sugars and milk and took a hard swig of instant buzz. His phone rang on the desk and the operator informed him that Wilson was on the line.

"Dr Wilson, I am the Chief Constable of Cambridgeshire Police. We have a situation ongoing of which I am sure you are aware. I want to meet with you as soon as possible, and I mean within the hour."

"Good morning Sir, yes, I am aware and we are already preparing to leave to offer assistance to you. Our helicopter is arriving in 10 minutes and we can be near you within the hour."

"Good, I will instruct our people to prepare to receive you at the Police HQ in Hinchingbrooke. Have your aircrew contact RAF Wittering and agree flight information and landing procedures. I will see you very soon."

Having finished the coffee, Foster went back to the control room and informed everyone to make ready for the arrival of the MoD delegation. He still had overall authority for the whole situation, and the MoD would dance to his tune on this one, for now at least.

The noise and clatter of the aircraft arriving was deafening, the front car parking area had been cleared, and more than enough space made available for a safe landing. No sooner had the rotors started to slow, than the doors slid back and four people emerged.

"Good afternoon, Gentleman, I am the Chief Constable. Please follow me."

A room had already been prepared; there was a large table, a large tray of coffee, overhead projectors, computer projectors and terminals. The curtains had been pulled and two officers stood like guards on the doors.

"Make sure we are not disturbed, unless it is imperative to interrupt."

Foster closed the door and sat at the head of the table.

"A Dr Coleman stole an amount of a virus from BBS this morning. The information I have from your own emergency standing orders is that this virus is, in fact, anthrax. Coleman has already killed one policeman, crippled another, and shot and almost killed another. We have two unidentified bodies in a local Travelodge, which are linked in some way to Coleman.

I now understand that Coleman has worked for you in the past, perhaps gentleman you could explain what the hell is going on."

Wilson looked up, and set his pen down very precisely at the front edge of his notebook.

"Sir, Coleman was employed by the MoD to work with us at Boscombe Down research facility. He is an eminent scientist whose previous work was of use to the aims of our facility at the time.

HM Government, following the 911 disaster, set in motion several, should I say, 'preventative' measures. In simple terms he was engineering different varieties of the anthrax virus. The results were then shipped to BBS where they would, in turn, engineer anti-virus.

The aim was to give us a counter-measure for any biological attack from terrorists, plus of course, although this would be denied, it could provided some new, lethal, biological weapons.

Coleman was fanatical about the Middle East; we know he had a Israeli girlfriend. Certain information came to us that put Coleman's security status in doubt. Nothing could be proven, but we could not take a chance. He was removed from the project. He was also prevented from working at any other scientific facility in Europe.

What he has stolen is the result of the last project he was working on. This was just about to start testing at BBS for the counter measures. He had inside help at BBS without a doubt."

Foster looked puzzled and interrupted Wilson.

"You just sacked this man and let him go, without any follow-up. Were you no longer watching him? Did you not consider he might react badly to being sacked in such a way, a man of his calibre?"

"Frankly, no. We expected him to go away and get on with his life. He was wealthy and had no problems in his life."

"So what exactly does he have, and how deadly is it?" Foster asked.

"What he has is very dangerous, very deadly, and beyond real description. It is the anthrax virus mutated with a cold virus to combine and form a new type of anthrax. It is spread just as a common cold would spread. Infect one person, he infects two, they infect two, they each infect two others. It will spread out of control. It will affect all animal life, not just humans.

He has the means to Armageddon in his hands." Wilson stopped and gazed at Foster.

"And…," Foster said, "is that it, what the hell do we do?"

"We have to get it back, without it being released. Without any press, whatever it takes. He must not be allowed to even open the flask."

Foster was now angry, he stood up and moved over to the whiteboard and grabbed a pen.

"Look, here is Abbotsley." He drew on the board a circle in the middle. He added Cambridge, Bedford, Peterborough, Stevenage, Hertford and Luton.

"These are all within 30 miles of the village. One million people in this area. They are all now in danger. Coleman has the village bugged in some way. He can detect movement. He is ruthless and will kill without hesitation."

"How is the virus packed?"

"It is in a flask, assuming he has not changed this, but I doubt that. The flask is designed to withstand most things, rather like the waste nuclear fuel containers. As yet we have not worked on the virus and so we are unable to comment on how to stop it."

"Unable to comment, this is not a press conference, Mr Wilson, I need to know what I have to fight, and how to fight it. Stop covering your arse and help me. If he allows this virus to escape, you are going to die along with us, and your family. Now let us get very real and you tell me exactly what is, and is not, possible."

"From previous tests, fire will destroy the virus in the atmosphere. No amount of explosion will destroy the flask. There is no anti-virus, nor is there a vaccine we can offer anyone. If it were to be released and could be contained, it would be destroyed by fire, or explosion. But how can you contain it?"

Suddenly one of the other people who arrived on the helicopter spoke. A tall Scottish man, smartly dressed, either service or ex-service man.

"There is only one option, go in and get it back. Use the military, I understand the SAS have been involved already and that reinforcements are on the way now."

Foster looked at the new voice very hard, trying to understand his background and position in all of this, not that it mattered as he was here with the MoD delegation, and supposed to be helping.

"Yes, your lads were involved earlier today when they stopped one of the vehicles that were running from BBS. The rest are due very soon and I am expecting a call from their CO within the hour.

So, to summarise, Gentlemen.

One – we cannot allow any chance of this virus being released.

Two – if it is released, there is nothing we can do to stop it spreading.

Three – fire will kill it, but not damage the flask.

Four – we have no way of containing it."

"Sir," new voice was talking again, "have any demands been made yet? Has Coleman said what it is he wants?"

"Well I don't think he wants his job back. But no! He insisted that we have this meeting and then I have to call him. I suggest we do that now, from this room, together."

Coleman was strutting around the main bar of the pub still. Jimmy had provided more brandy for them all, and they remained calm. The music was still going.

It was now over 2 hours since he last spoke with Foster. He expected a call any minute and, as if by magic, the phone rang.

"Mr Foster, I assume you have had your meeting, and now understand what I have. I am also correct in assuming that Wilson is still with you and can hear this conversation."

"Yes, that is correct; there are three other people from the MoD with us too. We all know the ability of what you have stolen to kill. What we do not know, is what are you trying to achieve, what is it that you want?"

"It is very simple actually. If you want your precious virus back, then in return you must persuade your Government to force the West to accept that the Palestinian people have a right to a land of their own.

The land of their forefathers, not the backyard they have to live in now, but the original land they once occupied. They must agree to remove Israel from this territory and restore it to its rightful owners.

This is not something that could be achieved in a matter of hours. I realise that this would take years to complete. However, it must start now. Your Government have to issue a declaration that it believes that Israeli state to be illegal, and founded upon land that was taken illegally, and that it intends to work together with the people from Palestine to restore it to them.

Such a declaration could be made tomorrow at the United Nations Assembly. Then the Government could start negotiations to bring about this great thing. Once it has made its position clear, to the world, then there can be no retreat, it would have to continue.

These are the demands that you must meet to prevent us from using this terrible thing your own Government has developed. If my demands are met, and I can see on the television that you have indeed made the declaration in the UN, then I will give myself up, together with my friends, and the virus. No one will be hurt.

I have friends throughout the world, and they will all report to me once you have addressed the UN. Do not be tempted to try to trick me. I am not stupid.

If you attempt to enter this building, attack us in any way, we will release the virus and then kill everyone, including us. I have brought with me the means to deliver the virus high into the atmosphere. This will disperse over a huge area, and then will be unstoppable. Within 7 days the entire population of the UK could be dead.

Now my friends, do you understand, are there any questions?"

Wilson was the only person who could talk, the others were struck dumb having listened to what Coleman had said.

"Coleman, this is Wilson. Are you completely crazy? You of all people know what you are playing with. Your demands are outrageous, I cannot see the Government agreeing to what you want."

"Then, Mr Wilson, I suggest you take your head out of your arse and convince them that I am deadly serious. 'You of all people' know that I never do anything that has not been thoroughly researched and thought through."

The line went dead.

"Gentlemen, I suggest you use this room as your base, do whatever you need to do, and talk to whoever needs to be involved. I want a reaction to his demands within the hour. I will be back then. Thank you."

Foster left the room and returned to his office. A small room on the far side of his office house a washroom and toilet. He closed the office door, ran to the toilet unable to stop himself vomiting.

13. Response to Pub

An hour and a half after the helicopter had left Hereford in the morning, the remainder of B Squadron left in four Range Rovers heading east. As they joined the M50 and headed towards the M5, they were joined by four police motorcycles, making sure no one got in their way.

Travelling north, they headed towards Birmingham, passing south using the M42 then joined the M6 and A14 towards Huntingdon.

One squadron of the SAS was always available for anti-terrorist work in the UK. The other squadrons could be anywhere in the world, training or on active duty.

Each vehicle contained a driver and three other SAS men, all wearing civilian clothes. In the back behind the rear seat was the equipment they might need to deal with any form of terrorist threat: their usual black uniforms used for anti-terrorist operations, body armour, and weapons; the famous Heckler and Koch MP5 submachine guns, Gilly suits and sniper rifles; explosives, flash bangs and an assortment of other gear.

Passing the scene where the Discovery had earlier been stopped, they were waved through the blocked road. Turning south onto the A1 they continued on towards their RV point, now the car park at Ernulf School. The police had cleared the school car park of any other vehicles, closed the recreation centre and prepared for the arrival of the military helicopter.

It arrived, landing centrally between the school art department and the town's indoor swimming pool. As the rotors slowed to a stop, the doors remained closed. The occupants sat and waited; they would not get out.

141

The small convoy had now left the A1 and was moving along the A428 bypass. Progress was slowed now as they had to negotiate the traffic pulling over to allow them through.

The four dark blue Range Rovers pulled into the school still being led by two motorcyclists, they pulled up and parked just to the rear of their own helicopter. Once again, no one got out.

The Cambridgeshire Police mobile incident unit arrived, and took its place in the growing mass of vehicles, now waiting. With it came three marked police cars: the two armed response vehicles, and a car containing the Chief Constable and his deputy. At this point in time, the problem was still one controlled by the police, and the Chief Constable had assumed direct command.

As the Chief arrived, one Range Rover door opened and a uniformed officer climbed down and walked towards the third police car, in turn the Chief got out of his car and met the officer half-way. There was no saluting, both men shook hands, and talked briefly.

The Fire Service incident control unit arrived together with two pumps and a normal car sporting the fire service blue lights on the top. They were shepherded into the far corner and stopped.

Almost immediately following them a fleet of three ambulances arrived.

The police control unit was now operational, the civilian driver and his mate were very good at deploying this trailer and commissioning it within minutes. The radio system was online and secure data terminals were operating.

The Chief Constable ushered his new colleague towards the trailer and went inside. They were joined by the Deputy Chief Constable, another non-uniformed occupant from the Range Rover and Kevin from the ARV.

Kevin and his driver were the only ones to have been in close so far, and at the time they were not too interested in what was going on, or the surroundings. They did take in some of it, probably through the rear view mirror on the way out of the village.

The Chief Constable started the briefing.

"They have chosen a very good vantage point within the village and can easily see any approach by a vehicle. They claim to have placed some form of detection devices that can warn of any approach by car or on foot within 500 yards of the pub.

One officer is dead, killed when his car was fired upon. His colleague is critical in hospital. Another officer is critical in hospital with a bad chest wound. Two further bodies have been found at a Travelodge, identity unknown.

These people are ruthless; they will kill without any conscience. They have in their possession the most deadly virus, or chemical weapon, ever developed. It is a modified version of anthrax combined with the common cold virus. If they release it, it won't kill thousands, it could wipe out the whole country.

We are in contact with Whitehall; they have an operational office, with scientific advisors at our HQ. The Prime Minister has been briefed on the situation."

The Chief stopped to allow for questions and to get his breath back. The five men with Foster in the room looked pale and very sick. Two of these men were battle hardened soldiers who thought they had seen everything.

"Sir, what is the closest point we can get to without being seen from the building? Where can we set up a forward operating point without risking compromising the situation?"

"The difficulty we have Major, is that we do not have any deep, good local knowledge of the village. PC Johnson recovered the wounded officer and has seen the layout in front of the building. There are no officers who live in the village, the nearest is Gamlingay, 4 miles away. We do not normally plan to have to wage war on one of our own villages. The best information we have is an ordnance survey map."

"The lads will want to talk with PC Johnson; they need to know everything he saw." The Major interrupted.

He looked at the map now hanging on the wall of the mobile unit. It was a few minutes before he returned to the conversation.

"Looking at the map I feel the best option would be to assemble on the road from the south, and use the farmyard on this road. This puts us about half a mile from the pub, to the south. It is also appears to be blind to the pub except for the last 300 yards."

"With your permission, Sir, this will be designated as our forward operating point. I want to start to move to this point as quickly as possible. We need to take a look." The Major turned to leave and returned to his vehicle.

143

"Take PC Johnson and his ARV with some of your team and check to see if it is suitable for use without any risk. Once you establish this, we will reconvene there. In the meantime we will work out where to deploy our officers as back-up, road blocks, and how best to get the fire and medical services in if and when required."

Kevin walked together with the non uniformed SAS man and got into the Range Rover where the officer was previously travelling. He in turn got into the ARV. They left the school and the Range Rover followed.

The roads approaching the school were now closed. No one could use the access between the school and Abbotsley. All traffic was being diverted around the area.

Overhead, Hotel 1 was hovering, but he had been ordered not to go within 2 miles of the village.

With the roads clear, the two vehicles made their way quickly along past the golf club and towards the south of the village. They turned left, north in towards the village and then left again into the farmyard. It was ideal.

Kevin got out and approached the farmhouse. They had been told by now that something bad was going on. Either the police or BT would have been in contact with them on the phone. No one was allowed outside. So the farmer was not surprised when the police banged on his door.

Kevin told him that they needed to use his yard to park some police and army vehicles. This was not problem, the farmer immediately offered all manner of help and assistance. They were back at the school within 15 minutes.

To anyone watching, the next 10 minutes would have been like something from a movie. The three police cars left first, followed by the four Range Rovers. The mobile incident room was next and two fire engines and three paramedic units, in turn, followed.

The roads to the village had been closed from the bottom of Potton Road in Eynesbury. Similarly, the road was closed at the T-junction on the opposite side of Abbotsley. Access to the road from Gamlingay to Abbotsley had been closed too. At each roadblock, armed Policeman now took up positions. All access by road was now controlled.

Over the next 30 minutes the control position was established and linked into the telephone network. The farmer offered a power supply from his main barn but this was not used, as mains power could be interrupted. Portable generators now provided power for the command vehicle.

The fire and ambulance service were sent to pre-agreed positions outside of the limits given by Coleman, and out of sight of the pub. If needed, they could be there in minutes.

"Coleman," the voice answered as the Chief rang the Abbot to re establish contact.

"Dr Coleman, we must evacuate the people from the village and need to bring vehicles in to move them. Could you agree to this?"

"We have already discussed this. No! My restrictions will not be broken. You will not disobey me. What has been done to meet the demands we have given you?"

"You will agree that what you ask is beyond my offices and has to be dealt with by Government. Government is not known for moving fast. This will take some time. I have no information for you."

"Mr Foster, I want you to call me every hour, on the hour and give me a situation report on what is being done to meet our demands. If you do not call me, I will kill one of the people here with me. If I have no information from your Government by midnight, I will start to kill people.

I have two children in here, they will be the very first to die. Have I made myself clear?"

A cold chill ran down Foster's spine and his mouth went dry; he knew the position he had been put in was almost impossible. The Government could not recommend this demand to the Western world, not without owning up to the true situation.

Now it was possible hostages would be shot if information were not given to Coleman of the progress being made. This man was no fool; they could not lie to him.

Foster sat quietly for 2 minutes, then made a call to Whitehall.

"Sir, in my opinion the situation is one that can only be resolved by the military. Any possibility of their demands being met is almost nil. They must know this. If no progress is being made towards meeting their demands, they will kill hostages.

I intend to evacuate anyone who is living in a property not in view of the pub. Any others that can be moved through the backs of their houses will be removed. The rest have to stay. Once that is organised, I will hand over to the military."

He replaced the phone and sat for another minute thinking.

"George, contact the control room, I want everyone in Abbotsley to be contacted on the phone again. Advise them there is still a problem and if they are not in view of the pub, to leave their house immediately. They must not use the roads, but walk across the fields.

Get more people down here; I need more officers out in the fields, collecting and directing people to safety. Open up the school and get someone in the kitchens, we need to have food and drink available. Whatever happens, they must only move if they are out of sight of the pub. What he cannot see will not bother him.

Set up RV points at each side of the village again, out of sight of the pub, then get these folks out of here. Advise anyone within sight of the pub to stay inside and close the windows and doors. I want contact with the remaining people every 20 minutes. Keep them calm and safe. You have 1 hour, after that no one moves unless it is one of us."

Out of his briefcase the Chief Constable took a set of documents and set them on the table in front of the Major. He signed each of the three pages, dated each and put the time on each. Then handed them to the Major.

"Thank you, time is now 16.30. We now have control of the situation from the police."

"Sir, I will co-ordinate our forces, I would be grateful if you would co-ordinate the civilian services. I need to know that fire and ambulance can be here within seconds if called on. Please keep all unauthorised people away from anywhere within a 2 mile ground radius of the village.

If, somehow, these terrorists were to escape, anyone within that radius risks being shot on site.

I intend to put one of my men in each of your ARV cars. They will be able to act on my instructions and co-ordinate the use of these assets if required."

The Major left the control vehicle and spent a few minutes talking with his men outside. As he finished, they all moved to the rear of the four Range Rovers and started to change. Within a few minutes, they had transformed their appearance and were ready to deploy.

"We have little or no good recon. of the village. We have no idea of access to the pub from either side, or behind. There are apparently some sensors around the building. Just what, or where is unknown, or even if they exist.

Coleman has demanded that no aircraft comes within 5 miles of the pub. We believe this is to stop us approaching with a helicopter either for recon. reasons or to drop men at the start of an assault. Again, we are unsure of any ability to enforce this demand."

Eastwell was now using the encrypted satellite radio link direct to Hereford and was updating the Commanding Officer. Together they would discuss options, before Eastwell would call the team together. Everyone would have their say in a situation like this. The teams were very highly trained and most of the men would be more experienced than the officers or Ruperts as they were called.

In Chinese Parliament everything was open for discussion, this pooled ideas and knowledge. The final decision, however, was made by the C.O. He alone would dictate the way he wanted the operation to be handled.

The result of their discussions was that they badly needed information on the layout of the ground around the pub and ways in and out. There was not time to send in a traditional SAS recon. troop. This normally would be done over several days, hiding away and noting down relevant information.

The SAS officer moved over towards Foster and spoke to him.

"Coleman may not have considered a fast jet flying over. He is worried about the possibilities of helicopters. If I am correct, the village lies within military airspace used for training and low-level flying. We could call in a low-level recon. pass from a Tornado. What do you think?"

"Can the aircraft give you the information that you need? If so, it may be worth the risk. Coleman may feel it is something we have overlooked if we pretend it was an ongoing exercise."

"I will run the request through to the RAF and get a response. We need this information soonest."

There were 16 men in the four Range Rovers and eight from the helicopter. Twenty-four men in total were now all crowded into a small barn that the Farmer had made available for the police and their staff.

He was unaware of the presence of the SAS. Eastwell was talking to his men.

"We appear to have very few options.

"To risk the release of this virus is unacceptable. If we feel they are serious, and could release it, then a full-on assault is not an option without better recon. and more information on the layout of the building.

"We do know, however, that somehow a crazy computer buff is flashing pictures from a computer inside. Apparently, they were planning a big party and the disco is a bloody computer. A link is being set up as we talk.

"The virus can be killed by fire, explosion, a bomb, but this means wiping out the other people, the hostages. Not much of an option either. Powers that be are thinking this one over. If we are asked, we will have to do it. Better to lose a few than half the county. I have sent for the extra ordinance required.

"We could try to sweat it out, but again we risk hostages and release.

"Finally, we have to cover the possibility of them making a break for it under the cover of darkness. If they run, we need to be ready for them.

"I intend to put two of you in the armed response vehicles with the police. If this goes mobile, I want SAS with them. They are very good people, but you will take charge and keep them alive.

"The police helicopter is now re-fuelled and standing by at RV2 back at the school. One will go with this. Our own is also ready to go, but the police have the better gear for tracking and following them on foot or mobile.

"Four more of us in our aircraft to deploy as required.

"If we carry out an assault, we need three teams of two. Six in total; that leaves ten plus myself in the control room.

"Using the maps we have, figure out points to lay up, take the snipers, kite sights, use your gilly suits and get hidden. If anyone comes out of the village, take them down. No one moves without us knowing, if they do, they must be considered hostile.

"Questions?"

There then followed a barrage of ideas, questions and answers, training and experience being moulded into the situation to find the best solution. Every possibility has to be covered.

Ten of the squadron separated off and poured over the maps they had. Mainly ordnance survey, but they showed the relief of the surrounding area well. The gilly suit is like an overall made of mesh, with strips of different coloured rags and material hanging off. It is used to break up the line of the man when lying or hiding. Perfect to help hide them tonight.

Once they had decided on their individual points, each man then sat with his weapon and broke it down, cleaned, checked then reassembled it. They were quiet, pensive, they all realised that, if the virus was released, they had no protection. They had their NBC suits, but all had elected to work without them.

It would take up to 1 hour to get all of them in position. Some may be within view of the pub and could not take up their position until dark. Moving as far as they could, they would wait.

Once in position, none would move until told to. They had to stay in position, regardless of how long this would take. Anyone moving could be shot.

Kite sight was their slang for the night vision goggles. They could use these to see in the dark; the background light was amplified. They were heavy though and would soon become a burden.

The time now was 5.07 pm.

Out of sight of the pub, the village people were moving away to pre-agreed meeting points. There, the police were shepherding them farther back and out to waiting transport. The RV point back at the school was now being turned into a support unit for the village folks to rest and wait. The large school sports hall was now their home.

Twenty-five houses were in sight of the pub, out of these five were able to move away protected from view by their own house. The rest were now in regular contact with the Police HQ, and as far from the pub as they could get, within their own homes.

"Major, RAF confirm two inbound Tornados ETA 10 minutes. Low and very fast should over fly at 5.17 pm." The police radio controller confirmed to the Major and the Chief Constable, who for the first time that day was trying to eat a sandwich and drink some more coffee.

"Please warn your people," barked the Major, "sergeant, tell the lads."

"Sir, one will pass north to south, the other will be west to east, the noise will be frightening, what about warning them?"

"No, we must seem as surprised as they are."

Foster stood next to the telephone and waited, he wanted to call Coleman as soon as the aircraft had gone over. Try to make him understand it was nothing to do with them.

Two seconds later the first Tornado rocketed over the pub, the aircraft was gone but the noise that followed was unbelievable. Ten seconds later the second aircraft passed over the top of the village. Everyone shook as they flew over.

"That must be what it is like when those crazy buggers come after your airfield." Eastwell thought as the phone rang and the Chief Constable picked it up. Even though the SAS had taken over, they did not need to spook Coleman. Foster would continue the dialogue.

14. RAF

Ipswich city centre is hard work at the best of times, but always worse when Ipswich Town are playing at home. The fans seem to get into town early, wander around the shopping centre and department stores, then head for the pubs.

The Club, now premier league, has in recent years gone from strength to strength. Today, they were playing Liverpool, and the journey from Liverpool is not an easy one. Fans had either arrived the night before, or had to set off very early to be sure of arriving on time.

Most of the clubs and pubs had reported a very good night, and there was little trouble.

In the shopping centre, however, it was mayhem. Saturday morning almost midday, and Will was not the happiest of husbands at the shops, standing outside New Look waiting for his wife and daughter.

Wing Commander Will Rivers was OC 2 Squadron at RAF Marham in Norfolk, and would have cut off his leg to be back in the flight office on camp, instead of waiting endlessly for the return of the big spenders.

It seems a duty that husbands are expected to perform each week, or on a regular basis at least. The female mind seems unable to understand that it is not much fun hanging around waiting, whilst they start at one end of the shop and move slowly to the other, checking every new item.

Reverse the situation and all hell breaks loose, "Where have you been? What took so long, I've been waiting ages?" Perhaps time passes differently when confronted with endless options of clothing.

The theme from Monty Python's flying circus suddenly sounded very loudly, and Will's mobile started to vibrate in his pocket.

"What do the boys want now?" he thought pulling the phone from inside his jacket. At least they were at home out of this misery. Both of his boys were back home in Saxmundham, lazing around doing nothing. Horrified at the thought of shopping, they had managed to escape, claiming mountains of homework that needed to be done.

"Wing Commander Rivers?" enquired the voice on the phone.

"Yes, who is this please?"

"Duty Officer, RAF Marham, Sir. We need you back on Camp within the hour Sir, and airborne as soon as possible."

"It's the weekend, and my first one for 2 months, where is the duty Squadron Commander?"

"Sorry, Sir, my orders are to instruct you to return to Camp immediately. Where are you now, Sir?"

"Ipswich, bloody shopping, it will take me at least 2 hours to get to you, I have to get home and change first."

"Standby, Sir, please."

There was a pause and the line went dead, for what seemed like a lifetime.

Will's wife Jean and daughter re-appeared looking very pleased with themselves. Several bags of clothing now attached themselves to the previous purchases.

"We haven't been too long have we, Will?" more of a statement than a question. "Oh, I really need a sit down and a coffee, I'm about had it," Jean admits.

"Something's up love, I have been recalled to Camp."

"Yeh, like a war or something, you just want to get out of town," Jean was not amused. "Why do they?…."

The phone came back to life.

"Wing Commander Rivers, Sir, please proceed to the police station in Ipswich, they have a car and escort waiting for you. You will be brought to Base immediately, and as fast as possible. Please contact me via secure police radio *en route* and we will brief you as to the situation. There will be no reason to change, Sir, your flight suit is on Camp and there is no need for your uniform."

Will made his way to the police station in the middle of Ipswich, and presented himself to the officer on the front desk. After showing his RAF ID card he was taken directly to a waiting police traffic car and motorcycle escort. Thirty minutes later Will was back in his office changing into his flight gear.

"Briefing will be in 10 minutes, Flight, warn the crews and get me the maintenance reports on both Alpha 21 and 22; they are ready I presume?"

Although the aircraft had been in preparation for over an hour, Will wanted to be sure his crews were going to be safe, and that meant checking and rechecking everything.

"Last flight, Alpha 21 reported a light failure on the right weapons console, has this been checked? No record of repair is showing."

Flight crews reported problems in two ways, urgent – likely to ground the aircraft, in more ways than one, and non-urgent, just for attention of the maintenance crews.

"Can't say, Sir," Flight Sergeant Holmes replied quickly. "You're not going to need weapons Sir!!"

"Get it sorted, Flight, this is not a drill."

In the briefing room 15 minutes later, Will and the Station Commander poured over charts and maps of the area surrounding Abbotsley.

"The airspace to the north of the village is all military space, so no problem here. The area to the south is commercial and runs directly into the approach path for Stansted Airport."

"We do not have time to divert traffic to allow our passage," comments the C.O.

"At 500 knots, the pass will take only 6 seconds over target, we then need to turn east and move away from the commercial guys."

The north–south run for the lead aircraft was no problem as most of the airspace was reserved for military use, taking in the RAF bases around Lincolnshire, Waddington, and Scampton and then, to the southwest, Cottesmore and Wittering.

There is what was a USAF base at Alconbury. To the west of Alconbury is Molesworth, the focus of so much attention when the Americans used the base to house their nuclear weapons.

No one knows if they are still there. Supposedly not, but there are regular drills even today for the convoys carrying something.

It was a very familiar site in Abbotsley to see various aircraft from these bases overhead. Waddington was now the home of the RAF Memorial Flight, a Lancaster, a Spitfire and a Hurricane. During the summer they were always overhead, *en route* and returning from the many airshows they attended, instantly recognisable by the sound of their Merlin engines.

The over flight into commercial airspace was not critical but it was a problem. This is normally not allowed, and avoided at all costs. On this occasion Air Traffic Control would be alerted to the situation and would be looking for the Tornado. At 200 feet and 500 knots, it would be very hard to track.

Commercial radar does not rely on the response or reflection of the radio waves back from the aircraft. It relies on the airliner's "Squawking". A small radio device transmits information of the aircraft's identification, height and direction.

If you turn this device off, the aircraft, to commercial radar, becomes invisible. Exactly what happened to the hijacked jets that attacked the Twin Towers in New York: Air Traffic Control just lost them.

The Tornado is equipped to squawk and it will need to today.

The second run will be from west to east and not as difficult, passing over the target and then on directly overhead Cambridge. The airport at Cambridge does fly commercial traffic, but is not as active as it could be. Stansted to the south has recently expanded and taken away any hopes the owners had of increasing short hop traffic.

Today, there were no flight plans filed for Cambridge, and as of 1 hour ago, the airport had been closed.

The flight out to the west comes close to East Midlands and Birmingham airports, both of whom, together with Air Traffic Control, were aware of possible military aircraft in the area.

It was believed, or rather hoped, that the demand from the terrorist that no aircraft were to come within 5 miles of the village, was more aimed at restricting the authorities in using helicopters.

This had limited the ability to approach for recce reasons or in fact to drop special forces with lines nearer to the building. The chance of the anthrax being released was too great; they could not push these people to test them, and the costs were too high.

The idea of a fast aircraft flying over may not have occurred to the terrorists, there was no way the authorities would want to bomb the pub, and if they were intelligent this would not seem to be a threat to them.

This was a gamble that Eastwell was taking. The terrorists had specifically instructed that no aircraft were to approach! To 'approach' in Eastwell's mind meant rotary wing, not a Tornado over flying fast and then gone.

Even if the noise bugged them a little, it could be explained away very easily with the village being in military airspace.

At RAF Marham, things were now in full motion preparing the departure. They could not go until they had launch authority, and that meant direct from Whitehall. This was, for intents and purposes, a hostile mission. There was no way Wing Commander Rivers was going to allow any margin for error.

He was a veteran of the Gulf War flying over 40 sorties against Iraq. He still keeps the voice tape of the first mission. More of a reminder of the fear and tension he felt on his first night, reminding him that he was mortal and could crash and burn like many others before him. That was his first sortie when anyone had fired back at him.

Will was a navigator. Having joined the RAF with a degree, he trained at the Royal Air Force College at RAF Cranwell and passed out with honours. Moving on to RAF Finingley in Yorkshire, he again finished top of the navigator training course.

Flight crew selection is very tough, and you all take the same route, some emerging as pilot trainees and others as navigators, the majority failing. The difference could be something as simple as not being able to cross your eyes.

Will worked hard through the next years, promotion and training pushing him to Wing Commander and his first squadron at one of the youngest ages on record. Obtaining his masters degree in the same year he took command of 2 Squadron at RAF Marham.

He flew again, against Iraq, whilst he was with the coalition forces monitoring the no fly zone to the south of Baghdad, this time as the Squadron second in command, based at RAF Bruggen in Germany.

He did not expect to be shot at this afternoon, but the mission was just as important to him as if he was about to bomb the Iraqis on the first night of the Gulf war.

The information needed by the SAS and police was so vital to the people involved. He cannot mess this up.

Alpha 21 and 22 stood ready in their hardened shelters, time was 14.24. Weather was very fine, little wind across the runway from the east, and about 20 degrees. Fantastic flying weather, and great to get the recce needed, which must go in during daylight to get as much information as possible. A night-time run would be useful, but not as good as the results they were expecting from today's sortie.

The ground crews were all over the aircraft, cables and hoses providing power and cooling for the sensitive electronic systems.

Powered by two Rolls Royce afterburning RB199-104 engines the Panavia Tornado GR4A is an impressive aircraft. It has a wingspan of over 45 ft with the wings fully spread; 28 ft swept to 68° and is over 54 ft long; a top speed of over 1452 mph and carries a pilot plus navigator in tandem.

A small window below the main cockpit houses the Vicon camera pod. The GR4A has no cannons mounted in the forward fuselage. Replacing these are a sideways looking infra-red system and a linescan infra-red surveillance system. It can still carry and deliver over 18,000 lbs of ordnance.

No ordnance has been fitted today; all that was required was high detail information on location, buildings, people, etc.

"Quiet please," began Will, "there are three crews operational today, Alpha 21 with Muttley and I are the lead jet, alpha 22 with Jones and Adams will fly the second run."

"Thompson and Wilf stand by with alpha 32 in case one of us goes U/S: you need to be ready to taxi within 10 minutes of a request to go."

Typical planning for the RAF, two planes going and one on standby. During the Falklands war, the RAF Flew a Vulcan down to bomb the airstrip at Port Stanley, this went U/S *en route* and diverted to land and was impounded. The second standby aircraft following behind went on to complete the bomb run.

"This mission is highly classified, The C.O., me and you five are the only ones who know of the true reason for today's mission."

The ground crew had been informed this was an emergency situation, set up to test the ability of Marham to provide air support at short notice.

"Unknown terrorists have somehow got their hands on weapons' grade anthrax that was being used under licence to develop anti-serum or vaccine following the problems in the US. How they came by it is not our problem.

They are now holed up in a village pub, why this pub is unknown, again not our problem. The demands are that there is a 1-mile exclusion zone on the ground and 5 miles in the air. Any breach of this will result in the anthrax being released.

This is not ordinary anthrax, this is weapons' grade, recently developed, held in a water suspension that will, and can, be dispersed by the weather, falling to earth as rain eventually. It will then spread like a common cold. This is the mother of all biological weapons. It was only developed to allow the production of an anti vaccine"

"What? We have to breach this no fly zone and risk these fucks letting the anthrax go?" This was Muttley, so called because of his strange laugh, just like the cartoon character.

"The lads on the ground, SAS, feel that the terrorists are referring only to rotary wing aircraft. They don't want choppers about. This has blown any chance of them putting in an airborne recce mission. Approach on foot is not possible because of the high position of the pub and apparent smart sensors put in place before they took over the building."

"So what can we do to help?" This time it was Jones.

"We are going to make two runs, from north to south, and from west to east. I want full camera scans, infra-red, and every possible way of picking up detail of location, buildings, anything that will help these lads go in and get this anthrax back. If a dog farts whilst you are passing, I want it on video."

"Alpha 21 will pass north to south. Problems – nothing to the north, Stansted approach airspace to the south. We will clear target and bear hard left heading 080 and back east out of the way. Other issue is the Sandy TV transmitter, 200 feet high, well lit."

The mast would be less than 3 seconds after the target, and this was a problem if it was overlooked.

"Alpha 22 will pass west to east. Problems – East Midlands and Birmingham airports to the west, full lighting and squawk as agreed with ATC. To the east, Cambridge airport now closed and, of course, inbound approach for Stansted."

"All other information and flight plans are ready, get set up and loaded, let's get on with it."

This was a simple mission for the crews, practised many times, and would be carried out over the UK without the risk of hostile action. There should be no reason for problems, and none were expected.

"Alpha 21 and 22 clear for taxi, runway 30, wind 5 knots, 200, climb to 3000 feet heading 290, confirm?"

Both aircraft responded, taxied to the runway and both lifted into the air simultaneously, climbing to 3000 ft heading northwest towards Lincoln. *En route* the navs in both aircraft were in contact with civilian air traffic control, making sure they knew of the situation and making sure they were aware of other aircraft in the area.

Both had their radar active looking for commercial traffic. No other military aircraft were up at this time so all contacts were commercial and to be avoided.

Climbing to 5000 ft, alpha 21 moved away and north to the Humber, circling over Scunthorpe, military air space and under their control. At the same altitude, Alpha 22 had moved off towards Wolverhampton where, under the control of the Birmingham airport tower, he would circle, both now waiting for the order to go, and this was in the hands of the SAS and Whitehall.

"Alpha 21 and Alpha 22, we have authorisation to commit, please execute," Control confirmed.

Alpha 22 was unable to go to low level immediately and had to descend slowly crossing from Birmingham towards Rugby, turning south towards Milton Keynes and then east, crossing to the north of Bedford, dropping to 200 feet just over Marston. Accelerating to 500 knots, the aircraft was hugging the ground, moving up and down as the ground tracking radar followed the contours of surface below.

They would pass over Abbotsley a clear 10 seconds before Alpha 21 came in from the north. Alpha 21 could go to low level sooner, but there was no real reason, holding 2000 feet until they were clear of Peterborough and then dropping to 200 feet and accelerating to 500 knots.

Will's aircraft was now committed to the run and on full auto-pilot. The cameras and infra-red equipment would spool up and run 15 seconds before the pass started. They expected only 30 seconds of information and it had to be good.

The noise of both aircraft passing over would be deafening for less than 1 second, and then gone. There is little noise on approach as the aircraft moving very fast was gone before the sound arrived.

At exactly 17.17 and 10 seconds Alpha 22 roared overhead the Abbot public house, and at 17.17 and 25 seconds Alpha 21 passed overhead, and both were gone.

The noise took the whole pub by surprise, shaking it to the foundations. Coleman became wild with anger.

"How dare they disobey me," grabbing the telephone with one hand and waving the ozi with the other.

"I am sorry about that," pretended Foster. "The RAF use this for low-flying training, and there are training missions taking place this week end. With the news blackout you insisted on, we were unable to inform them. We will ask them to avoid the area if they can."

Complete crap thought Foster; God I hope he goes for this. "Surely you don't think that this is anything to do with the police?"

"Mr Foster, please inform whoever it is that is controlling the armed forces you have working with you that, if you disobey me again, we will attack any other aircraft. Have I made this clear?"

"Oh, right," thought Foster, "what are you going to fire at it?"

The data was already being streamed to RAF Marham, where the technicians would decode it and forward it on to the SAS head quarters in Hereford. The pictures should show everything needed to locate points that are unseen from the pub, and possible ways of attack.

RAF Marham 20.30

"Wng Cmd Rivers, C.O. on line one," Flight called.

"Yes sir, have you got the results yet?"

"Good run, Will, but the ground guys want another run using thermal imaging, we need to know if there is anyone outside and if possible try to pick up some sensors on the ground. I need to see you immediately; I will be with you in 5 minutes."

The C.O. was a Group Captain of over 25 years' experience in the RAF. He had seen action, like Will, in the Gulf, he had taken part in the NATO attack in Bosnia. It was his job, and he did it without question. After the conversation he had just had with Major Eastwell, he was now a very disturbed man.

"Will, sit down."

Will sat in the chair nearest the window, overlooking the airfield, the C.O. took Will's chair.

"I have just finished talking with the Major who is controlling the problem in Abbotsbury. They have requested another run to get better thermal and infra-red pictures now that it is cooler."

"OK, Sir, Alpha 21 has gone U/S; defective panel lights; Muttley and I will take 22 and get some more shots."

"That's fine, Will, please ready two more aircraft. I am authorising you to arm them with two 500 lb HE laser guided bombs."

"Why?" was all Will could say. He knew the answer, but "why?" just came out.

"The virus is contained in a special flask, it can with stand fire, and will survive an impact. If the virus is released in the building, fire will kill it. The feeling on the ground is that they will release the virus. Major Eastwell has just received permission to bomb the pub."

"How many are inside?"

"Three terrorists, two kids and five adults, that's all."

"That's all, they were planning a party!! And I am supposed to go bomb them?"

"Not you, Will, you will do the thermal run, the other two will do the bomb run, If needed. The better your information, the less chance we will have to drop anything."

Will waited before replying, agreed, and stood to leave the room.

"I want you over target at 2115. Let me know when you're ready to go."

Fifteen minutes later, briefed and ready to go, the C.O. gave his authorisation for the flight.

"This time, Will, go to 5000 feet Scunthorpe and wait for clearance to proceed."

The evening was clear and the sun was slowly disappearing, a fantastic orange glow was growing across the sky, it was now 21.35, in 10 minutes it would be dark. Will was in holding pattern above Scunthorpe, enjoying the evening.

"Alpha 22 you have clearance to start your run, please execute," control informed Will.

"Wilco control, we're are on the way now."

They went to low level much quicker this time, even with the best training and absolute faith in the terrain following radar, it is scary at night and easier if you get used to it over a longer period. Muttley went low level just north of Stamford, dropping to 200 feet as they passed Cottesmore to their right.

"We are inbound, ground 45, ETA 2 minutes 30," Will advised the ground personnel so they are aware the aircraft is about to over fly their position.

It had been agreed that, by now, Foster will have told the terrorists that one final aircraft was passing over, the last one of the exercise. He was to use the excuse that it would have caused concern to stop any over flight. What Will was unaware of is that the terrorist had made threats against any aircraft within the area. Using what was unknown. Coleman had repeated this threat in no uncertain terms. Plus he had been told another aircraft was due to fly over.

Will had no reason to be at all concerned about any threat and, as they were to fly into commercial airspace, had all of his navigation lights working.

"767 should see me," he thought.

"They believe we are stupid," Coleman said to one of his men. "They do not believe we can threaten an aircraft. But we have the means to attack them and we will, now go and prepare."

Five miles out of target and with all the imaging systems ready to go, the Tornado now thundered into the night, at 3 miles out the cockpit went mad with alarms sounding.

"Fuck, something is looking for us, we have been lit by something." The aircraft's system had detected a radar, a SAM radar.

"Firing chaff, and decoys called, Will," no response, "firing failed, re-trying now." Years of training had now taken over.

"No chaff or decoys loaded, this was supposed to be a friendly day out." Muttley said, strangely calm.

"Control Alpha 22, we have SAM threat request abort."

"Negative 22, continue course and mission we believe no threat, no risk, continue."

"Fucking hell, what are they saying, boss," Muttley said, now breathing a little harder.

"We will be gone in 15 seconds, it can only be a shoulder launch missile and, unless he is bionic, he has no chance." Will was trying to reassure himself as well as Muttley.

The night was clear and cool and the view from the pub was great. Standing at the front of the pub on the west side, Shaviv had the stinger on his shoulder waiting. The large golf bag that had been brought into the pub had hidden the weapon. Coleman expected that he might need it for helicopters, just as Eastwell had guessed. In this case, it would be a good demonstration of his resolve.

As it was so clear, and he knew that no air traffic would be in the area, when he saw a fast white light approaching in the sky, he guessed it must be the incoming aircraft.

"Boss, kill the lights, we have navigation lights on still."

"Good call," and the plane went black.

The stinger had already powered up and was making a high-pitched whining noise. The green glow of the targeting screen lit his face in an eerie way. Pointing the cross hairs on the screen at the moving image, the system had acquired the aircraft remarkably quickly, and the tone changed to one of a beep, beep, beep, meaning he could fire.

As he pointed the missile forwards toward the bright light in the sky, the light went out but the stinger had detected the Tornado.

The warning tone in the cockpit changed; missile lock.

"Control, they have lock," Alpha 22 reported.

A white flash about 4 feet long leapt from behind the Arab, and the SAM screamed skyward chasing the Tornado into the night.

"Incoming missile, Muttley, stinger is away and tracking us 4 miles to the south."

If the aircraft were to stand still in the air, it would take less than 14 seconds for the missile to strike. Every extra bit of distance was extra time.

Muttley reacted by instinct pushing the aircraft's throttles fully open into afterburner.

"Control, this is alpha 22 we have incoming missile threat 6000 yards, taking evasive action,"

"Break left, come round 180, go vertical, let's lose this fucker."

The big plane's wings came back as it rolled over and came to the left, the afterburners were now fully engaged, the Tornado accelerating as fast as it could, at maximum power. The crew's G suits inflated, pushing blood from their legs and abdomen into their chests and heads.

"If that bloody thing misses us, it will fly straight into commercial airspace and pop an airliner," Will informed control, "we have to lead it away from any other risk."

They completed a 180-degree turn and then going almost vertical, climbed straight up to get some moving space at 20,000 feet. The maximum speed of the aircraft depended on height; it could fly faster at higher altitude. As close to the ground as they were, there was not enough room to fight the aircraft against the threat.

"15 seconds to impact," counted Will.

The boom was heard over a radius of about 30 miles as the aircraft accelerated through the sound barrier, now moving at almost mach 1.2 due north and jinxing the aircraft on the way.

The missile was closing, very fast, and they had no countermeasures to fool it, not enough speed to out-run it and, if they could not dodge it, they were dead!

"12 seconds to impact," Will had put the comms on to open circuit; everyone on the ground and at control had a full commentary of the problem overhead.

"11 seconds to impact, lose this fucker Muttley, I'm ready for home now."

"Alpha 22, Alpha 32, you are ahead of our position, we are inbound east to west across your path, speed 600 knots, on my mark break left, dive away from threat and steer heading 280 degrees, will converge in less than 5 seconds."

Out the darkness, Thompson's voice now gave Will a little hope; Alpha 32 together with alpha 14 had been standing off to the northeast waiting, carrying their deadly cargo. As the aircraft was armed, it had also been supplied with chaff and decoys on the orders of the C.O. at Marham. Standing off only 6 miles, it had been monitoring the problem and left the station to try to intercept the missile.

"Bullshit 5 seconds, this thing will be over in 2," Will called mocking the Top Gun film.

"Will, there is water to your northwest, Grafham water, head down fast, and if you need to get out, go out over the water. Keep the risk of aircraft impact minimum."

Out of his starboard side, Will now saw the Tornado hurtling its way towards them, it was already popping flares, huge magnesium balls lighting the sky, flying out in pairs from just below the cockpit on each side. The aircraft was about 400 ft above them.

"10 seconds to impact."

"Break left," Thompson called.

Muttley dropped the left wing of the aircraft and, less than a second later, Alpha 32 crossed their position at 600 knots, dropping flares in front of the oncoming missile.

Diving and turning onto the heading towards Grafham water, now only 8 seconds in front of them, Mutley reduced speed and cut the afterburners. If they had to eject following the missile impact, they need to know roughly where the aircraft will impact. No pilot will leave the wreckage to fall onto a populated area when he still has some control. The water offered a safe possibility and Thompson had realised. If his pass did not work, Alpha 22 was going in.

Even if Thompson had cannon shells loaded, these were too big and too slow to stop the missile. Defence against a missile threat using a gun normally meant a gatling gun and the ability to put up a wall of lead, not a few hundred rounds. As it happened, he only had two hi tech cameras.

The missile changed course and now targeted a flare, Alpha 22 turned northwest revealing her exhausts to the missile; a bigger target. The missile re-acquired Alpha 22 and the gap between them closed again, but they had gained another few seconds.

"Missile still inbound, nice try Thompson," Will advised.

"Eight seconds to impact," Will called. "Dive at the water, Muttley, bring this bugger in close, and then pull up bank left on full power. Maybe, just maybe, it may impact on the water."

"Five seconds to impact." The aircraft was now diving, the missile chasing their exhaust.

Four seconds, 3 seconds, no one on the ground said a word; they knew what was about to happen; by hanging on to try to save the aircraft and keep the missile out of commercial airspace, if they failed, they were dead.

"Pull up, hit the burners, get the fuck out of here."

Muttley pulled back and right on the stick, pushing the throttles as far forward as they would go, the wings came back again, controlled by the airframe computer. Their suits re-inflated and they both began to pull high G and hold very tightly.

The missile impacted the surface of the water, as hard as concrete at that speed, and exploded into a mass of flame and shrapnel. The aircraft was only 400 yards away and banking hard right.

Seven lights came on, on the right console next to Will's leg. The aircraft lost speed and started to judder.

"Control Alpha 22, we have cleared missile threat but have taken damage, stand by for sit rep."

Muttley was already half-way through checking his systems.

"We are losing fuel from the port side tanks, I have no hydraulics to the port side, rudder function is almost gone, and can't be sure gear will come down. Plane's fucked, boss."

Parts of the missile had passed through the structure of the aircraft, ripping the flying systems apart on the way. Without rudder control, they cannot steer the aircraft, even if they could land without hydraulics and wheels.

"Control, we are declaring an emergency, aircraft is badly damaged from missile explosion, no direct impact secondary damage. We have no rudder, no hydraulics, fuel is leaking from port side. Port engine is now down for safety."

They now had three options, RAF Wittering at Stamford, only 10 miles north, or RAF Cottesmore, 20 miles north. He would head for one these bases. The third option was to bang out, and he did not want to take this option.

On the ground at the RAF stations, staffing levels were minimal as it was the weekend but both stations were now suddenly on full alert and both runways were being prepared to recover a crippled aircraft.

Muttley could not turn the aircraft easily, but was bringing her very slowly onto a flight path to line up with Wittering. If he could not make the turn in time, he would turn slower and line up on Cottesmore.

"Can't get the wings forward, boss, system is down." This meant the swing-wings were locked in the swept position. Lift developed at this position may not be enough to keep the aircraft up a low landing speed. " We have got to go in faster."

It was now less than 2 minutes after the impact, Muttley had the Tornado lined up on Wittering, 5 miles down range. In delaying the landing, the fuel was now gone from the port tanks. His height and level were good, and he knew the airfield was on full alert, ready to recover him.

To the northeast of the runway, if he overshot, was the A1, full of traffic on any other Saturday, but now it was completely empty. To the north and south he could see blue flashing lights, the RAF police had closed the road, while Muttley tried to land.

"Great," he thought, "they don't expect me to make this."

"Undercarriage lights are good, it looks like they are down, can we get a visual?" Mutley asked.

"No time, mate, and it is too dark, go for it, we are going to land."

400 yards before the end of the runway was a net, strung over its full width and 100 yards each way beyond. 500 yards before this was another identical set-up.

To the left and right of the runway stood the RAF Fire service.

"Muttley, if you are not happy at any time, shout GO!, I will pull the lever and get us out; there is no risk except for a hole in the tarmac."

Muttley was fighting the airplane and it was taking all of his strength. If he needed to, he could not pull the lever to eject the pair of them.

"Alpha 22, you're at 1000 feet, speed too high, flight path is good, lose speed."

"Negative approach, wings jammed will stall at a lower speed, we have to land, and we are coming in now."

The big foam spraying engines were already moving, flashing orange and blue everywhere, moving parallel to the runway, building speed for the chase. Two other engines were spraying foam onto the nets at the end of the runway.

"500, 300, 150, 100, 50, " Muttley called. With a backbreaking bump they hit the runway and sped onwards. Muttley hit the airbrakes and wheel brakes, but the hydraulics were out on the port side. The effect of the braking was not enough and started to slew the aircraft to the right, Muttley corrected and started to jab at the brakes.

By now, the two nets at the end of the runway were themselves buried in deep foam: a huge white mass kids would love to play in. "Go for the foam, Muttley."

Three seconds later spinning sideways they disappeared into a white mountain, and did not emerge. They knew the drill. The aircraft had been jerked to a stop and pulled back on itself by the huge nets. The first gave way under strain, but slowed the speed down. The second held.

Sitting in this unreal world, they checked for fire. They could evacuate by blowing off the canopy in the event of fire. There was no fire, they waited. They were down, they were safe, and they were OK or would be when they stopped shaking.

"Bastards."

15. SAS

"Major Eastwell, if you disobey me again we will attack any other aircraft."

Eastwell pondered on this statement for a few moments. Could they have anything that could threaten an aircraft? Gunfire would be almost ineffective unless they were really lucky.

"I need hard copies of all of the pictures that are being sent out from the pub. Get a message to the computer geek, ask if they have seen any large weapons in the pub, or if the bad guys have bragged or mentioned anything big."

The link set up from Neil's House to the Police HQ was via the internet and very fast; they, in turn, blasted the pictures direct to Hereford to the SAS Control room. The relay to the satellite and back to the control room at Abbotsley was instant. Within 5 minutes of the request, the pictures as they were taken were beamed half-way around the UK, up to the satellite and down to the people who needed to see them.

Hard copies were being printed and examined in minute detail. Nothing in the pub seem out of place. There were three adults and two kids sitting against the fireplace. Three other men, the terrorists were talking near the bar, and one further man stood behind the bar.

The only weapons visible were on the bar near to the three.

"Major, we have a response from the pub. He says they have machine guns and small guns. They have seen a knife. Three bags have been put in the other side of the pub. Not in view, plus, a golf bag.

The leader keeps playing with a silver flask, rather like a vacuum flask."

Things then went very quiet; all eyes were on Eastwell as he considered exactly what the terrorists might have in their possession.

"How long before Hereford get the pictures from the RAF? I want to see them now; we need recon. on that building now, not in an hour. Chase it, immediately."

Activity returned to the control room, Eastwell pulled on his, now cold, coffee and moved to speak with the Chief.

"Why would a terrorist bring a golf bag with him? There are three bags, plus the golf bag. I guess one for the flask containing the virus, one for their weapons, and the other could have contained the so-called sensors plus ammunition possibly. The golf bag disturbs me.

There are several possibilities. One, it is a golf bag, and the bloke is nuts. Two, it contains some form of weapon. Three, it is some form of delivery device for the virus.

Hopefully it is one, but my instincts are telling me it is either a weapon or some means of delivering the virus to a target, or dispersal here. We have to assume the worst and they intend to use the virus.

They have the virus; this is without question. Coleman told us about it, no one outside of the Cambridgeshire Police, BBS and us knew it was missing. It now seems he may have the ability to deliver the virus. But where and why?

He could just open the flask, but dispersal would be minimised by containment in the building. He would not risk opening the flask outside because, as soon as he stepped outside the door with it, we would kill him.

We need a shooter watching the pub from high ground. We need to be able to seal the pub within seconds if required."

The major called in two of his men, two of the team preparing to take up sniping positions around the village. They came into the control room, completely kitted up, and ready to go. They looked frightening but at the same time comical.

"Take your gear and get on the top of the church tower. Do not trip any of these sensors. Take the long way round and in. The vicar is not there, he has gone with the rest of the villagers, so you have to climb.

From the pictures, we know there are four adults, all of whom have T-shirts on. We have no visual of the computer geek. The pictures show the terrorists wearing thicker clothes, which makes sense, and shows they have planned ahead. If they run for it, they need extra clothing to keep warm at night.

Anyone comes outside, check with us for instructions."

The church tower would allow a very good view of the eastern side of the pub, plus a limited view of the front. It would not give a good view of the very back or the west side.

The western side of the pub had an old wooden door, only used on rare occasions when the disco was set up at the opposite end of the pub, the opposite end to where it was today, and adjacent to Coleman's bags.

He then turned to the Chief Constable.

"Sir, if he opens the virus flask inside the pub, we need it contained inside. I want a foam spraying fire tender here, ready to go, and waiting as soon as possible. I suggest we get a military one; where is the nearest RAF flying base?"

"Wyton, RAF Wyton. That's about 15 miles away. I will deal with it immediately."

The Chief spoke calmly to his officer and arranged for RAF Wyton to despatch one of the foam spraying crash tenders. AV 1 was sent to guide the big vehicle into place. If the virus were released, the engine would cover the pub in thick foam. The hope was it would prevent any virus that leaked out from the building becoming airborne.

The information from the two aircraft had now arrived. The Major with three of his men sat looking at the pictures. They showed the pub and its surrounding buildings, the church, and neighbouring houses. Together with their own maps, they went over the pre-arranged sniping positions, and closed up the two gaps that had now been created by moving two shooters to the top of the church tower.

They could see nothing out of the ordinary, but were able to see a way into the area, if they had to go in, or now, when they went in.

It had been a beautiful day, very warm, and the thermal pictures were not as good as they needed. If anyone was posted outside the building as a sentry or watcher, they needed to know, and the information was not good enough.

"Contact Marham again, I want another run as soon as possible, this time full thermal scan and infra-red. It will be cooler and the results may be better. I also want to discuss something with the Station Commander, please make contact soonest."

170

Major Eastwell spent 10 minutes talking with the Commanding Officer at RAF Marham. He spoke quietly and, when he was finished, turned to the Chief Constable.

"Sir, I want to convene a meeting for my lads, this is to include both yourself and your Deputy. After it is finished, I would then ask you to brief your own people and the civilian service commanders. Let's go into the barn."

The SAS men all stood up and waited whilst Eastwell sat down. The two Police Chiefs sat amongst them and listened.

"We have to assume that these people have every intention of releasing the virus into the atmosphere, the results of which would be catastrophic. It would kill thousands and could not be contained.

"We also have to assume that there is no way we can talk them out, nor is there any way, certainly quickly, that Government could try to meet their demands.

"It is obvious that we have to go in, and take them out, to recover the virus and destroy it.

"Looking at what recon. we have already, I have changed my mind and we will now use two assault teams of three men. I have ordered two of the lads on to the church tower, but they can only cover two sides.

"I have called in another run from a Tornado, there was too much background heat earlier and some points need confirmation. Also, after discussions with Hereford, I have placed two further Tornados on standby, each armed with a 500 lb HE bomb.

"Should we judge that the assault is not possible without risking them releasing the virus, we have no alternative, the pub goes. This is not something that has been decided lightly. Four people and two kids will be killed along with the terrorists.

"Questions?"

A brief discussion took place about the rights and wrongs of planning to solve the problem by bombing the pub, the morality of hitting six innocent people preparing to celebrate a 40th birthday party. Should they let them know through the computer geek, or is it better not to?

By now, everyone inside the pub would have known what it was the terrorists had, and that the demands they had made were impossible to meet. They would be frightened and no one dared to try to imagine how Tom would feel being there with his two kids, and powerless to help them.

"From what we know, can see, and have seen on the pictures from the pub, there are three doors, one door on the east side, one on the west. Both open into the main pub area.

"The front door has an inner door and is unsuitable for attack entry.

"Team one will work their way around the back of village and in towards the pub from the east side, approaching over gardens and buildings. Stay off and away from pathways and roads.

"Team two will do the same from the west.

"We have to assume they have these sensor devices. The tech guys feel it cold be a simple passive infra-red device, which means we could see it. One in each team will use infra-red goggles.

"Things could turn to rat shit after the next aircraft comes over. The data link has been established direct and we will receive feed within 15 seconds.

"Time now is 19.30, the over flight is due at 20.15. I want everyone in position by this time. We will be ready to go at any time after this point. Is everyone clear?"

Nods of agreement from the gathering signalled that everyone understood. The two senior police officers looked very pale, and stood to leave.

"Let's get this right and get those people out if we can! If anyone sees anything that could indicate imminent release of the virus, call it in, we can take no chances; the strike aircraft can be over target in less than 3 minutes from their holding point."

Two had left earlier and were now well on the way to the church. They had moved out of the RV point and east around the back edge of the village. Each man would move forward 10 yards, stop, crouching down, and wait, listening for signs, sounds, anything that could spell danger. When he was satisfied, he would wave the other forward, and so it repeated.

Slowly they progressed to a point at 4 pm on the clock looking at the village facing north. Behind a mesh fence, with leylandi trees forming a garden boundary, they could see the church tower over the top of the houses.

Cutting a hole through the mesh, they left their equipment and one by one pushed through. Lying silently, watching again for sign. Nothing.

The first moved forward to the back of the house, checked slowly for life, clear! The second brought the small burgens, moving forward round the house, across the road, round the vicarage garden, and then on into the graveyard and to the back of the church. It had taken 60 minutes, 45 minutes left.

Two grappling hooks caught on the roof of the church and fixed. The line on one immediately became taut as the first climbed up the side of the building, rising to just below the apex. He pulled the second rope, which then copied the first. Another 10 minutes later both were at the top of the tower looking out over miles of countryside, but more importantly over the pub.

"Rifle 1 in position, nothing to see."

At the same time as the first two left, the RV point eight more followed and spread out, moving to their pre-arranged points. If the terrorists did make a run for it, they would almost certainly go across country and avoid the roads. From the layout of the village and surrounding land, it was assumed they would move south as this was the easier route and provided cover more quickly in the woods to south of the village.

Five of the snipers moved south and spread across the village. They were about 600 yards away from the edge of the first buildings, and had each found a place where, using their camouflaged Gilly suits, were now laid up and invisible, their weapons up on the small two-legged support.

The arc of fire from each position was such that it overlapped the next position. Each man knew roughly where his mate was, but knew he could only fire into his own killing ground. Outside of this, he was unable to fire to avoid any risk of killing his team member.

To the north of the village, 600 yards from the first houses, the other three men were now crawling along the edge of a hedge leading them out into the open. From there, they would separate and continue to their own positions.

It had been decided that this part of the open land was easier to cover as it was flatter and the route likely to be taken from the pub was more obvious. To avoid crossing deep ditches and getting wet, they would need to use one of two small farm bridges.

Again, they set themselves into their positions with overlapping arcs of fire. If they came, they should be seen. They were dressed in sports-type clothing and would be easily spotted.

The two assault teams had prepared their own equipment and left 30 minutes ago. They had been instructed to get within 50 yards of the pub, to the south. They had no idea where the sensors had been placed, but hoped they might show up with infra-red goggles.

A small domestic movement sensor, such as the trigger for an outside security light can be defeated, but only by very slow movement. As soon as they identify the sensor, they would have to inch past it, very slowly, making no sudden movements. It could take 15–30 minutes to get everyone past.

Keeping off of the road surface away from pathways, each team now made its way towards the waiting point. They crawled through the front gardens of the houses bordering the road leading to the pub, over the walls or through the fences, slowly and deliberately.

One hundred yards south of the side of the pub, a hand went up and all three of the first team dropped onto their haunches. A signal indicated that a light source was registering in the infra-red goggles worn by the first man. Moving right and into the next garden they continued crawling alongside a low wall, shielding them from the sensor.

It left 20 feet of open ground to cover and it had to be done, extremely slowly, crawling on their stomachs, moving six inches, waiting, moving and waiting again.

Both teams were now in place.

If they were given the order to go, they would have to cover the final distance as quickly as possible, and then hit the building. It was about 50 yards. A sportsman could race this distance in less than 10 seconds. In 10 seconds everyone inside could be dead. They had to move like the wind, when the time came.

Racing the final distance would almost certainly trip the sensors that remained. Coleman would have a few seconds' warning of what would be going to happen. Depending on what he was doing, they might succeed, or fail.

At eight o'clock Eastwell had made contact with Coleman, as he was required to do. He informed him that he could not report any progress in meeting his demands, but could tell him that an emergency cabinet meeting had been convened at 1930 hrs. They were still in the meeting and there had been no word from them.

"There is still an ongoing RAF exercise and we have information that one or two aircraft may over-fly the area. We have complained to them about the noise, pretending to be residents. I cannot be sure it will stop them."

"Major, I have ordered you to stop any aircraft. I will attack any aircraft that approaches this building or area. Have I made myself clear?"

8.10 pm Abbotsley

The Tornado was now inbound towards Abbotsley, The crew had been in contact with the ground forces already. When the missile was fired, it took everyone by surprise. The two in the church tower only saw the flash as it leapt skyward.

"Where the fuck did that come from, rifle one?"

"West side of the building, they guessed we might be here. Are the crew OK?"

The tactical radios used by the special forces are encrypted to prevent others listening in, the system can be connected to the other radio system and Eastwell now patched the conversation between the Tornado crew through to his men. They could hear exactly what was going on.

As the tension fell away, the anger began to grow; everyone was now becoming a little frustrated with the situation. They could not go one way or the other.

Major Eastwell was in the command centre when the telephone rang.

"Major, I did warn you. There was no reason for another aircraft to fly over this area. I am sure you could have stopped it avoiding breaking our agreements. Therefore, it was sent for a reason. Reconnaissance I would imagine."

"There was no need to attack the aircraft, what did you expect to achieve?"

"Exactly what I have achieved, my friend. You now realise we are deadly serious. What news from your Government?"

"Nothing I am afraid, we have no news for you."

"It is now 8.15. At 9.00 pm I will kill a hostage unless we hear that your Government is starting to act. Is that clear?"

8.30 pm The Abbot

The tension in the pub was electric; everyone was scared, Jane kept crying, whilst the others stared into the room, looking at nothing.

"You have nothing to fear, your Government has been pushed up against the wall, and they will have to give in to our demands. I believe very soon you will be home.

Put the music back on, and I want it loud. By now they may have some form of device installed to listen into our conversations."

Tom moved back towards the disco to start the music.

"I need the toilet," said Ant in a very low sheepish voice.

"What," bellowed Coleman, "speak up, boy."

"I want the toilet," he repeated. "So do I," Jane said.

"Go then! Go together, and be very quick, no games."

Ant and Jane moved towards the toilet in the far corner of the room, walking past Tom as they did so. Jane was crying and she hugged her Dad as she passed. Tom held her tight and whispered in her ear.

"Use the toilet seat, it's broken, smash the window and run, run anywhere, get away, hide, get out of here. Wait for the beat of the music, go!"

"No talking, get on with it and get back here."

Coleman struck Tom hard on the side of his head. He was now angry but did not suspect a thing.

Jane looked at her Dad again and he winked, she pulled Ant by his sleeve and they both went into the men's toilet. Tom returned to his computer and put a record on, very loud, and very banging. The three terrorists now moved towards the far end of the bar, discussing something.

In the toilet, Jane told Ant what Tom had said.

"Dad said to use the busted toilet seat and break the window, smash the glass out and get out. Then run like hell. Wait for the beat and hit it in time."

As with many men's toilets, the seat was broken and hanging off. This was a solid pine wood seat. Ant grabbed the towel, and then picked up the toilet seat. In time with the music he swung practice swings at the glass, then called to Jane.

"Ready?"

The next swing hit the pane of glass dead centre and smashed it outwards in hundreds of pieces. He hit again and removed the spikes at the top and bottom. Then put the towel over what was left.

"Go, Jane, go, get out."

Jane was small, very thin, very fit. They both were. Dancing, PE and other sporting activities kept them very fit. Jane was through quickly and on the other side; Ant went through a little slower; being bigger it was more difficult. He caught his arm on the glass at the side and ripped his top, cutting his arm deeply.

The music was still banging, both were now on the ground outside the pub.

"Which way, which way do we go?" Jane screeched.

"Into the dark, over there into the graveyard."

As if joined at the hip, they both took off and ran for the dark area beneath the trees at the side of the pub car park, racing into cover and then stopped. They looked back at the side of the pub and Jane, sobbing, said,

"We can't just leave Dad in there."

"Yes, we have to , now let's get out of here, and stop blubbering, run."

As they both rose and moved to start running again, a hand reached out and caught Ant, pulling him down onto the floor, and a second hand covered his mouth. Pushing hard, he could not breathe. Jane was brought down in the same way and both lay facing up, on the ground staring at three people.

They were dressed in black, wore jackets like the police, they each carried a gun, and wore a balaclava.

"Shut up, lie still and listen. We will not hurt you. Quiet!!"

Ant was struggling big time and the one holding him had his work cut out. He took a big bite out of the hand forced into his mouth. But it did not move away.

"Fuck, he bit me, lie still, and shut up, we are on your side, and we are the good guys." He released some of the pressure on Ant's mouth.

Ant slowly calmed down, and stared at the dark figures holding them. Slowly, they released their grip and relaxed.

"Listen carefully, we are here to help, answer carefully, this is important. How many are there?"

"Three," Jane replied.

"Where are they now?"

"At the bar, talking."

"What are they wearing?"

"Hooded fleeces and dark trousers. They have guns."

"So do we, where are the others?"

"There are only three of them."

"No, your friends, where are they?"

"Near the fire against the wall, except Dad, he is at the disco, and Jimmy is behind the bar."

"Where are their bags? Have you seen a flask like a thermos?"

"At the far end of the pub, on the table. The flask is there or he has it."

"Who is he? Coleman?"

"Yes."

The three then spoke quickly between themselves. Jane was shaking and Ant grabbed her away from the one holding her.

"Stay here, stay in the dark under the tree, we are going to help your friends in the pub. Do you understand, don't move, OK?"

Ant and Jane agreed and shuffled back more into the shadows. The three dark figures moved away around to the rear of the pub, and then pushed themselves up against the wall. They were about 50 yards from where Ant and Jane lay.

"Let's go, run, run past the church and keep going, run like hell. Keep in the dark bits. There must be policemen just around the corner. Run until you meet them."

Ant pushed Jane forward and out from the darkness. Running for their lives they rounded the corner, down the side of the graveyard and headed east away from the pub.

Coleman suddenly stopped talking, realising that the kids had been some time in the toilet. He stormed over to the disco and yelled at Tom.

"Turn it off, turn it off. Where are your kids?"

"In the toilet, they went to the toilet."

178

Tom knew that, as they had been a long time, there was a good chance they had got out. He was very relieved, more so when Coleman confirmed it. Storming out from the Gents, he lunged at Tom.

"They have gone, they have escaped. Now I will show you what we meant when we told you to obey us."

He grabbed Tom and punched him again; then as Tom recovered from the force of the punch he hit him again with the butt of his gun and smashed him to the ground, opening a deep cut along the top of his eye.

He ran to the bar and grabbed the Ouzi machine gun and started back towards Tom.

Tom looked at him, saw the anger in his eyes and knew he was dead; he was only glad his kids were out of the way and would not have to see this happen. He closed his eyes tight and held his breath.

"You people will not disobey me, I am in control, you always have to learn the hard way, you never take notice of history, I'll show you the cost of this stupidity. They may have escaped, but I will still kill them, later along with everyone nearby."

Coleman raised the gun and pointed it at Tom, just as a huge bang blew in the door behind Tom, next to the toilets. The room filled with dust and the stench of explosives.

Three dark figures rushed in to the room, one went down and to his right and fired a three-round burst directly into the side of the first Arab's head. It exploded, trailing a mess of blood, bone and brain on the brick pillar behind him.

Jimmy saw immediately what was happening and reached behind the bar, whilst the remaining Arab started to move, Jimmy hit him full in the face, as hard as he could, with a baseball bat, kept just in case there was trouble. There was trouble, and Jimmy, like a man possessed, hit out at his attacker.

The second Arab dropped to his knees, blood gushing between his fingers as he held his face. The next controlled burst from the second figure rolling in the door going left went straight through his hands and he fell onto his side.

The third dark shadow fired once, hitting Coleman in the upper arm that was holding his gun. Luckily for Tom he dropped it. The second shot hit him just above his stomach and took him down in agony.

"Where is it?"

The voice was calm and gentle. Only Coleman recognised it, immediately, and looked deep into his attacker's eyes.

"Ella?" he thought. "Ella, why is Ella here."

"Where is the flask? Where have you put it? We will take it now."

"It's on the table at the back, in the green bag," Tom yelled.

"Fuck you," Coleman yelled.

"Fuck you," Ella said as her next round drilled a hole in the middle of Coleman's forehead, and blew the back of his head away.

"Clear." "Clear." "Clear."

The first two raced to the back, grabbed at the bags, located the flask and ran back. They stood with their backs to each other, weapons raised, and each scanned the room, quickly, efficiently, then each again repeated,

"Clear."

"GO."

Then they were gone as fast as they had arrived.

The two on the church tower heard the bang of the small charge taking off the door, then the first shots above the music, and recognised the signature of the Heckler and Koch.

"Rifle one, door charge and gun fire from the pub, sounds like one of ours."

This threw everyone into confusion. The two assault teams were in position waiting for the order to go. They got it. Eastwell ordered in the Tornados. They had less than 3 minutes before the building would be ash.

"Teams one and two GO. You have 2 minutes. The strike aircraft are on the way. We can take no chances. I want immediate feedback, who is firing at who. It is not us!"

The two teams raced up both sides of the pub and, on the word go from one of the leaders, burst into the pub. Three men each side, each moving to his agreed position.

"Down, down, get on the floor, armed police, armed police."

"Hold it, hold it, they're dead, it's OK, your lads just shot them."

"Down, down, get on the floor, armed police, armed police."

Jimmy shouted at the SAS but they ignored him. Everyone was forced to lie down, face down, hands and legs spread.

"Clear, Clear," six times.

"Three dead terrorists, sir, no injuries to hostages, flask is gone. Whoever did this was good, and quick, and bloody clever."

"Stand by."

They moved in pairs now, to each of the villagers, forcing them down, kicking their legs apart, one held their weapon pointing simply at the head, the other frisked the person, with little respect.

"Clear" again, for each of the now, very puzzled, frighted, and pissed off locals.

"It was your lot, they were dressed like you, black, masks, vests, guns. They shot the lot and took the bag. How were we to know?"

"You weren't, mate, don't worry. We'll do that for you."

Major Eastwell was now numb.

"Who were they? What were they, how did they get in, why did we not see them. Where are they now?"

"More to the point," commented the Chief, "how did they know about the flask?"

16. On the Run

"Chief, get your men into the pub, and my men out. Once in the pub stay there, do not evacuate. I want no movement in or around the village.

Teams one and two, get out, police on route, RV back here soonest.

Get someone in to talk to the hostages, debrief them. We need to know what went on in there."

The Major ran back to the large desk, spreading the maps out across the table. He too was fitted with a tactical radio and immediately started barking orders.

"A special ops team just attacked the pub, took down all three terrorists and have taken the flask containing the virus. Heads up, on the open ground, they have to cross somewhere to get out.

Indications are that they are very good. They must have been good to get in through the village without us seeing them, or tripping a sensor. They are dressed like us.

No one is moving on the ground, we have the pub secure, the police are on the way now. Our two assault teams are back at RV. Static shooters are in place. No one moves, otherwise they are to be considered a target. Shoot on sight."

A crackle of comment came back but one comment made sense.

"Maybe they were here already, or followed the terrorists in. Waiting for an opportunity. But who are they?"

"God knows, but we will find them."

He then turned to the Chief Constable.

"Sir, get your chopper up and over here, my lad is already there and ready.

Teams one and two, get back to the school, get airborne. Load the minimi on the police helicopter and one of you pair up with the one on board. We are taking no chances."

Two of the four Range Rovers shot out of the farm and back towards Ernulf School. Already, both helicopters were spooling up, starting the engines.

When they arrived at the school, they ran from the vehicles, under the rotors and into the dark military helicopter. The SAS men at the school had broken out with a minimi light machine gun and put it in the back of the police helicopter together with plenty of ammunition. They had to assume that they could come under fire.

Likewise in the back of the military helicopter the four men who had been detailed to wait at the school had two further minimi machine guns ready. They also had two type 66 rocket launchers available.

Five of the six joined the first four in the military aircraft; the last one ran and joined his mate in the police one.

Exactly 7 minutes after both teams left the forward RV point, both helicopters were up and moving towards Abbotsley.

"Hotel 1 airborne, ETA 3 minutes."

"Military 1 airborne, same ETA."

In the distance the sound of aircraft became noticeable, and at the same time Eastwell remembered, the radio came to life.

"Ground control, this is Alpha 14, 45 seconds out, commenced bomb run, please confirm, we need permission to fire."

"Fuck, abort the RAF, I forgot they were on the way in."

The Major had forgotten that he had authorised the two Tornados to attack the Pub; there was no longer any need. He spoke with the crews himself.

"Alpha 14, abort, I say again abort bomb run, situation has changed, confirm."

"Roger that. Confirm abort, bad idea bombing a pub anyway."

"Situation has changed, still critical, does not now involve building. Have you time to switch to carry out a full thermal imaging run? Confirm?"

"Need to go round again, back in 2, ready to run."

"Be advised two helicopters now overhead village."

183

"Confirm two helos, advise them to move east, and stand by."

Both Tornados were audible and the sound changed as they moved away to turn full circle and back in again, giving the crew time to set up the cameras for the run. The thermal cameras would find any heat source, moving or not. The two helicopters now held their position hovering over the far edges of Eynesbury about one and half miles from Abbotsley.

"Alpha 14 ETA 40 seconds, inbound north to south, stand by to receive the data."

Both aircraft crashed over the village within seconds of each other, low, but not as fast this time, they needed better results. The noise was unbelievable and again they were gone. The helicopters bowed their heads gracefully again and moved forward.

The data showed the village in black, any heat source was lighter depending on the intensity. The pub was lit like a fairground and some houses near to it, also showed heat sources. Beyond that, except for the street lighting, it was black.

The snipers were just visible in an irregular ring around the village, and two heat sources could be seen clearly on the top of the church.

To the edge of the village at approx 4 o'clock as you look north, was a large heat source, static. This was where the rifle team, now on top of the church tower, had come through into the garden of a house. Their choice of route in towards the church and pub could be the choice made by the intruders to escape. If they were trained in a similar manner to the SAS, they might see this route the same as the SAS would.

If the heat source was the intruders, it should show three sources; it only showed one. Unless they heard the aircraft inbound and huddled together.

"Possible contact 4 o'clock on village perimeter. Not moving, showing as one heat source, could be huddled, or hiding."

"That's the way we came in!" Rifle one commented, "If it is them, they are retracing our steps to get out, they know what they are doing!"

"Follow them up, get down ASAP, and follow. Do not move past the edge of the village, we have no way of identifying you. Stay within the village. Follow up in case they come back."

The two men grabbed their small burgens and fixed one rope to the roof. They strapped their weapons over their front, stepped out into the blackness and dropped down.

Andy was the first to go, moving out over the side of the tower and leaning back with total trust in his own ability and that of the rope to hold him. He dropped two feet, squatted in towards the wall then pushed off with his legs into nowhere, dropped another 15 feet, and did the same again, abseiling down the tower.

They could drop all of the way to the bottom this time; there was no need to stop on the church rooftop.

Andy hit the floor; fell flat with his weapon in front of him, ready. He waited and listened. Without a sound he gently pulled the rope to signal Chinky to follow.

The rope was left; it was not needed and could be recovered later.

They knew where the targets were, and how far away, they also knew this time that there was no reason to worry about the sensors. Still moving with extreme caution, moving, crouching, waiting, and then moving again, they advanced back towards the garden they had first cut their way into. If the intruders were as good as it seemed, they would notice that someone had passed this way previously. They might have even watched them.

As they reached the front of the house they stopped outside the front wall and waited again. There was not a sound. The distant sound of the rotor beat from the helicopters was getting louder and would soon drown out any possibility they had of detecting sound.

Careful deliberate movements around the edge of the wall allowed them to see there was no threat, it was clear. They moved again towards the edge of the house along the front pathway. Each side of the pathway small dwarf conifers were neatly trimmed into an ornamental hedge, making it look rather regal. As Andy moved forward he felt the gentle pull on his boot at the same time as his peripheral vision picked up the glint of the steel wire in the moonlight.

"Trip wire! Move, get out."

The wire was obviously a trap, and Andy had walked right into it. It would almost certainly be attached to one of two things; a grenade or an anti-personnel mine. They knew that it would be at one end of the wire or the other. This meant it was pointless to go to the right or the left, any blast might catch them. They had to go forward or back. And very quickly.

"Go back," Andy yelled.

Both men leapt backwards, through the gate and dropped flat behind the small wall.

From the time Andy had tripped the wire, there would have been either an immediate blast or a 3–5 second delay. There was a delay; this meant that it must have been a grenade.

The blast was enormous, a huge noise and a blinding white light. The two experienced soldiers knew they had messed up, and should be dead. The fact that they were still alive meant it was not an anti personnel mine. The delay meant it was a grenade; but there was no shrapnel. In unison, they both said the same thing:

"Flash bang? That was a fucking flash bang. These people are fucking with us."

The huge bang was heard at the control centre and both helicopters noticed the flash. The SAS teams in the air knew what it was, they had used them many times both in training and in anger.

"Sit rep rifle one," Eastwell called, "You OK?"

"Stepped into a wire, boss, thought we were dead, but they set a flash bang. Why? Early warning, or are they trying to teach us a lesson, maybe avoid hurting anyone?"

"They took the bad guys down, and without hesitation."

"So would we have done, but we wouldn't take out a policeman. Are these guys on our side?"

Andy and Chinky lay still for a few minutes, caught their breath, and counted their blessings for a few moments. Then moved out again. This time on their bellies. At the corner of the wall they split and went forward in parallel, one each side of the path. Sliding carefully.

Andy moved right into a thick hedge at the side of the garden. He moved underneath, crawling backwards until he was hardly visible. Chinky went right and moved into the deep shadow between the side of the house and a large green oil tank. Their instructions were to wait in case they came back and that is exactly what they would do.

From the noise, both helicopters were now over the village and had heard the conversations over the radio. Hotel 1, the police helicopter was now approaching the area where the heat source had been seen.

It too had thermal imaging and was now searching for the source the aircraft had seen.

It was hovering at around 200 ft, closing sideways towards the heat source and had picked up something. There were now two sources, and they were moving out of the village.

"Target moving slowly, have two heat sources, they are past the rear garden of a house, heading south."

"Sniper 4, that is my area, I am scanning with the kite sight, nothing seen."

The military helicopter swung south and came around at 90 degrees to the police and held its position, south and in line with where they were expected to move. The police closed the gap slightly more and turned on the big million-candle searchlight on the front. The response was immediate.

Automatic fire shot up from the ground, complete with tracer arcing up into the night sky.

"Back it off, Hotel 1, kill the light."

They pulled the aircraft away from the threat, and switched off the light. From half way up the hill to the south, a bright muzzle flash was seen as Sniper 4 fired.

"Sniper 4 contact, three people, had view for second only when they fired. Engaged one target result unknown."

"Major, the fire from the ground was not aimed at anything. If these guys have a light machine gun, complete with tracer they could have downed the police easily. They aimed to miss. What's going on, this some sort of exercise?"

"Fuck knows, your orders are clear, recover the flask at all costs, shoot to kill, no excuses. I want these fuckers."

Judging from the change in language, things were now becoming very confused. What appears to have been a highly trained team had just killed three terrorists who happened to have a very deadly virus, which no one was supposed to have known about.

They somehow managed to get into the village when the SAS chose not to for fear of the consequences, for fear of them releasing the virus, then make their escape. On the way lay a deadly trap for any follow-up, but only used a flash bang. Just to scare anyone who may follow them up.

Engaging the police helicopter with automatic fire, but to miss deliberately was even more confusing. The lads in the helicopter were right; it could be an exercise. But it was not. Eastwell had all of these points going round and round in his mind.

1.   How did they know about the virus?
2.   How did they get into the village?
3.   Why lay a booby trap with a flash bang?
4.   Why deliberately aim away at the Chopper but still fire?

Lying flat on the ground, half under a hedgerow, three blackened figures huddled together to allow their heat footprint to look as one. They were motionless, the only thing moving was their eyes.

In a quiet whisper they discussed their options.

"They did follow us, we heard the bang. They will wait now, as they cannot risk mixing their people with us.

There are guns above us on the hill, the one that fired almost killed me; the round hit the mud 3 inches from my side.

The helicopters can see us as heat, and the second one holds more troops. What do we do?"

Ella spoke this time, calmly and with as much authority as the others.

"They expect us to move, let us disappoint them. Use the thermal sheets and we will hide underneath. Then wait for 2 hours. This will use the fuel from the helicopters, they need to refuel sometime."

Each of them carried an emergency pack containing first aid equipment, and survival gear. One of the things they all had was a thermal blanket. This was like the silvery sheets you see marathon runners wrapped in as they finish their race. These, however, were matt black and non-reflective.

Out of Ella's Pack one of the others pulled a sheet, they moved close together and pulled it over themselves. Lying quietly, not talking, just listening. From the air, the heat source that the police were watching slowly died away and was gone.

"Hotel 1, we have lost contact with the heat source, it has disappeared."

"Hold your position, keep looking."

The intruders lay deadly still again, waiting, for 2 hours they lay. The helicopters were moving around seeking, looking for some form of sign they were still there.

After a further 20 minutes the police helicopter moved away and headed off northeast.

"Hotel 1, refuelling, back in 30."

"Major we need fuel too, the lads want drop, take up positions on the edge of the woods behind the snipers?

"Negative, I will not risk hitting our men, refuel and get back here."

Both aircraft moved off towards RAF Wyton where the ground crews were already waiting with fuel. They would be back on station in under 30 minutes.

11.30 South side of Abbotsley

The intruders now moved, slowly crawling on their stomachs along the edge of the field, following the old hedgerow. They knew there were guns waiting for them, but knew where one of them was, roughly, having seen the muzzle flash. Their best option was to head for this gun, and the box round it, staying close and quiet.

It made sense that the other snipers would not be too near him. More importantly, would not fire towards him.

Before they left, they fixed a remote radio controlled detonator to another flash bang. Wrapped it carefully with tape, and tossed it hard to the southwest of their position, deliberately in the area between the sniper that had fired and the possible position of another. It made a dull thump as it hit the ground and rolled into a furrow.

From where the shot was fired by the sniper could have been no more that 300 yards away. They had to clear those 300 yards and more whilst they boxed around, in the time it took for the helicopters to re-fuel and return.

It was still a clear, crisp night, a great night for party, but no one in the pub would be feeling in the mood. The moon was high, and working against the intruders.

Slowly, they inched their way along, covering the ground very deliberately, moving twigs, stones out of the way, still crawling on their bellies. At a point where they estimated they were within 50 yards of the gun, they turned left and moved off at right angles. In another 100 yards they would turn right and then head straight again.

By now they were almost level with the sniper, but 100 yards away and continuing. Ella was leading the three; she was lightest and would have less impact on any loose or insecure ground. She still frightened the pheasant the same as any fat guy would have. It made the most frightening screech and flew off towards the moon, still screaming.

Instantly, two guns turned into the noise, and the kite sights the SAS were using picked up a slight movement.

"Contact high ground between sniper 4 and 5, we cannot fire, out of arc. Where is the chopper, instructions control?"

As the intruders had now moved south between the two snipers, they were not in any of the snipers' killing fields. This meant that, if one fired, he risked hitting his mate, or even worse starting a firefight between them. Blue on blue. They could not fire, they could not move. The intruders were using the SAS's own safe practices against them.

"Sniper 4 hit the ground, stay low, 5 toss a flash bang, get as close as you can with it, see if you can see anything."

He threw the flash bang as far as he could in the general direction of the contact; it went off with a huge blast and lit up the whole area. In the light two of three were visible. The flash ruined the night vision of the intruders, and the SAS.

The intruders took the opportunity of the snipers being blind for a few seconds, and raced along on all fours heading in the same direction. Sniper 4 had hid his eyes and bounced back up to see the three shapes moving for the first time against the horizon.

"4; Contact, engaging."

He knew that the movement was not one of the SAS, they were all still, their orders, and standing operating procedures for this type of deployment were to stay still. The muzzle flash leapt a yard out of the gun as the round found its target.

With a yell, the third intruder stopped and bit hard into his hand. His other hand reached down to his thigh. He was bleeding; the shot had hit him above his knee in the flashy part in the middle of his thigh. It had passed right through, leaving a clean hole. He fell from the slightly raised side of the field down into the edge rut where the plough had been.

Seeing his mate go down, the second man pressed the remote he had in his pocket and 400 yards away the flash bang went off between rifle 4 and 3. Both snipers dropped to ground; then came up turning the guns in the direction of the blast.

Ella was on him immediately; she rolled up his left sleeve to reveal an IV butterfly, already inserted and taped down. Breaking open her kit she took a pre-filled syringe of diamorphine, broke off the seal and pushed it and the contents into his arm. At the same time the second intruder had wrapped a field dressing over the top of his fatigues, sealing the wound tightly.

The wound was not critical but he was losing blood very fast. The shot had missed his artery, but it was a big 7.62 round and it had made a mess passing through. They wrapped another field dressing around the wound, and Ella now strung a fluid bag on the hedge and connected it to the IV. He started to go into shock.

"You can't go on, you realise that? We will have to leave you. Wait as long as you can; then release the flare and two or three of the red marker flares."

Ella knew they could not carry him, or expect him to keep up. His best option, particularly as they were in a "friendly" country was to stay put, and give himself up.

"OK, go on," he said, "I am OK. The second bang confused them and the helicopters will not take long to re-fuel and return, you must move now, and rest when they are back."

All agreed, in spite of his injury and the pain. Ella pulled another thermal sheet over him and they moved off, leaving him behind. They left their own saline bags for his IV and their own morphine.

Slower, but still making ground they moved as quickly as they dare, away to the south and past the two snipers they now knew about.

The field began to flatten out; the backdrop of the woods hid them as they moved. Changing direction slightly, they headed in towards the complete darkness of the trees. They needed to make it through and get hidden again before the helicopters returned. In the distance the thump thump could once again be heard.

Sliding finally over a small single-track road the two intruders entered the edge of the woods. Now knowing they would be hidden well, rose to half height, and ran deeper into the trees.

In a small hollow, they grouped together again, and covered themselves once more with the sheet. Now they could rest.

17. Caught

12.15 am South of Abbotsley

The two helicopters were now back on station over the fields to the south of the village and once again seeking the intruders.

"Last contact was 300 yards south of the point they were first seen. One shot was fired at them and was a possible hit.

"A flash bang went off to the west of this position at the same time we had the contact. This could mean they have split up."

The Major turned back to the Chief and sat down next to him at the table.

"I believe we hit one of them and they are now trying to E&E with an injured man. He could be hit badly, or it could be a walking wound and not bad at all.

If I were in their situation; I would now go for a vehicle, which means moving on to another location, or back-tracking into the village to lift a car. How far is the next village?"

"Waresley or Gamlingay; both 2 or 3 miles. Unlikely they would head that way. We have no one in the village except for your team from the tower and the armed officers at the pub."

"Yes, I know. I am going to drop the other men back into the village, they will have to go down in the playing field."

"I will move both armed vehicles out a little. I want one in Gamlingay and one on the road out towards the A428. We have the main through road either side of the village covered. We can block the road outside with a truck."

The military helicopter came down briefly, hovering 6 ft above the grass in the middle of the cricket pitch. Five of the nine men dropped onto the ground, in kneeling positions, formed a small circle facing out.

Behind them into the middle of the circle the remaining four dropped their small burgens. The helicopter rose and moved away, leaving the five men motionless, each getting accustomed to his new surroundings and situation.

Two then moved into the centre and sorted the kit, picked up their own burgens and returned to the edge. Another two did the same and finally the last man. They moved out away from the centre of the field towards the houses in Hardwick Lane.

Separated by around 8 feet they patrolled up Hardwick lane and crossed into Peppercorns Lane.

It made sense that, should the intruders come back to the village to lift a car, they would approach in a rough area near to where they left. Two SAS lay in wait already, and they were now in contact with their comrades who had just landed.

They separated into one three-man patrol and a two-man. The three found a position in the shadows and waited. The other two left to carry out a reccy on Peppercorns Lane to find good positions to lie up and wait. If the intruders did return to take a car, they would have the road covered.

It had now been over 60 minutes since he had taken the round in the thigh. He knew his friends would be well concealed, and he also calculated that both helicopters would be low on fuel again. If he was going to do it, then now was about the best time.

The pain had returned to his leg, and he needed more morphine. It could send him to sleep, which might mean bleeding to death. The white flare was by his side, ready to fire, but first he pulled the ignition cords on the red marker flares. He tossed one about 3 ft from each side of him. This would mark his position.

Sniper 4 just caught the red flash as the marker was thrown. He immediately brought his gun to bear.

The sight of the white flare going airborne was unexpected.

"4, someone has just fired a white flare from the ground midway between 4 and 5, the area where I engaged the target. I have also seen a small red marker flare. It looks like the one we hit wants to be seen."

"Stand by 4."

There was a silence for 15 seconds, then the Major came back.

"Military 1, did you see theflare?"

"Affirmative, there are also two red markers on the ground."

"Anything on thermal?"

"Negative control."

"Hotel 1, use the searchlight, take a look."

The massive light on the front of the police helicopter lit up the ground clearly with a white circle about 20 feet across. Outside of the circle, it was still clearer. Within a matter of seconds they saw the wounded man.

He was lying in the same position and was very still. From the air they could see the IV bag hanging on the hedge. Covering him was the thermal blanket.

"We have a casualty on the ground, he is not moving, but must have fired the flares. Instructions?"

"Stand by."

"Military 1, move in to the south of the position, approach with caution and recover the casualty. Hotel 1, provide cover with the minimi."

The two SAS men opened the rear door of the police helicopter on the right side, and pushed the barrel of the minimi out into the night air. It is a big gun, but not too heavy and can be manoeuvred in tight conditions.

The two front legs rested on the edge of the floor, the ammunition now loaded was fed from the belt magazine slung underneath.

"Hotel 1, ready."

"Military 1, going in now."

The dark green helicopter dropped rapidly and hovered again 6 ft from the ground, Four dark shapes dropped, and stayed down; this time flat. The aircraft was gone. They were about 50 yards to the south of the position where the intruder lay.

Advancing in twos, covering opposite arcs, two forward two backward, scanning for any sight of a threat. Above them the police were scanning with the thermal camera and could see the four of them clearly.

Slowly, they advanced a yard at a time, waited and moved on. Stopping, crouching and moving on.

When they reached the intruder, he was in a bad way, the IV had run out, and he did not have the strength to set up one of the bags his friends had left him. He had managed to administer the morphine, and he was anaesthetised. His pulse was weak.

One of the SAS moved in to help him; all are trained to a high level of first aid, some even further. Luckily for the intruder, this man was a fully trained medic and had spent many weeks working in accident and emergency.

The other three formed a protective circle around the point, 10 ft away, and 20 ft apart. Ignoring what was going on with the casualty; they looked into the darkness.

A second bag was attached to the IV and more field dressings were applied to the wound. A brief search of his clothes and pockets revealed nothing. No identification, no dog tags.

"Control, 1 casualty, alive, but only just, need immediate casevac to hospital. Bring the helo back. He fired the flares; the remains are here with him. He must have done it as a last resort to attract attention."

"Military 1, move back, recover the team and casualty."

The Major turned once more to the Chief.

"Where can he go?"

"Addenbrooke's is equipped to accept the helicopter and can provide a secure ward, if he makes it. I will arrange armed guard and reception to meet the aircraft. No problem for your guys, they just stay put and fly out."

As always, no SAS soldiers would want to be identified. Either at the time, or possibly later by chance. They would need to know they could remain on the aircraft.

The big helicopter came back in on the position, both side doors open. Two of the SAS picked up the intruder, and walked the few feet to aircraft. As they did so, their mates followed them up, and backed into the helicopter. As fast as it came in, it now left and headed due eat to Cambridge.

"If he says anything, I want to know! OK!"

The medical attention continued *en route* to Cambridge, they cut away his black trousers and his boot revealing the extent of the wound. Without worrying about cleanliness they stuffed more field dressings into the holes, then bound them tight with bandages. They had to slow the bleeding. The new IV bag had drained; the last one was now in place and emptying at an alarming rate.

Within the space of less than ten minutes they pumped two IV bags of saline into him, and he was now moving slightly. He did murmur but no one understood what he said.

The noise and distraction caused by the evacuation of their comrade gave the other two an opportunity to move. They too had decided it might be time to find a vehicle and get mobile.

In the darkness of the night, a silhouette of a farm building had appeared on the horizon to the west of their position. They hoped that, if they could make the farm, it might be possible to steal a vehicle of some kind.

They were now 100 yards into the woods away from the road, giving them about 600 yards from the edge of the village and at least 300–400 from the snipers; who were still there, as far as they could tell.

The road was also the top of the rise, and once over it, the land became more flat. It was unlikely that the snipers would see them, provided they kept low. Moving again on all fours, they crawled slowly along using the bottom of a dry ditch.

"Major, your helicopter has left Addenbrooke's and has gone for re-fuelling. It will be back on station within 25 minutes. The police helicopter has around another 10 minutes before it too needs fuel."

"OK, continue the search of the area to the south of the place where the casualty was found. They must have gone on, and not back."

As the helicopter moved slowly towards them, the two intruders once again hid beneath their thermal blankets. Ten minutes later they heard the sound of the rotors change and the aircraft moved away. They started to move again.

The farmyard was now less than 400 yards away and more defined against the dark sky. There were no lights anywhere to be seen. There was the most awful stink though; rotten onions.

Fifteen minutes later the two lay against the outer fence of the farm, a wooden livestock fence. The stink was now unbearable, how anyone could live next to this was beyond belief. To inflict the smell on a local community was even more unreasonable.

None of the intruders had radio communications. They had agreed that they would operate without them tonight. If one of them were caught, they could not risk the mission with the possibility of compromise because of the radio.

At this stage of their escape Ella was wishing they had not made that choice. Splitting up, they moved into the farm. They did not expect any threat from the security forces, but did not know who might be about. The farm was dark, suggesting that the occupants had been evacuated.

There were muffled sounds and bangs from the farm buildings, animals of some kind. Hopefully, the onion stink would prevent them picking up any scent from them.

They agreed to separate for 10 minutes. They left the backpacks, one containing the flask, at the fence. If one got caught, the other went for the flask. They would rendezvous back where they started.

It was quiet, the sound of the two helicopters gone for now. Ten minutes later, the pair lay again next to the fence.

"There is a small van on the far side of the farm. It is parked at the front of the house. So far as I can tell it is useable, we may have to hotwire it."

Major Eastwell was now faced with a problem; he had to re-deploy his men on the assumption that the intruding team had not gone back to the village for a car, but had, in fact, continued south out of the village and away.

It was now almost 2.30 am.

He called back four of the seven men in the village, then re-deployed the northern snipers in to positions between the others on the south. They would fire towards the village, the others away from the village, covering all possibilities.

Three vehicles were allowed into the area, a police forensics team, a minibus to move the people in the pub, and a dark van to move the dead.

Ella now moved away once again from the fence, together they were crawling towards the north side of the farmhouse. Staying flat on their stomachs, it took them 20 minutes to reach it, where they stopped and rested. In the distance they could see clearly the many flashing blue lights in and around the village.

After a short respite, they continued to the far corner of the house, and Ella went forward to check it was clear as she looked around the corner to the west side of the building. In the half light she could just make out the white van.

Moving again, they skirted the yard to the north and found the van.

For the first time since they started their task, followed Coleman, found their way into the village and stormed the pub, the intruders were about to get it wrong.

Ella crouched watching their rear whilst her friend opened the van. There were no keys, so he wrenched off the steering lock, popped the bonnet and hotwired it quickly enough to make the local gypsies proud.

The van did not roar out of the farmyard, it moved slowly, with no lights, but fate moved against them. The farmyard had floodlights, typical domestic types, just like you buy in B&Q, activated by infra-red sensors. Suddenly they came on, all four wired on the same circuit and lit up the front and north side of the farm, just like a fairground.

"Sniper 1, the lights in the farm above you to the southwest have just come on."

His response was immediate, it had to be them, or there was every chance it was them.

"GO!, you four take the Range Rover and get after them."

The four men who had just been taken out of the village ran and took the first of the vehicles they got to. Throwing their weapons into the back, the driver pulled away before the doors were even shut.

Out of the farm and turning left, the van sped up the road towards the farm. The van had about 3 minutes' start on them.

The problem of the virus still existed. Could they risk it? Could they take it out like the discovery earlier in the day? That situation was more controlled; they were in the open, miles from anywhere.

Eastwell turned to the Chief Constable once more.

"Sir, I will control the aircraft and my men in the Range Rover, you co-ordinate your two armed vehicles and other police vehicles. He is running, and we have him. The trick is going to be forcing him into an area where we can deal with the threat.

Use the ARVs in close and the other vehicles to block roads. If we work together, we can lead him where we need to."

Both men moved to separate parts of the table, looking at the same map. The Chief using police radio and the Major his own tactical radio.

"Hotel 1, sit rep please."

"Re-fuelling has been aborted, we have enough fuel for another hour, already on the way back your aircraft is with us, ETA 5 minutes."

The Major continued and, at the same time, the Chief brought his own resources into play. This was now looking like a huge game of chess.

"ARV 1, head into Gamlingay B1040 and block exit from village in your direction. There is a Bedfordshire unit heading to block the road their side of the village.

He will be forced through the village which will slow him down and on towards Little Gransden.

ARV 2, come back into Abbotsley, follow up the SAS and the white van, stay back, go around Gamlingay to the west into Potton and then follow B1042 towards Cambridge. Seal off his right turn, should he decide to go through Hatley."

The Major was not listening to any of the commands being sent to police units. He was now talking with the SAS team following up the van. Behind the Range Rover in the distance, the flashing blue lights of the ARV were now visible and their SAS mate was talking to them.

"Hotel 1, close in on the van; make sure he turns the right way, do not fire on him, even if fired upon."

The intruders were not familiar with the area and were driving on instinct. As the van sped into the village of Gamlingay and stopped at the first junction, they could see the roads blocked to the left and right; blue flashing lights both sides.

It drove straight on, through the village and out the other side, heading towards Little Gransden.

"He has gone straight through the village, signposted to Little Gransden. We are closing on him now."

Immediately, the Chief broke in to the conversation.

"ARV 1, move through the village past the fire station, out along the Hatley Road. Block any chance of a right turn back towards Gamlingay. Move it, you have little time."

Looking at the map the Chief could see that the van might turn right in about 1 mile. This road linked through to the Gamlingay–Hatley road. The van could turn right and double back. ARV1 would have to move very fast. But they were good at that.

The van sped on approaching the junction, it was travelling east, and instinct took it right and south again, away from the village and the pub. This was a short road, no more than ½ a mile, and they moved as fast as they could. Approaching the junction, visibility each way is good, and they saw the flashing blue lights of ARV1 racing towards them. They turned left, and floored the little van.

"Van has gone left, left at the junction, he must have seen the police car. We are following at a safe distance."

"ARV1, back off, let the Range Rover through, then follow up."

"Hotel 1, do not engage target, do not fire unless you are fired upon. We want this van to stop, or continue south on the A1198. Bassingbourn Barracks is 3 miles south, a good place to finish this."

The Major then talked to the Chief; together they consulted the map, and moved their pawns once more. The Chief was the first to begin again.

"ARV1, turn left through Croydon into Arrington, then right on A1198. Prevent left turn to the north. There is a Herts police van blocking eastbound on A603. They have to go right, to the south."

After this the Chief, in direct contact with Hertfordshire and Bedfordshire Headquarters requested further support from Hertfordshire in blocking the right turn from the main road towards Wendy.

At the same time, Major Eastwell was speaking to the two helicopters and the Range Rover. The trap had been set, and the two aircraft were the main pieces in the closing part of their game.

"Military 1, head south, and land on the A1198 in front of the main gates at Bassingbourn barracks. They are expecting you, confirm?"

"Confirm, we are turning now."

"Hotel 1, keep on the van, hassle him, let him know you are there, make sure he goes where we want him to."

The big green helicopter peeled off to the southwest, away from the van speeding along the road, its course now taking it down towards Royston. It then circled into the east and landed in the middle of the road.

The police helicopter closed on the van. It was now approaching the T-junction with the B1042, Sandy to Cambridge road. The approach was downhill and the main road was clear in the distance, again to the right side; they saw the ARV flashing towards them.

At the junction they went for the right turn. ARV1 was still 400 yards away, and they took the chance. Before they could even complete the turn, the ARV saw the change in headlight direction, immediately hit the brakes, spun sideways and blocked the road. As they did so,

Hotel 1 swooped from the right and forced the van to change direction once more, they headed east.

At the roundabout at the junction of the B1042 and the A1198, ARV 1 was already waiting, the car blocked the north exit, and both the policemen, together with their SAS companion, had their firearms raised, ready to fire. On the far side of the roundabout, the police van had every light it could flashing; they needed to be seen.

The intruders' van now raced up to the roundabout, saw that their only direction was south, they knew they were being trapped, but could do nothing. They moved to the opposite side of the road, turned right, went the wrong way around the roundabout and south.

"Hotel 1, close in behind and follow, reduce your airspeed, and be ready to land. The road ahead is blocked by the SAS and they are ready to engage the van. When the van stops, land 100 yards behind, ready to support if needed.

"I want the Range Rover behind the aircraft and the team deployed for protection and if necessary to engage. All units confirm?"

The major moved closer to the Chief and they talked quietly for a few moments.

"If Coleman had succeeded, he could have passed the virus to be used in defence of the Palestinians. We cannot be sure he would have surrendered the flask. Their only target would be the Israelis. They alone.

Maybe, just maybe, this team is an Israeli special ops team, sent to follow Coleman. They could have been on to him for a long time. Somehow, they might have had information in advance and went after him."

"Aren't they supposed to be on our side? Should they not have informed us?"

"If they had let us know, we would have taken Coleman out ourselves. They wanted to get their hands on the virus for the same reasons we developed it. They want the anti-virus, or serum for their own protection. These people are Israelis, that's why they did not try to hurt us, or shoot directly at the helicopter."

The Major leapt up and contacted the teams now approaching the van.

"All units, we believe the targets to be an Israeli special ops team. This could end up as a serious engagement. Do not fire unless fired upon. We need to let them know, we know. Does anyone have any knowledge of Hebrew or Yiddish?"

"A little, Sir, what do you need?"

"Just a few words, stop, or halt, or give up. If they hear their own language, they will realise we have them figured out, and may give up without the fight."

"Ophaltn or Farhaltn, try those, that's all I know."

The van raced along the road and slowly picked up the shape of the helicopter across the road in front of them, as they closed in they could see clearly two pairs of men, either side of the door, on the ground.

One man was shouldering a 66, at his side, lying prone on the ground was another man with the minimi machine gun.

They slowed but still approached the barrier. Behind them 200 yards back, Hotel 1 stopped in and hovered in sideways above the road. The back doors opened and two SAS pushed the minimi out once more, and brought it to bear on the van still moving away.

The Range Rover had already stopped and the two pairs of men were now moving along the edges of the road, in the darkness. The big light from helicopter was blinding a rear view from the van and, while it was on, they ran forward, closer to the van. Then the light was gone, and a silence fell on the road.

The flash of the 66 would make anyone's blood run cold. It was fired from the right-hand side of military1 as the van approached. It flashed across the front of it, only two to three yards ahead and impacted on the roadside bank. The blast was just far enough behind the van to avoid any serious damage, but the nearside window shattered.

The van swerved to the right and lost control momentarily, then straightened up still facing the helicopter. Its lights went out and the van stopped.

"Hotel 1, use the PA system, tell them to stay where they are, use the words Ophaltn and Farhaltn. Inform them we are asking them to surrender."

The PA was seriously loud and there was no risk that any occupant of the van would not hear. Several times, over and over again, the message was repeated. No one in the van moved, it was still.

"Repeat it, Hotel 1, tell them we will attack if they do not respond."

Again, they issued their threats to the van, but this time there was a response. The lights on the vehicle flashed on, then off, and from where the SAS were it appeared that the engine had been cut. Then it was still.

A gun appeared from the side window. It was not threatening to anyone, so no one fired; it was pushed further out, and then fell with a metallic clatter on to the road. The same happened on the right; a gun was pushed out of the window. Then again, it was still.

Slowly, the driver's door opened and two hands appeared over the top and then went up into the air. The upper part of a dark body pushed out, still with its hands in the air, it turned, and put both hands on the top of the van and stopped.

When it had been in the same position for 2 minutes, the PA system sprang back into life.

"Move away from the van, walk ten paces forward. Lie down on your front, legs spread, hands above your head, spread. Do not move, do not talk, otherwise you could be shot."

The person did exactly what he was told, and he lay on the floor for 10 minutes. Nothing moved, no one said a word.

"There is only one?"

"Go." The Major sent his men to take the intruder.

Both of the pairs had worked their way down the road on the verge, they had been in position for 5 minutes. Nothing had moved in the van, nor had the suspect moved.

Swiftly, they approached the prone soldier on the floor. A gun was put to his head, whilst he was secured with cable ties. Hands forced hard down his back, and tied to his belt.

Once secure, the prisoner was searched. No weapons were found, not even a knife.

Whilst this was happening, the second pair cleared the van. There was nothing inside, no weapons, no nothing.

"Control, one prisoner only, I confirm one prisoner only."

From the gate of the base, a Landrover and a black bomb disposal unit moved forward to the van. The prisoner was put into the Landrover and taken away to the safety of the military base. From the back of the Transit, four uniformed soldiers jumped out and starting to examine the vehicle in great detail.

Panic had again returned to the control at the FOP in Abbotsley.

18. Not Beaten Yet

Even Ella had not thought about the lights in the farmyard. As they drove around the corner to the side of the house, the lights came on and lit the place up like a football ground.

Her instinct for survival locked in immediately as she realised the situation. They would be seen, and followed and caught.

"Stop the car, quickly; stop the car." She screamed.

"Let me out, and you go, get as far as you can then give it up, do not fight, they will kill you."

She took the small bergen and ran putting it on as she went, running around the west side of the house and to the north, into the barns, into the stink of the onions. In the far corner, away from the lights, she sank on to her haunches and thought for a few moments.

She heard the van move off; it went onto the road and sped towards Gamlingay.

Eastwell was not stupid by any means and had ordered his men to the farm just as quickly as he sent the others after the van. He had to be sure they had taken the flask and not abandoned it. Had he considered however, how many were in the van?

In her view the best place she could be right now was close to the village as near to their own operation control as possible. She had seen the Range Rover responding to the van leaving and where it had come from. She was now on all fours crawling behind huge stacks of hay towards that exact same place.

They would not look in their own backyard.

The second patrol was on the farm in minutes and they were following their own strict operational regulations. The farmhouse could be rigged with any type of booby trap, anti-personnel mine or similar. Until it was cleared, they followed the book. This all gave Ella extra time, but she knew that.

She reached the back of the farmyard where the both police and SAS had set up home for the day. She found her way into an old broken-down, very dark, tin barn, and crawled up to the side facing east and facing the assembled police and military.

Through a crack in the broken wall, she could easily see the whole area. If this had been a war, they would all be dead. But it was not a war, well at least not in this country, or against this country. What Ella wanted, she had, and was not going to be caught; she would escape with it.

E&E, or escape and evade, basic training for any special forces. When it comes to having to do it, there is a doubt in your mind as to whether you can actually avoid being caught.

Ella lay prone on the floor facing the FOP area established in the farmyard. She was breathing slowly but deeply, getting her breath back and fighting away the adrenalin.

The old barn was in a slightly elevated position to the south of the village and Ella could glance left and look down across the fields towards a children's play area. This was just visible in the glow from the street lighting. Further to her left was darkness, what appeared to be trees and through the trees she could see a few small lights. She could now only go forward into the village or left into the trees.

Not too much of a choice and Ella moved off to the left, following a small hedgerow, keeping low and moving slow. She had to move forward for about 200 yards, then turn left and towards the trees in the distance.

"Hotel 1, we need thermal scan over the area surrounding the farmhouse, get back over target area soonest."

Eastwell was bringing back the police helicopter just in case anyone had stayed behind. For all they know if could be the farmer in the van. Time would tell. It was unlikely as he knew that the farmer should have been evacuated along with everyone else.

The helicopter was now going to look for Ella. The thermal imaging would certainly be able to spot her, if she was there.

"Hotel 1, less than 4 minutes and we will be over the farm. We will start to look on the way in."

Ella needed to get as much space between her and the farm as possible. In the distance she could hear the helicopter returning and when it did she knew it could see her in the dark. The time had come to break cover and run. It was very dark and, if she could run a little, it was going to save her life.

The field was flat along the hedgerow, she was on pasture land, it was flat and grass. Also very open, and dangerous; she ran as hard as she could.

As the dark shapes of the trees grew and started to become more recognisable, Ella tripped on a clump of mud and fell hard onto the floor. She fell with her hands out in front, but hit her head on some hard mud to the side. It dazed her, and knocked her wind out.

She sat, 100 yards short of the cover of the trees, and breathed hard, pulling wind back into her. Her head hurt and a warm trickle was running down from her temple on the right.

Two minutes passed and she ran again, this time clearing the field and into the bracken. In the distance she could see the lights of the farm now ½ mile away and see the soldiers looking for her. The helicopter was overhead the main barn.

Moving out from the farm in circles, it too was looking for her. Increasing the diameter each time it went around.

She rested, and thought of her options. She still had her weapon; she still had two flash bangs, two live grenades and trip wire. They would eventually follow up her route; they thought as she did. They would analyse where she would run to, and do the same.

Working quickly in the dark, she taped a flash bang to the roots of a large tree, exposed from the ground to the left side of the track she was using. There were about 5 yards of space between the track and the tree. She fixed one end of the wire to the flash bang and stretched the other across the track, securing it around the base of a hawthorn hedge tree. Removing the safety, she moved on.

A hundred yards on and she turned right and went into the field 50 yards. On all fours she dug a hole only 6 to 10 inches deep and placed a grenade into the hole, attaching a radio detonator. Then piling the soil back on top; she pushed a full magazine of rounds into the soft soil.

Scrambling back to her feet, she turned and ran back towards the hedge behind her, heading towards the lights ahead still visible through the trees. As she reached the edge of the track where it met the hedgerow from the field, the helicopter flew over 200 to 300 yards away.

Ella pulled herself behind the trunk of a large tree and hid from it.

"Hotel 1, we have just seen a very small heat signature in the trees to the west of the farm, 600 yards approx north northwest. It may have been wildlife as we only just caught it."

"Acknowledge that, Hotel 1, stay on station just to be sure, keep looking."

Eastwell also advise the men on foot around the farmhouse of the possible sighting. They considered the area, the possible exits, the route, and also came to the same conclusion that Ella had earlier. This was the best way out.

She could see and hear the helicopter now. Although hidden behind the tree and more or less undetectable, she could not move without being seen. Ella had to think and think quickly.

A follow up would be sent on foot, and soon. She could not see any lights heading this way, but they would not use torches anyway, they would use night sights. She still had her heat blanket that would shield her, but she needed to move on, not hide.

The aircraft could not land or land troops because of the trees, nor could they deploy using drop lines without risk of injury. The helicopter might see her, but it could do nothing. She had to move on, regardless of the helicopter.

Ella pulled out the heat blanket from her belt pack and pulled it over her shoulders and down her front, rather like a woman's shawl. It would not hide all of her, but what was seen would look very strange. Then she ran again, heading deeper into the trees. What she needed was a diversion to distract the helicopter for a few minutes whilst she either hid, or changed route to lose it.

"Hotel 1, we have another sighting difficult to ID but it is moving away to the west, it could be shielded by something."

It was now approximately 10 minutes since the sighting had been reported, time enough for any follow-up to have been nearby. Ella was now concerned that she would be caught.

A huge flash followed by a very loud bang filled the air. The follow-up team had tripped the wire and set off the flash bang. Ella grinned inside to herself.

The four SAS men hit the ground hard and rolled into the darkness, waiting for any incoming fire from the position of the bang. But none came.

Hotel 1 came about and hovered over the scene directly above the four prone men. From the field 50 yards to the north, the grenade exploded. This time it was a live grenade. It showered shrapnel and mud everywhere. It also set off the magazine of rounds, which fired off in all directions like a crazed Chinese cracker.

The soldiers hit the floor again, very flat this time.

The magazine was at ground level and most of the rounds went to safety in the mud. Two or three shot across the heads of the men on the ground, much to their relief, and one round went straight up into the air, right through the rear section of the tail of the helicopter.

There was only minimal damage; the round had broken one of the control systems for the rotor on the rear. It had a back-up system built in for safety, but this was enough to warrant the aircraft returning to base.

"Hotel 1, we have taken damage to the aircraft; request return to base immediately."

"Acknowledged Hotel 1, sit rep please, what the hell is going on, who is firing on who?"

"It appears your lads have taken fire from two positions to the north and south of the track they are on. We cannot see anyone on the ground except your lads.

Turning to the Chief, Eastwell now asked him to call in one of the armed response vehicles and put it on the road nearest to the position of the firing. This would put the car somewhere on the back road between Abbotsley and the golf club. He also sent his remaining men to a position on the road where it crossed a direct line from the village to where the sighting and firing were.

Within seconds, the big Volvo was flashing its way back from the pursuit of the van, now stopped and the driver in custody.

Hotel 1 peeled off to the north and slowly moved away towards RAF Wyton and its base. It would have to avoid flying over the village and any other built up areas on route. It was also much closer to the ground than usual. If the rotor did go badly wrong or fail, then the less distance they had to drop the better.

Ella saw the helicopter limp off and ran, this time as she had been trained. Run and stop, crouching to see what was in front and behind, happy? Then run again. She was alone, no back up behind her.

She decided to put in a box detour as it would be obvious she was moving in a straight line, she turned right and ran a further 500 yards down a slight hill, almost to the road, then left and on towards the old farmhouse that sat near the double bends. Then Ella turned left again heading back uphill towards the lights again. The ground was uneven this time and harder to run on. She had to slow her pace or risk falling again; back towards the cover of the woods.

As she turned left, she dropped her last flash bang, this time with a radio detonator attached. It had a limited range of about 700 yards, but that would be enough for the diversion she wanted. As she reached the edge of the trees, she stopped and dropped to the floor behind a small clump of undergrowth.

The four SAS soldiers quickly regained their composure and regrouped in two sets of two, one to the front and one to the rear. Concerned that there might be more traps set for them, and even more concerned that, for the first time, a live grenade had been used.

They advanced together in pairs, slowly, and Ella knew they would take more time, giving her some extra space.

With a push of the control, the flash bang went off, lighting the area around it. A second or so later the sound of the boom was heard.

The follow-up team had now progressed farther into the trees and was still looking for sign of anyone passing through. The flash bang had them all on the floor again, this time only by pure instinct. It was obvious the bang was some way off. They decided to split up. This could be a diversion and they were not going to be fooled so easily this time.

Eastwell had ordered his men into action from the far road. They would converge together, meeting in the middle and where their prey should be.

Two patrolled down towards the area where the bang came from and the others pressed on forwards.

Ella moved out again and through the trees. The lights in front became bigger and she could make out some large buildings, a hotel, and a golf course.

As she cleared the cover of the woods, the tended grass of the golf course was in front of her and she could run faster. To the right was a small rain shelter used by the golfers in bad weather. She headed for that and, once inside, crouched again looking back for the follow-up.

Then she had an idea. There are no serving women in any of the 'western' special forces. They would not be expecting a woman!

On the left of the rain shelter was a large area of grass, much more finely tended, and there was a sign marking the tee for the seventh fairway. She had never played golf in her life, but she knew that, where there was a golf fairway, there would be sand. Bunkers!

She ran up to the tee and then followed it along its length. On the right side after 100 yards there was a bunker. Kidney shaped and about 10 by 4 yards in size. The bunker was very uneven and had obviously been played out of, at some time during the day.

"Perfect", she thought to herself.

Laying flat in the middle of the bunker she began to dig again, this time a deep and bigger hole. When she was satisfied, she stopped and opened the Bergen, taking out the flask. Carefully she opened it and looked inside. Another flask within. When she was finished she replaced it into the Bergen and dropped it, together with her belt kit and her weapons, into the hole. Then buried them, smoothing the sand as best she could and making it look normal for a used bunker.

The hotel had been evacuated, together with the staff. It was secure, but still lit both inside and out. Ella moved to the main hotel bedroom area, a separate building. Walking along the outside of the building, she peered into each room, looking for signs of clothes. On the bed of the fourth room she looked into was a half empty case and women's clothes.

There was no time to mess around, she smashed the window and climbed through into the room. Having cleared the bathroom, she checked the locks on the entrance door, killed the lights, then grabbed the case of clothes and closed the bathroom door behind her.

Ella was filthy, she had spent the last hours crawling around in every filth she could find. She rushed, turned on the shower, stripped and not waiting for hot water, very quickly cleaned herself.

Less than 2 minutes in the shower, and she was out, drying herself.

The clothes were luckily a little too big, better than too small. She did not need to bother with a bra, but pulled on a clean pair of pants, and then pulled a neat, plain shift-style of dress over her head.

Ella then bundled up her own uniform, climbed on the chair, and stuffed it into the highest part of the cupboard over the wardrobe. Covering it with a blanket, she closed the doors.

Her hair was short, it had to be in her line of work, so the hair dryer took no time to get it dry. She was transformed. No longer the soldier; who would suspect anything?

Before leaving the bathroom, Ella stood in front of the mirror and with the finger nail on her thumb re-opened the cut on her head. It was deep and blood soon started to flow again, helped this time by Ella digging her nail deep into the wound.

It covered the side of her face quickly, and she made sure it was on her dress. Turning off the light, she went back to the room, in the dark and waited.

Within a few minutes she had regained her night sight and was watching out of the window for signs of movement.

The three teams, one of four men approaching from the west now, and the two teams of two men approaching from the east had reached the boundaries of the golf club. They were using the tactical radios, the 'net' and were making sure they announced their progress to each other as they moved forward.

By the book, and carefully, they were advancing on the main buildings of the golf club. Clearing each part, advising control and their mates heading directly at them. They could not risk a blue on blue fire fight.

They met, without a problem on the far side of the club house, in the area where golfers emerged from the changing rooms. A quick discussion and they re formed into two teams of four. The only place anyone could hide now was in the hotel building.

If that was clear, they had missed them.

One team went to the front and right, the other team went to the front and left. They would clear the perimeter of the building first and then move inside.

At each corner, two men went forward, one of them stood, the other crouched and waited.

"Go."

Standing man moved around the corner, crouching man rolled low and covered him.

"Clear."

The second two overtook them and moved to the next corner.

"Go."

And it repeated.

It was the first four who saw the broken window, and called it in on the net. Two either side of the frame, they crouched looking up.

"Team 1, flash bang in from the window, take no chances, Team 2, go to the front and cover any exit."

Eastwell thought he had his prey cornered.

"Team 2, ready."

"Team 1, stand by, going on three, two, one."

As he hit one, the flash bang went in through the window. Ella knew it might come and had now positioned herself on the floor, looking as though she had been knocked down, away from the window and the flash bang.

Her night vision was gone, along with her hearing and any orientation she had left. Ella was now a mess, but she did not care, it all added to the effect.

Stepping on the cupped hands of their mates, the first two went in through the window, rolled on to the floor, one going left, one right. And waited. No movement, through their kite sights all they could see was a body on the floor.

"Body on floor, no other sign, stand by, moving."

One moved, the other covered, his weapon raised and ready to fire. He moved past the closed door of the bathroom, to the far side, standing astride Ella on the floor.

"Go."

He did not need to say anymore. Standard building clearance. The first man now kicked in the door and rolled through, his mate following him to cover.

"Clear, room is clear. Team 2 get in here."

Team 2 moved to the main door. A double tap from the Koch and Heckler opened the lock, and they went in.

They checked Ella for a pulse. It was good and strong. No other wounds, only the head wound.

"She is fine, plasticuffs. Let's go"

Having secured Ella and eliminated any chance she could be a threat, they moved off and, over the next 12 minutes, the two teams cleared the whole building.

"Control, building is clear, one female casualty, head wound, secure. Advise."

"Secure the area, we are on the way."

Ella was pulled to her feet and taken outside into the main car parking area of the Hotel. The SAS men treated her head wound and stopped the bleeding. She could not hear much, and was still seeing flashes in front of her eyes.

They were all very kind to her, asked how she had been injured. Ella claimed that someone forced their way into the window, hit her and ran off through the building, not stopping.

She expected to be questioned further; about why she was there, what had happened and was already preparing herself. She saw what appeared to be an officer approaching her.

It was not until he was about 10 feet away that Ella saw a second soldier just behind him, carrying her uniform. They had already searched the room and had found the clothes she had hidden.

She turned and moved slightly backward, straight into the chest of one of the two men that now stood behind her.

"Re-cuff her." He barked.

"Name?"

"Ben-Yehuda." Ella snapped back at him.

"Nationality?"

"Israeli."

"You have something that was taken from the pub in the village. We want it back, where is it?"

"I am unwilling to discuss this with you, Sir, please advise your Government that I wish a representative of the Israeli Embassy to be informed of my capture."

"How about if I just shoot you here and now? I want to know where the flask, that you have stolen, has been hidden."

"Don't play games with me, Sir, I will only reveal this under the supervision of my own Government and only then against assurances of our safe passage back to Israel."

"Take her to Bassingbourn."

Epil☙gue

Ella was bundled into the back of one of the Range Rovers. Each side of her squeezed an SAS member, and the front passenger seat was occupied by another. They were polite, and did not mistreat her.

They knew Ella was Special Forces and they had respect for that, more so that she was female. The journey to Bassingbourn was very quick, ARV1 led the way and two brought up the rear.

Eastwell brought in as much manpower as he could and began to search the golf complex. He needed to find the flask, but it could be anywhere, it could take years to find it. It had to be found as the risk of someone unearthing it in years to come was far too big a risk to take.

The military police took charge of Ella and within the first 10 minutes had her in a secure complex at the heart of the base. Outside the entrance, two armed guards were stationed and the whole base was now on full alert.

Unknown to Ella, her colleague was in the next room. The last thing they needed was for them to escape again.

The SAS had asked for Ella to be stripped searched, but had conceded that this should be carried out by a female officer. She was completely stripped, and then, using a field decontamination tent, washed and washed again with disinfectants and other anti-chemical weapon fluids.

Her clothes were bagged and kept for forensic examination. These were sent immediately back to Huntingdon to the police laboratories where they joined those of her two friends. They would be looking for signs of the virus.

When the SAS Major arrived at the base, he was shown through to the secure unit. The Chief Constable was not allowed to pass through. The matter had now become a full military one and their rules applied.

Both the intruders were shown into separate interrogation rooms. Each room allowed them to be clinically isolated, without risk to any interrogators. They were both informed that the Israeli chargé d'affaires was en route and would be allowed to act as their representative. Over the next 8 hours, they co-operated and informed the British authorities exactly how they had infiltrated the terrorist organisation.

Ella became Coleman's girlfriend because she was instructed to do so. It had taken her 2 years to become accepted as part of the Palestinian group, 2 years to be accepted as one of them.

She had killed her own countrymen to become accepted; it was not enough to just eradicate these terrorists. As one died, another took his place. They would never stop. Their defence was to become them, see what they were doing, and interfere where they could. They had achieved more in this way than Bush could achieve in 10 years of a war in the Middle East. She told them that now she felt she had failed. The virus had been recovered, but it still existed, and so presented a threat to Israel.

The British government were in a no-win situation. They could not prosecute these people, as it would surely mean this information becoming public knowledge. They could not imprison them without trial. If they were held with no charge, then Israel would seek their release, and this too would cause problems. They had to reach a deal with them to recover the virus.

The chargé d'affaires explained the terms of the deal to both soldiers. He offered them a way out, and back to Israel, together with their wounded friend. They accepted. Ella informed them where she had buried the flask. It was recovered and returned to Boscombe Down.

Eastwell had done his job; he had recovered this insane fluid developed with the blessing of the HM Government. He returned to Hereford wondering what they hell he was doing this job for.

The Chief returned to Abbotsley to clean up the mess left behind in the pub.

The Government had agreed to repatriate the three soldiers back to Israel.

Twenty-four hours after they were captured; they were flown out of Bassingbourn on board a military helicopter and taken to RAF Brize

Norton. As far as the army was concerned, all three represented a biological hazard and they were treated as such.

There, on the tarmac waited an Israeli Air Force Hercules. It had been on the ground for less than 1 hour. No one had approached it, as was agreed. The helicopter landed 100 yards away from the big plane, and two figures carrying a stretcher moved across, ran up the rear ramp, and were gone.

The loadies pressed the button and the rear started to move. Each one had an NBC suit on. At the front, the aircrew too had NBC suits on. As the two sat down on the benches at the back, they were handed their own suits.

The results from the lab at Huntingdon showed tiny traces of the virus on the clothes worn by the female. The other clothes were clear.

The virus that had been returned to Boscombe Down was destroyed on the direct orders of the Prime Minister. No records of the experiments with the virus were kept. As far as the government were concerned, they now had a lid on the whole episode. The man who had dreamed up this dreadful virus was dead, and so too now were his records.

Two thousand miles away in a military hospital isolation ward, Ella lay on a bed. Her fever had developed like a cold and was now very severe.

At her side, her mother and father looked on at their daughter. They too were dressed in suits designed to protect them from any biological threat. Through a thick rubber glove, Mum held her daughter's hand. In the other hand was a postcard from Jerusalem.

Ella had less than a day to live, but she knew that her sacrifice was worth it. Israel would have her anti-virus..... Ella made sure of that.